The First Pat

By Mark Rengel

The First Pat

This is a work of fiction. Names, characters, places, events, and incidents are either the product of the author's imagination or used fictitiously. Any resemblance to actual persons, living or dead, or actual events is purely coincidental.

Published by Rengel Books

ISBN: 978-1-7637663-4-1

First published in 2026   Printed in Australia

Cover design by the author.

Cover timber-wolf image by Michael Cummings Wildlife Photography: www.worldwildlifephotography.org

Interior design by the author.

Author website: markrengel.com
Author email contact: rengelbooks@gmail.com

Other Books by this author

- *The Nomadic Shrub*

THE HOWLING MOON

- *Eurasia / Late Stone Age*
- *Upper Palaeolithic Period*
- *37,000 years BC*

...Somewhere west of present day *Kaktolga Кактолга* near the Ergun River border region of China and Russia...

...The old man and the boy stood looking out across the valley, admiring the view.

Their two, large, hunting dogs by their sides, sat restfully on their haunches, alert yet relaxed, panting quietly.

Not far from their little village, returning home from a busy day, they'd taken a moment to rest, pause and take in the magnitude of their world.

A huge full moon hung high in the early evening's sky, bathing down its brilliant light onto the endless, expansive vista before them.

Earlier, there had been the warmth and the splendour of a lovely sunny day –and now, there was this cool, eerily lit, glowing wonderment of otherworldly effervescence to behold and enjoy.

Both of their dogs were making slight, suppressed vocalisations in response to the loud chorus of wolves nearby in a neighbouring valley, who were all busy howling away at the moon. The two hunting dogs had been sternly trained not to join in with their noisy cousins in the wild, they knew they needed to keep themselves quiet.

Yet an autonomic stirring in their souls kept urging them to try and sing along. Something was pushing its way through with their subdued murmurings and whines.

The young boy spoke in a language that would be almost untraceable by most modern-day, anthropological linguists –words that have long been lost to our species, heavily eroded by the sands of time, vanished vocab, phonetics and a syntax belonging to an incredibly distant human past...much, much longer than most of us would even realise...

 Turning to his father, he asked:

"Papa, why do they howl at the moon?"

The father's smile faded slightly, a sad understanding could be faintly seen in his expression as he looked up into the dead centre of the glowing moon.

"My Grandfather told me once, long, long ago, when I was just a small boy,"

He looked down to his son "smaller than you are now" pausing, before looking back up again at the moon again,

"He said that there was never a moon in the sky to begin with, back when he was only a young boy, there just wasn't any moon...nothing...just the stars"

"Really?!? –No Moon?!" the boy asked quizzically.

 "That's right, that's what he told me. He said it just suddenly arrived years later when he was a grown man, one night –out of nowhere it appeared up there in that night sky, glowing away like it is now...And he said, when it did first appear, a great sadness fell over everyone's hearts and souls.

He said it felt like a horrible thing had just happened. Everyone felt like something had been stolen away from them. Although they couldn't quite say what it was exactly, they just knew they'd been robbed of something very precious.

When the moon first appeared, my grandfather said everyone looked up at it and cried too, the same way the wolves do now.

For some reason, it made everyone's hearts and spirits feel crushed and heartbroken, like they were no longer free to roam the World and the Universe anymore. People had this dreadful feeling they were all caught in a terrible, circular trap. They hated the moon to begin with.

But, as the time slowly passed by, most people forgot about how badly it made them all feel at the start of its arrival, and they grew accustomed to it being there. They accepted the sad sensation it caused them and learnt to ignore the terrible way it made them feel.

The sorrow of feeling horribly trapped here on Earth forever, faded away. People accepted it. After a while, they came to forget they were now prisoners here and had lost their true, cosmic freedom."

He ran his hand through the thick furry mane of the dog sitting closest to him.

"These guys have been our closest friends for a long time. Many of the elders believe they can see things which we cannot.

They say, all dogs, including the wolves, are able to see something going-on up there in the moon that is so horrible and so wrong, it causes them to cry out in fear and sorrow.

They are calling out in sympathy for what is happening to their best friend's souls up there.

They are howling for us – trying to warn us – trying to protect us, as their true sprits always do."

"What do you think they can see up there Papa?" Asked the boy

"The elders who can speak with the animals in the spirit world say, the wolves can see all of our souls being trapped up there together in the moon, like a school of fish being caught in a large net, our souls are being collected and caught by the glowing moonlight."

The father sang loudly up to the moon:

"DON'T GO INTO THAT LIGHT MY HUMAN BROTHERS AND SISTERS! –DON'T BE FOOLED – IT'S A TRAP FOR YOUR SOUL –DON'T GO INTO THE LIGHT!"

He looked down to his son, "I think that is what the wolves are trying to say to our spirits when they howl up at the moon."

"They cry out for our freedom. They howl for their best friend, and they lament for all the other spirits of the world as they are taken-up, caught and collected by the moon – they are crying out to warn the souls of the dead, trying to save them from being trapped up there and fed upon by something evil."

"Will I get trapped up there when I die Papa?" he asked in a very concerned tone.

"So long as you can hear the dogs barking and the wolves howling up to you, warning you.

So long as you know what they are trying to tell you –yelling up to you, trying to get you to turn around and listen to them –listen to them as they sing up to you:

"HEY, my friend - Turn around and look at us down here! Don't go into that light, turn around, resist it, face the other way!

–face freedom and observe the wild open expanse of the universe before you –You must ask the Universe to take you back to your true home…Tell it that's where you want to go! That's where we'll be waiting for you, waiting patiently to be by your side once again, like we have always done throughout time

– For when our spirits are together, that's when we have truly found our way home again in the Universe!" –As long as you can remember this and can hear them warning you and helping you to not get trapped up there…Your soul won't be harvested like a fish, and you will be free to roam the Universe with your best friend by your side forever."

"Wherever our true home is, out there in the universe, there's a dog waiting patiently for us to get there, waiting to be by our side once again and to shower us with all the unconditional love that they always have in their hearts to give to us.

And we long to be by their side too, to pat and cuddle them with all the unconditional love that we also have to give to them.

And then the father and son, without saying another word, in a moment of much needed levity brought-on by the heavy nature of their deep and melancholy conversation, both looked up at the moon, cupped the sides of their mouths with their hands and started to howl, pausing to have a chuckle as their two furry companions immediately took this as their special cue to also join-in and have a good and long howl with their human friends, as well as their cousins in the wild.

A few minutes later they stopped howling, but kept laughing, as they turned to walk back home to their village.

Some 39,000 years later, their bones would be discovered resting beside their two dogs, after another day's hunting trip that sadly had not ended as well as this one had.

A fossilised testimony to the bond we have always shared for so many endless years with these beautiful, furry, gifts from God, our spiritual guardians wrapped in fur, that have literally been our best friends forever, and a day.

THE FRACTURE POINT

The air split open like a glass sheet shattering across infinity.

Sherri ran for her life.

The ground beneath her wasn't ground at all really anymore—just a constantly shifting kaleidoscope of fractured, spluttering time distortions, each step warping through *centuries in an instant*. Her foot landed in a snowy Ice Age plain, then a neon-lit cybernetic city, then a pristine meadow untouched by human hands—reality was bending and unfolding back in on itself, and they were at the epicentre of it all.

"KEEP MOVING!" Jake roared, hauling his brother forward over the raging chaos surrounding them. His younger brother, Byron, desperately clutched at his side, bleeding—from a wound that flickered in and out of existence. One second healing, the next gone, erased, then suddenly gaping open again and haemorrhaging...time itself couldn't decide if it had happened to him yet or if it had not.

Sherri's lungs burned as she vaulted over a collapsed, rusty metal girder—or what had *been* a girder. Now it was the exposed ribcage of a Woolly Mammoth. Before she could register any of this confusing turmoil, it *shifted again* becoming a chrome beam extending from a futuristic skyscraper beneath her feet.

Everything was collapsing down, into, and back onto itself, over and over again in a confounding, rapid flux.

And in the very centre of all this, standing paralysed by the storm of the surrounding chaos, was the juvenile wolf.

A small, furry, golden-eyed anomaly in a war between two splintered realities.

Sherri did a baseball slide, coming to a stop, dirt and fermion-sparks flying up around her. The wolf was frozen, its paws flickering—one moment standing in a prehistoric tundra, the next in the middle of a suburban highway about to be run-over by the oncoming traffic, then a quiet, deserted beach.

This was it – *This was their moment...*

"Sherri!" Hannah's voice cracked out through the storm of chaos. She was grappling with the dog-flag, the same old one they'd made back home an eternity ago—but now *the paw print was gone*. Just a blank, white, canvas square on a bamboo pole –the only thing that was left of it, whipping wildly in the wind, as another flickering eruption of subatomic, lightning particles and ionic tendrils fractured across and through the space-time-continuum. Then came the angry, malevolent claws of spaghetti-like plasma that soon followed, fiercely trying to snatch-onto and tear-away at the flag that she was so desperately holding onto firmly with all her might.

"We're losing it!" Jake gasped, his voice raspy, distorting within the unstable soundwaves caused by the prolapsing timeline.

No. No, not now!

Sherri's mind burned, flashes of Uncle Frank's theories detonating through her thoughts—Die Glocke, the Linear Displacement Generator, the Mandela Effect, all collapsing in real-time. The enemy had reached the fracture point first, trying to erase all of it, trying to overwrite history before the connection could be forged...or "re-forged"...or "pre-forged"—or ALL three versions of forging, smudged together as one.

The wolf should not really exist now – But it still DID!

There it stood, with its tail wagging, doing that smiley panting-face that we all know and love ever so well.

LOVE can NEVER be destroyed!

LOVE will ALWAYS exist!

If she didn't act now though, it quite possibly *wouldn't*.

Jacinta, who was struggling on her own at the very end of the group, turned around, her pupils shrinking in horror. **"THEY'RE COMING!"**

Sherri spun around to look.

The Riftwalkers...

Shadowy, humanoid blotches not of this world, slipping through dimensional cracks like living afterimages. Their forms hideously twisted and gruntingly bent, their bodies almost humanoid, but disturbingly not quite, their movements like glitches in the universe itself.

They weren't just here to stop them.

They were here to *erase them*.

Jake screamed as one of them lunged toward him—it just missed grabbing him, recoiling back in a spasmodic, snapping motion. Yet, by coming that close to him, it had caused his entire body to become momentarily distorted, flickering between past and present versions of himself all at once. A baby / an old man / a foetus / a toddler / a nothing/ an everything –then back again to his normal self.

"SHERRI!" Byron roared. "DO IT NOW!"

The wolf.

Its tail wagged again...

Everything else—**the storm, the collapsing multiverse, the creatures hunting them, the screaming past and future—**none of it mattered.

Only this precious moment did...

Sherri stretched her hand out, reaching, waving, reaching.

She needed to touch it—she had to pat it with all the love in her soul, projecting our entire specie's collective love for them that we have. And in that impossible moment, she also needed to feel its love and loyalty reflecting back at her, forming a universal, cosmic bridge connecting humans with our furry best friend.

Her fingers brushed the wolf's head—

And the universe exploded...

THE GOLD COAST

Kirra Beach, Australia

Saturday, November 16th, 2024

(In an alternate Universe & timeline where COVID 19 never damn well happened, and an avoidable housing and cost of living crisis hadn't come about either…)

Half a dozen lawnmowers steadily thrummed their chorus-line choir of furious buzzing that erupted out from different yards, at various volumes. ALL roaring-away at different tempos in their quarter-acre blocks.

The monotonous stream of their rapidly purring two-stroke engine revs, blended with all the other atmospheric sounds of this early-spring day's afternoon to create an ever so subtle, yet distinctive, ambient feel that was the ever-typical Saturday "arvo" in an Australian, weekend, suburban landscape.

It was a slow and timeless, same-old-same-old here, *as it always has been*, with a nice, relaxed, chilled-out pleasant feel to it that went into creating this classic, urban-utopian ambiance.

Seabee Close, where all the lawnmowing was taking place, was a classic text-book example of this laid-back, coastal, Aussie suburban weekend afternoon vibe. Situated just two blocks away from Kirra Beach proper. You only needed to take a short five-minute stroll, crossing over Coolangatta Road, to find yourself standing on one of the most beautiful, semi-tropical, white, sandy beaches in all of Australia – or the World for that matter.

Everyone who lived here in this Southern end of Queensland's Gold Coast, completely loved it.

Glimmering aqua and turquoise seas, long white beaches stretching for miles, easy surf spread across a range of breaks, and a relaxed, unpretentious atmosphere gave the area a yesteryear feel that drifted back into the surrounding residential suburbs. The place carried a quiet sleepiness — a breezy, sandy, and unmistakably Aussie, coastal vibe.

And with the daily sea-breeze, came huge amounts of beach-sand that would blow-in lazily trying to recreate new sections of beach and sand dunes here-and-there, trying to cover over the man-made landscapes.

Grains of beach sand skip-scotched with the breeze as they went skittering over roads, footpaths, parks, gardens and grass. Everywhere patches of white beach-sand, sometimes many months and years in the making, had formed mini swatches of beach.

Along property fencelines, shop doorways, alleyways, front gardens and carparks, there was always enough collected beach sand to let you know, at one quick glance, the Ocean wasn't too far away and was trying its best to make more beach than it already had.

On the small, vacant patch of Council land that formed the corner leading into Seabee Close, the beach sand had completely covered over the weed-grass with a decently sized, white, wavy, miniature, sand dune.

In the middle of this almost ten-cubic-meter mound of accumulated beach sand, tilting over like a short, stubby, four-foot high Leaning Tower of Pisa, sat an old, mottled and peeled, white wooden post. A relic from the 1970's. It was slowly being swallowed-up by the growing sand-dune.

Bolted to the top was a very rusty Main Roads sign that read: "NO THROUGH ROAD".

The residents of Seabee Close hated this sign every time they unavoidably glanced at it while turning into their street.

Most of the parents, at one stage or another, had considered putting the sign out of its misery by completely kicking and stomping it over all the way.

They had calculated it would only take one swift kick to do the trick, but obviously, they figured, this was not a task to be done out in the broad daylight for the world to see – it was after-all an act of vandalism of sorts, of council property, and was probably better done under the cover of darkness, discreet-ish, in a very covert, "special-ops" kind of night-time, stealth mission way.

But, you know how it goes with parents, nothing much gets done in the evenings, not when they sink into their comfortable sofas, after dinner and after the dishes have been done, with their wide-screen TVs and their cold beers or chilled (or warm) glasses of wine firmly glued to one hand and the remote control in the other – can anything be expected of them?

Inevitably the sofas would get the better of them, causing them to sink-down further and further into their beloved, comfy items of furniture.

Venturing-out into the darkness of the night to destroy an old, annoying, eye-sore of a Main Roads sign was never really going to happen, especially not by any of this street's mums and dads.

And so, the old, leaning-tower-of NO THROUGH ROAD sign survived—year after year—right where it was.

It kept on leaning.

It kept on irritating people.

It kept on being ignored by the council.

And for reasons no one could ever quite explain, it never got fixed or replaced by anyone. It just stayed there.

It was an impossibly permanent and timeless fixture.

And, unlike the parents, the kids all dearly loved and cherished the rusty old sign on the corner of their street.

The reason why it annoyed the parents so much, was not because it was an old, decrepit eyesore of a sign. It annoyed them because, in their minds, their lovely street they lived in, wasn't a "NO THROUGH ROAD".

They didn't see it that way. Their street was a "cul-de-sac". That's what everyone called it. Just like every other group of residents in Australia who lived in a "cul-de-sac" called their lovely, "sealed-off" street.

A cul-de-sac is considered to be a lovely, quiet and safe, family friendly slice of suburban Utopia. It's like a sandy cove on a rocky and windswept coastline.

Over the years, with the passing of time, homes in cul-de-sacs have become one of the most favoured and sought after types of suburban properties you can hope to buy in Australia – a small patch of suburban heaven for an Aussie family to live in.

Cul-de-sacs have always managed to keep that old-school, yesteryear feel and quality about them. Kids can play safely in the street (like their grandparents did), ride their bikes and skateboards without any worries and everyone seems to form a closer bond with their neighbours. The stress of the busy, endless speeding traffic and "hoons" racing around everywhere, all becomes a worry for other people, living on other streets to have to deal with, but not when you're living in a cul-de-sac.

On this particular Saturday afternoon in Seabee Close, a small group of kids and their dogs, were busily making full use of their cul-de-sac's greatest quality: They were happily playing right in the middle of it, right at the very end of it, where the road stopped, terminated and formed a perfectly round, bulbous, modest, bitumen playing field for them to run around on.

Their laughter and their shouting, combined with their dogs all barking away, mixed with the reverberations of the lawnmowers, birds singing in the trees, as-well-as all the other vibrant sounds of nature, merging to form an overall feeling of a classic springtime, weekend afternoon in Australia.

The whacky and unique game the kids were so immersed in playing, was currently responsible for having inspired a new generation of kids all around the country, and the world, to discard their screens, their video games, their computers and their next-to-sedentary lifestyles and actually start going outside again to actively play in the fresh air with each other, face–to-face.

They were now playing an actual, proper, real, physical game. After generations of kids before them, who had become so physically inactive playing video games and almost having lost the ability to socialise face-to-face with each other, this was a phenomenally new and positive change.

Although this super popular, new game hadn't been invented here in Seabee Close, it was very close by, only just a couple of blocks away in another location, where the game craze had originally begun.

Some of the kids in this group, two brothers and their younger sister, had created the game one wintery, Saturday afternoon.

The story of how the game came-to-be, was by now a legendary tale known throughout Australia, and the rest of the world too.

And like all stories that are retold and retold, over and over again, there will always be factual additives, untruths and variations applied to the tale, as part of the retelling process.

The story of how Scoot-Skittles was invented, was by no means any exception to this word-of-mouth, tale-telling tradition. Nevertheless, the following account is probably the best, most detailed and the most accurate you could ever possibly hope to find:

The Creation of Scoot-Skittles
– Kirra Beach – Sat 22 July 2023

One slightly cold, winter's Saturday afternoon, in the South Gold Coast region. Most will say it was Kirra Beach, a well-known fact, but regardless of this, many folks still insist it was Palm Beach (mostly Palm Beach parents trying to big-note themselves, their children and their suburb...as they have always had a tendency to do so...forever!)

But the truth is, it was two brothers and their younger sister who lived in the Kirra Shores residential complex who actually invented the game and kick-started the global craze.

And it was a yellow, recycling bin, left standing alone on the curb from Thursday's collection day that became the key component in helping to sprout the creation of this new game.

The younger sister had only one task to do each week for her pocket money. She needed to remember, on Thursdays, to wheel the garbage bin out to the curb in the mornings, and back in again later that same afternoon. Two bins - if it was a recycling day, or just the red bin if it wasn't.

But like most weeks, she would conveniently forget to bring the bin(s) back in again after arriving home from school in the afternoon. Watching TV or gaming on her laptop had a much higher priority to her than stopping to wheel the bin back in from the curb and re-positioning it neatly around the side of the house.

She would regularly saunter past the bin sitting on the curb on her B-line trajectory to the front door and the lounge room that lay beyond it. And if she did happen to manage to remember to bring the red bin back in, she would conveniently "forget" to bring the yellow, recycling bin back in.

She did however, remember, without fail, to ask for her pocket money to be paid-up in full, on Fridays, and not a day later.

The yellow recycling-bin was the ignored and neglected bin of the two bins, always left alone, regularly marooned out on the curb. It was almost a permanent fixture there at the front of their unit, standing like a guard at the end of their short driveway. The sunlight would highlight the war-wounds and gashes, scratches and missing chunks of plastic it had on it from always getting hit, unavoidably, by their mum as she madly reversed her old, 1971 VW Kombi, named "Flossie", out from the garage.

Like an old, retired, boxing champ, the yellow recycling bin had been continually smashed, pulverised and KO'd by a superior, heavyweight opponent throughout its career!

On this day's impact however, Flossie had struck the poor bin so hard that it was completely bowled over, disgorging its entire recyclable contents all over their driveway, adjoining grassed area and immediate road. Plastic bottles, cardboard boxes, paper waste and items too small and too many to identify, were strewn everywhere.

Their mum was now looking at this *"save the planet"* scene of plastic, environmental pollution all over their front lawn and driveway with dismay and rage: *"dis-rage-may"*— (Mums get it a lot!).

The combination of bikes, scooters and random sports gear items that were already laying around on the grass, added to the complete and absolute totality of this mess.

There at the end of the short driveway, already late for her Saturday afternoon shift at the Aldi store in Coolangatta's "Strand" shopping mall, she was forced to stomp down hard on the brake pedal like a body builder pumping his quad muscles on "Leg Day" at the gym.

The old drum brakes of the rusty, lime coloured, oversized bread-loaf on wheels, brought Flossie's bulky, metal frame to a lethargic lurch, coming to an almost sudden stop.

With Buddhist beads and shells on strings swinging intensely from her rear-view mirror and the obligatory, dashboard Hula dancer going into epileptic sways. Mum hastily rolled down Flossie's window and wrestled her head out of it, as far as it could go, then proceeded to roar at the top of her lungs like an enraged T-Rex– (a feat she did so well, and so frequently, that she had recently started to wonder if she had somehow reactivated some kind of ancient, T-Rex gene variant lying dormant in her human DNA?...a "Jurassic Mum" of sorts)

Having just "chain-drank" three cups of super-strong coffee, back-to-back, along with her two obligatory guarana tablets for good measure, her yelling now took-on an intensity and power that could have made a Boot Camp Drill Sergeant screaming abuse and profanity at his new Marine recruits seem like a nice, kind and dear, elderly grandma giving some caring, gentle, soothing and loving advice to her young grandkids.

Mum wanted action to be taken right away. And she would not *spare any quarter* this time if her demands were not met - *immediately*, she said to herself...*immediately!* – then, she paused for a moment to contemplate exactly what she would actually do if she did happen to not *"spare any quarter"* on her kids, just like she was always threatening them repetitively that she would do?

.... Perhaps, she speculated, it would most likely involve the neighbours trying to intervene and get involved, there would no-doubt be passers-by calling the police – and possibly human-rights organisations around the world getting involved too. She nodded assuredly to herself, *"Sparing no quarter"* would definitely be her A-bomb of ultimate, A-game disciplinary moves, one worth saving up for, if-and-when she ever needed to use it.

Like so many mums worth their weight in Woollie's rewards points, she held a 10th Degree Dan – a Grandmaster, (if you don't know the martial arts ranking system too well, a 10th Dan is 10 levels higher than a black belt) in the very, not-so mysterious, yet ancient, highly calculating art, known only to every parent – *everywhere* – called:
"Leverage-and-Threat Tai-Jutsu".

"IF ALL THREE OF YOU DON'T GET YOUR ASSES OUT HERE IN THE NEXT FIVE SECONDS, I'M COMING IN THERE AND TAKING THE MODEM WITH ME TO WORK – NO INTERNET!!! AND YOU'RE HAVING BEANS ON TOAST –
- COLD BEANS! – ON TOAST– FOR DINNER –
***I WONT EVEN BOTHER TO WARM THEM UP!* -**
INSTEAD OF YOUR SATURDAY NIGHT CHINESE TAKE-AWAY FOR DINNER!!!   YOU GOT THAT?!?!

Pausing, she huffed, then pulled her head back in through Flossie's window, like an angry tortoise in a big, lime green shell. With her arms outstretched, clenching the bus-like steering wheel of the Kombi, she braced herself, took a slow, voluminously deep breath in, reloading herself with lungful's of air like an entire gunnery crew on-board a naval destroyer reloading their cannons, she then repositioned her head out of Flossie's window again, took aim at the front door and blasted it with two deafening rounds of...

YOU HEAR ME!?!?

YOU HEAR ME IN THERE?!?"

People further up the coast in Surfer's Paradise could hear her!

Everyone in the Gold Coast region could hear her for that matter.

Incoming planes to Coolangatta Airport could hear her over their two-way radios.
"COME OUTSIDE AND CLEAN THIS BLOODY MESS UP NOW! – OR NO CHINESE TAKE-AWAY FOR DINNER!"
Many people felt compelled to go outside and clean-up the bloody mess –even pilots (whatever the bloody mess was?) even office workers doing Saturday, weekend overtime,

some of them 40 floors up, just knew that there was a mess outside, and it needed tidying up...immediately! *...or else!*

By now the two guarana tablets were having a caffeine party in her tummy with the three strong coffees she'd just chain-drank.

The caffeine levels combined with her special "*Mummy-Tanty-Moment*" made her wonder if she just might start turning green and transforming into the Hulk, rapidly gaining weight and bursting out through her clothes. (Although, come to think of it, she'd already been performing those last two feats quite easily for some years now, due simply to being a parent, raising kids and eating the same carbohydrate-loaded, starchy foods the kids ate, being too tired to fix anything healthy for herself. Plus working two sedentary jobs and having no time –or energy- - or motivation to exercise didn't help either.....But *why?* She wondered...*Why* wasn't she turning green just now?

Her imaginings about changing into the Hulk suddenly stopped when the two boys slowly emerged from the house first.

Sloth-like in speed, stepping like newborn foals, their walk and movement tottering, blinking and cringing, dazed and dazzled by the harsh, brutal, mid-day afternoon sun that assaulted their poor eyes. They were followed by their younger sister in the same fashion. Like subterranean, cave dwellers that had been driven out of their dark and peaceful habitat by some brutal and unforeseen force in nature...A furious mum!

"**MOVE IT!**" She barked. They jolted back a little as if they'd just been poked with an invisible, electric cattle-prod by the soundwave of her voice.

"It's not fair!" Complained the two brothers in unison... (*Everything in life isn't fair for boys at this age when they are required to do something that involves getting up off the sofa... or at any age for that matter?*)

"Jacinta's supposed to take the bins in! That's her job! She's the one who left it sitting out there!" both of them saying the words and pointing to the bin at the same time as if they were a well-rehearsed, song-and-dance duet.

"I DON'T BLOODY CARE! – THE THREE OF YOU GET TO WORK CLEANING THIS MESS UP – **N O W!** – OR NO CHINESE TONIGHT– I MEAN IT!

Then she lowered her voice dramatically, and proceeded to speak in that fearsome, foreboding, staged whisper that all mums are quite often predisposed to do, gaining an incredible, cutting effect,

"If this isn't cleaned up by the time I get back from work......it – will – be – cold – beans – on – toast!!!....Her voice then lowered even more, *" Do - you – hear – me ??"*....She paused, waited a few seconds, then instantly dialled-up her voice to a powerful "11" in nanoseconds and bellowed at the top of her lungs,
"B E A N S!!!!"

The three siblings reflexively jumped-back in unison.

And with that, she turned to face forwards and allowed Flossy to gracefully roll out of the short driveway, running over and squashing several plastic containers in the process. She revved the egg-beater VW engine to its breaking point and dropped the clutch in an attempt to smoke-it-up.

In any normal car it would have caused a screeching and burning of rubber as the vehicle rapidly accelerated off.

This was the dramatic effect their mum was after, as she wanted the kids to know that she was seriously, bogan mad.

However, in Flossie's case, the old car just lazily lunged forward a tad while belching-out copious amounts of oily, black smoke from her poor old vintage VW's overworked engine. Some mild acceleration did happen, very mild to be exact, as she headed off down the street, burbling away like a big, shoebox-shaped, land-torpedo, carrying a partly detonated, explosive payload of TMT (Total Mum Tantrum) inbound for Coolangatta Aldi and all those ever so lucky customers who would pass through her checkout that afternoon.

The three kids were left standing there awash in a misty sea of Kombi smoke surrounded by a flotsam-jetsam of recycling bin rubbish as far as the eye could see.

Jake, the eldest of the two brothers, watched Flossie travel down the road and then he "Huffed", then he sniffed, then he casually lent down and picked up a small, plastic yogurt container and tossed it at the back of his sister's head.
"This is all your fault –you lazy, little cow!"
The yogurt container bounced harmlessly off Jacinta's head making a "bonk" noise. She spun-around to face her brother and yelled,

"*Lazy*?!! – *Lazy*?! – **What about you?! You** *lazy* **hypocrite!**" She snatched-up a plastic 3-litre milk bottle and hurled it at him in one lightning-fast act of retaliation, "**HYPOCRITE!**—*You're* the laziest pig I've ever known!" She stomped her foot down and pointed at him, **"When's the last time you've ever picked up after yourself? Hey?** *Never!* **—you slack** *bum!*" The empty milk bottle struck Jake squarely on his nose and bounced-off, causing him to rile-up in anger.

That particular plastic milk bottle was actually quite pivotal in saving every living creature on the planet, although the three siblings had no idea of this at the time.

Byron, the middle child of the three, quickly leapt in-between his brother and sister before they started ripping each other apart. He knew the drill, "**Oy! Oy! ...–Com-MON! Watch yourselves, just watch-it Ay?! – What'ya think you're doing here?!**' He shoved the two of them apart with a mild force.
"Just **CHILL-OUT! ...*Both* of you—Chill-out!**" he manoeuvred, rotated and shuffled quickly to hold them at bay, **"keep-yah bloody heads-on, will you?!?! Yah pair of crazy galahs!"** he felt the energy and force that was trying to squash him in the middle, slowly begin to cycle-down. Any second now and they would switch-over to a reasonable logic and sensible mindedness, instead of blinding-rage. He watched to see it in their eyes, that's where the change would take place first. "Common man! – Don't be saying that nasty, psycho stuff to each other! ...We're a family!" he felt the tension drop like a bowling ball with his last three, salient words.

"What if Dad were here now? You reckon he'd be proud of the way you two are acting?!?

"I swear, I'm gonna smack-the-**snot** outa her one of these days for being a **mouthy little cow!**" Jake growled.

Byron knew it was just words now, he could see he'd calmed down. "Yeah, yeah ...give it a rest *tough guy!!!* ...Big hero that's gonna make you Ay?! Slapping your *sister*?! *Seriously!?* Quit being a psycho twat!" Byron looked straight at Jake and held his gaze, "You threw that at her first," he pointed to the yogurt container on the ground, **"What'd'yah expect her to do?!—Turn around, smile and curtsey at you?!?! Don't be a massive**

jerk! ...quit being such an agro bogan all of the time!"

Byron was the "old soul", the voice of reason, the cool-headed one of the three kids who always kept them in-check with his mature and peaceful outlook on everything. With his arms still outstretched, he continued keeping his brother and sister apart with an almost Kung-Fu-Master-like force, "You guys really don't wanna start bashing the crap out of each other and causing a damn scene here in the middle of this bloody huge mess –do you?!".

He looked around at the neighbouring villas, "Think about it!" Then he looked back at the two of them, "You reckon the neighbours are gonna be happy about seeing this pigsty here, and then see you two knuckleheads fighting away in the middle of it all? – They'll be ringing mum up straight away – or the Police!"

Jake looked at Byron, with just a hint of a smile starting to emerge on his angry face, "Think I'd rather deal with the Police more than I would Mum! –Wouldn't you?" he asked.

Byron and Jacinta began to smile too. Then the three of them took pause for a moment to look around again at the abysmal mess they were standing in the middle of.

"Flossie sure did a number on the recycling bin this time!" said Jacinta allowing a small laugh to escape.

"Knocked-it for a six, is more like it!" added Byron. All three of them burst out laughing at how ridiculously messy the area actually was.

Jake stepped over to Jacinta, "Sorry Sis," he apologised, patting Jacinta on the shoulder a few times and nodding his head, "I was well out-of-order for tossing that at you.

You're cool," he paused, "and you're not a cow. Maybe a bit lazy, but not a cow—No harm done?"

"No harm Jakester," she laughed, "I was out of order too mate," she pointed to the 3-litre milk bottle, and in her own way of apologising back, she gave her brother a light punch on the arm, then added, "No hard feelings, we're cool. Although Byron here looks like he's gonna have *fifty-kittens!*"

"Hey! —I'm stressing here!" as he worriedly waved his hands around at the mess, "look at all of this! How're we ever gonna get this pigsty cleaned away before she gets back?! It's gonna take us ages!"

"Nice *Jazz-Hands* Byro!" teased Jacinta, as she jokingly copied his hands going everywhere. They burst-out laughing again.

Byron didn't mind laughing at himself. He knew he was kind of animated and overly expressive when he was emotional or stressed-out, "We've each got our own stupid ways of dealing with stressful situations," he replied, "at least I don't get angry or violent." He trailed off.

Jake looked around not knowing really where to start, "Oh man! This is such a crazy mess we got ourselves here!" He looked around at the landfill that was their front lawn, then looked at his watch, "well, let's get cracking-away then, or we're gonna be in a big, steaming pile of Brad Pitt if it's still here when mum gets back!"

Jacinta then blurted out in a loud, mimicking voice, raising her pointer finger up and pulling a silly face "BEANS! – IT WILL BE BEANS! — I TELL YOU! - BEANS – NO MODEM and BEANS – BEEEANNSSS-SAHH!" and they all cracked-up laughing again.

And so, very slowly they got to work tidying-up the mess up. They made a good team. They started to refill the recycling bin of its contents and one-by-one they packed-away their bikes, scooters and sporting gear into the garage. Some throwing and catching and horsing-around started to take over their activity, until that's all they were doing, just playing around, (but that's how it goes with kids of any age when they're tasked with tidying-up)

By the time they had actually finished tidying up the mess, they were immersed in combining and mixing sporting items together with recycling rubbish. They were mirthfully playing fun, made-up games and mimicking TV sports commentators as they clowned around. They tried to use the most ridiculously mismatched combinations of equipment they could find.

An old, plastic bowling-pin set, called Skittles, was introduced, and then discarded in favour of using 3 litre milk bottles in the same way as the pins. They partly filled the milk bottles with water for a more challenging play. Before long they had a really fun game going on. They decided to move it over from the small, grassed area they were playing on to the harder, concrete surface of the quiet, closed-off, residential road in front of their villa.

They had hit upon a game that was so much fun they couldn't stop playing it ...or laughing. They were improving on it as they went along, testing each other out by throwing different items while hurtling around on their scooters trying to hit the milk bottles, or "Skittles" as they were calling them now. An old skateboard came into play after a short while. A couple of tennis balls along with a lot of plastic milk bottles became the game's mainstay of "equipment".

Pretty soon they had organised the game's layout and rules. They had formulated a true mash-up of half a dozen different games all rolled into one. Part cricket and baseball, some lawn balls, they included bacchii as they always played that at the Italian club, some elements of badminton and tennis were also woven into it. They kept fetching different sporting items to experiment with and to see if this racket or that bat, or this type of ball, would make the game any better.

Discarding anything that didn't "flow" with the play of the game, they soon narrowed it down to a dozen, plastic, 3-litre milk bottles, 2 tennis balls, 1 old ping-pong racket and 2 old skateboards or scooters (they couldn't decide which was better, so they left it open to the player to choose) this became the final set of equipment used in their game.

Oh, and there was one final, very essential piece of "*equipment*" that had not been included in the game at this particular point in time.
This very essential "piece of equipment" was introduced some 30 minutes later after they had started playing the nearly final version of the game.
He came happily plodding up to them all, tail wagging, panting away excitedly alongside his owner, Marvin, just as the first few rounds of the new game were underway. He was a Golden Labrador and his name was Scoot.

As a puppy, Scoot was always getting into clothes baskets, into the pantry (or anywhere he could find food...Labradors!!!) and was always making a big mess everywhere. He was forever being told to "SCOOT" by Marvin's mum. There was no question as to what Marvin was going to name his dog thereafter. Scoot soon learnt his new name well. Although a lot of confusion did follow in the ensuing months, every time   Marvin's Mum yelled "SCOOT" because she'd found him making a mess somewhere or ransacking the pantry again.

Even though he was getting older now, Scoot still had tons of energy, good cheer and a lot of go-go-go still left in him yet.

It was Jacinta's turn to be "in" and as she threw the ball, Scoot instantly dashed off after it. He crashed over milk bottles and nearly knocked Byron off his feet chasing after the ball like a freight-train on legs. They burst-out laughing and bent over in noisy hysterics.

"Hey, does that count?" asked Jacinta laughing, "– I just knocked-out three Skittles in one go!"

"Only if we get to use him when we're in on-base next – does that sound fair?" asked Jake. They all nodded in agreement with big, excited grins on their faces. They couldn't wait to have a go at using Scoot! It was a classic example of a "lightbulb moment" that happens by accident...Except this lightbulb weighed 40-kgs and was covered in fur.

They hurriedly explained the rules of the game (*so far*) to Marvin, with one major change; Scoot would be included as a piece of equipment. The player who was "in" could now use him. Just like a big, four-legged "ball" that could be moved around by the player who was "on base", Scoot would take the game to a whole new level of fun.

Just then, Jake looked over and spotted the empty, 3 litre milk bottle that Jacinta had tossed at him. It gave him another idea.

He walked over to it and picked the bottle up, looked at it, then stopped to think for a moment, then he carried it over to the centre "run" or "pitch" of the game and said, "This bottle will officially mark the "Dog Base", this is where Scoot has to come back to and sit after he chases the ball, Ok?...is that cool?" They all looked at each other and laughed, then agreed before excitedly starting to play the very, final version of the game.

They did make one further, small adjustment. Marvin suggested that they place a cricket stump (a wooden, cylinder pole about 28 inches long) into the Dog Base's milk bottle so that it would have a counterbalance to offset the small amount of water they'd put in it to stop it from blowing away. It could now be knocked over more easily, and if it did get knocked over, then Scoot was "out" and he had to go and sit-down for the rest of the round, over on the sideline.

This was quite a clever idea because it gave the dog a well-deserved rest, and each time this did happen, which was quite often, the player who was "in" or "on-base" had to change-up his play-technique because he no longer had a dog to use.

They tied an old bandana to the top of the stump, just for laughs, and named it the "Dog-Flag". It gave the whole layout of the game a fun, unique look to it. But it also seemed to more clearly help the dog to know where he or she needed to run back to. A longer, bamboo gardening stick was then used instead of the cricket stump, and the bandana was swapped out for a larger square of canvas. It was now a proper flag.

They began playing with their new four-legged "piece of equipment" and they continued to roar with laughter and delight. Scoot had never been so engaged in playing with his human friends either.

They didn't stop laughing and they didn't stop playing until their mum had arrived back home from work with the Chinese take-away for their dinner late in the early evening, just as it was getting dark.

As she climbed out of Flossie, they could smell the delicious aroma of the lemon chicken and special fried rice and all the other dishes wafting out from the two, large bags she was carrying in her arms, (and they exhaled a quiet, mental sigh of relief knowing they wouldn't be eating cold beans on toast for dinner – with no internet).

Once she'd stepped down from Flossie, and had surveyed the area, she said with a smile "Well done guys! Good to see you've tidied that mess away!" then she looked over and asked, "What's that game you're playing there?" she was definitely in a much more relaxed and happier mood now than when she was before leaving to do her shift.

"It looks quite interesting, what's it called?" she commented as she closed the car door.

They shrugged as they hadn't really thought of a name for it yet. Then they looked over at Scoot sitting down on the grass cooling-off, looking very exhausted and panting away.

Jake replied, "Hasn't got a name yet mum, we just made it up. But it's a ton of fun that's for sure!"
"How about we call it Scoot?" Said Byron, looking over at Scoot.

Jacinta looked over at Scoot too. On one side of him was a large drinking bowl of water which he'd been thirstily lapping away at. On the other side was the old, plastic Skittles bowling set box that had the word "SKITTLES" written across it in super-large print.
Looking at the box and then at Scoot, Jacinta quickly said, "Let's call it *Scoot-Skittles*?!??" she looked around at the others for approval.

"YES! – That's it Sis!!!—that's an awesome name for it!" and they laughed and repeated the name several times over to each other.

"Scoot-Skittles Hey?" said their mum as she looked over at old Scoot and smiled. She talked to him directly, "Have you been teaching them how to play a new game beautiful? — Hey?" He looked at her panting and wagging his tail. She walked over to where he was sitting to give him a big pat and a smooch and he slowly climbed to his feet to return the attention.

"Who's a beautiful dog, yes you are! And a clever dog too! Giving the kids some exercise, aren't you clever!?!" She patted and rubbed his side, then patted his head, "Awww, I wish we had a dog like you!" Scoot was now sniffing the bag of Chinese takeaway expectantly. "No, not for you sorry. Not for dogs, but maybe you can have a few treats." She turned to face the kids.

"Come on gang, time to call it a day and have some dinner?"

"For sure!" they all replied in unison. And with that the first day's play had come to a close for the new Aussie sport of "Scoot-Skittles" ...that would soon spread throughout the world.

They continued playing the very next day, showing more kids in their street how the game went. They kept it crazy-fun, simple and uncomplicated. More kids and more dogs eventually joined in and with a few adjustments and modifications to the rules, such as the option for 1 to 3 dogs being allowed to join into play at any one time, a seriously awesome new game started to take-off.

Within a couple of weeks, it had exploded in popularity around the South Gold Coast area.

Kids, and their dogs, suddenly began to get a lot more exercise than they normally did.

That was how the game of Scoot-Skittles was created, and that's how it got its name.

And unbeknownst to everyone involved in the creation of the game on that day, they had each played a vital role in saving the human race, saving dogs and the world as we currently know it...

This crazy, fun, silly and simple kid's game would go on to spread throughout Australia, and eventually to the rest of the world.

...And yet, there was an even greater, unimaginable and unforeseen, hidden importance to it.

Scoot-Skittles would smash a crack in the wall that we are normally oblivious to when changes are secretly made to our current timeline by malicious time-travellers.

Scoot-Skittles would become a warning message.

It would become a cautionary note written on the shoreline of a sandy beach for humanity to decipher, while further out to sea, a gigantic, horrendous storm was brewing and beginning to make its way towards land.

As the storm crept closer to the coast, some would see the message written in the sand and would begin to bravely contribute in their own special way to saving everything that we hold dear in this life.

A Game Changer of a Game

Like a nuclear, chain reaction, friends began to introduce the game to other friends and other kids in their family. Learning how to play the game was easy (for kids) and practicing with other kids who lived nearby was absolutely necessary to developed better skills in the game.

It advanced into a healthy obsession. Street after street, block after block, empty car parks here and there, ovals, grassed areas, backyards and school playgrounds, kids everywhere started playing Scoot-Skittles with a newfound, outdoor, sporting obsession.

The spread of the game happened so fast in that ageless and classic kind of way that kids have for sharing something that's fun, new and unique.

It spread like gastro, or an outbreak of head-lice at a primary school, or a nasty strain of strep-throat in a high school. When kids are sharing something around, they waste no time. And when something becomes the next big "new thing" with kids, it explodes outwards and takes-off rapidly. Wherever the epicentre might be, it travels great distances in almost little to no time at all.
Scoot-Skittles became the next, big, *new sensation*. It was like the hula-hoop; roller skates; skateboards, yo-yos, pogo-sticks, ping pong, paddle-pops, Pokémon, skateboards, slinky craze – *you-name-the craze* – of the day. Scoot-Skittles was all of these crazes, all through the decades, all rolled-up into one for the kids of 2023.

The funniest part about it, the part that caused most adults to chuckle away to themselves, was that this particular craze hadn't been incubated and hatched-out by some oily, slick team of self-promoting marketeers in some profiteering, toy company somewhere; it hadn't been fabricated as a cruddy, hack-kneed, slapped together

Japanese kids animation that was nothing more than 30 minutes of lame advertising for some gimmicky, plastic – "gotta grab'em all!" toy line –or overpriced – "gotta buy the set!" of playing cards; or brittle, over-priced, break-easy, miniature, spinning-top set with a flimsy-thin, plastic "arena" lid to spin the crappy, little toys in, or some such similar junk — No rubbishy, animation-cartoons masquerading as TV shows that were actually just adverts, were responsible for promoting this craze.

This craze was started by kids, for kids and with just one aim in mind: to *have as much fun as possible playing the game,* and nothing else.

No corporate greed, no profit-and-loss margins, no "*Bottom-Line*", no sales strategies, *nothing* had control over Scoot-Skittles.

It belonged to kids everywhere, they collectively owned it and they controlled it.
The "*suits*" were shut out from profiteering from it. No matter how they tried, they just couldn't devise a way to get-a-foot-in-the-door to monetize on it.

Kids purposely boycotted any commercial competitions set-up by businesses and corporations. In almost a religious kind of way, they shunned any organised sponsorship or attempts to set up clubs. Organised, commercial competitions and being sponsored was looked upon as super-lame, dorky, crappy and very uncool.

Like a puritanical movement, the game could only be played by teams of friends or classmates in a not-for-profit format. No prizes, no trophies, *nothing*, just a good, sporting handshake at the end of it and the fun of having played the game against another group of kids who knew the game too.

Parents really had a good laugh about this. Empty, plastic 3-litre milk bottles, old scooters or skateboards of any sort, some chalk and a few cheap, old tennis balls and a dog (or three) of any breed were all that kids needed to play this crazy game. Parents didn't have to spend diddly-squat

It could even be played at school without using scooters or skateboards –or a dog –as school rules mostly prohibited these three things on school grounds.

Kids just ran on foot instead of riding scooters, while someone would be the "the dog" (which made it quite funny) –The game still went on at school, but not nearly half as much fun as the dynamic "proper" version played with dogs, skateboards and scooters.

Independent dairy farmers couldn't have been more stoked. In a neat twist of good karma — that's kids for you — the cheap three-litre milk bottles used by the big corporate supermarkets were *not* the ones children preferred for Scoot-Skittles. Those bottles belonged to the very chains that had driven down the price of milk per litre by underpaying producers, causing years of grief for independent dairy farmers.

Instead, the bottles that worked best for the game came from small dairy collectives. Their milk cost a little more, but it was sold in a unique bottle shape that turned out to be absolutely perfect for Scoot-Skittles. Sales surged to record highs. As a bonus, kids developed a taste for milk that was fuller, creamier, and simply much better.

Parents were also happy because they witnessed their kids going outside and playing in the fresh air. They didn't have to spend a cent in order for their kids to be part of this new craze, aside from buying a lot of milk, which kids started drinking a lot more of as a net result.

Even though it had been almost a year since this new game rapidly took-off in popularity, not many adults could truly follow the logic of the game.

Mums and Dads didn't have a clue really as to how it actually was played. There was no apparent logic to any part of it. You sure couldn't get an understanding just from watching it.

Most parents figured it would probably be the same for an American person trying to figure-out what was going on in a game of Aussie cricket or an Australian trying to figure-out what the heck an American NFL game was all about.

Even though they were clueless about how it was played, the universal appeal to them was that it got the kids away from those execrable screen tablets and phones that they'd all been so worryingly glued to for so long.

Finally, something had snapped and the spell of computer games and social media and of burying their heads in their screens all of the day, was broken. Social media and the "digital world" had no more influence over the lives of younger kids.

Suddenly, all of that digital stuff wasn't cool anymore and they just didn't want it – didn't want to use it – didn't want to have it – didn't want to be a part of it. It was so absolutely and *totally* **uncool**.

All of that online stuff was just for "*uncool twats*" now.

All of it was *lame* and it was so "*hipster daggy*" in the eyes of the youth.

No one wanted to have a smart phone, use their computer (much…except to do homework and send basic emails) and all of this made their grandparents and all their "old-world" retro activities and things that the elderly seniors did, seem totally avant-garde, cool, refreshing and new.

In the eyes of this new generation of kids, their elderly grandparents were the coolest, full-on, totally "hip" & switched-on "with-it" people around…They did all this cool, awesome stuff and they knew about all these totally unreal things, and they'd been on all these different, real-world, awesome adventures during their lives.

Kids started looking at hipsters, millennials and all the other slightly older generation of wannabe-cool, drop-kick grown-ups populating the ranks of the over 18 to 30's age-group as just dumb, delusional, herd-minded, digitally-addicted sheep trying to be cool—but failing…in every, pretentious, stupid, fake thing they did.

They were so laughably caught-up in their dramatically structured online world of fakery, finding whatever contrived narrative and dramatic horse-crap they could align themselves with and position their social-media presence into for the sake of virtue signalling to the rest of the world…online.

They lived in their false, social media echo-chambers, feeding on the shallow nutrients of commentary, addicted to taking selfies, *thinking* they were *so-so-so-cool* doing whatever the "in" thing was to be doing at that "trending" moment in time…Or setting trends as "social influencers" –who were, to the younger kids, the most disgusting, uncool "dweeble-snots" to walk the face of the planet.

Although many grandparents did use the internet –and phones, it was always just used by them in a very limited, minimal, pragmatic kind of way…which was now the coolest way to use it…Kids had come to hate the overuse of smart-phones – it was disgustingly uncool and so cringey to be seen holding onto a phone like it was a bottle of life-saving medicine that the person could urgently need at any given moment.

To these young kids, paying in cash and having coins in your pocket, and having proper purses and wallets was hip –and nothing was more uncool than paying by using a card or paying with a phone. Kids were given phones by their parents, and the phones were left in their boxes. They just didn't want or need to use them anymore.

It was also **so *massively uncool*** to use the internet full-on and spend time on it, socially or otherwise. Young kids just didn't want anything to do with going online at-all. **They just hated ALL digital activity** and adopted a global Zeitgeist for their age group where they just didn't want to use any social media, "smart" devices or screens of any sort anymore.

They developed a strong, group aversion to having screens, tablets or any other smart devices – including digital games and game systems. Communicating on the internet or by digital phone became *totally lame*– even text messaging someone became *mammoth-lame*! – Instagram (or X as it was supposed to be called) was *a* massive joke to these younger kids who laughed hysterically at all the millennial, Instagram "Hipsters" viewing them as complete, pretentiously false and *daggy, old,* poncy tossers – whom they referred to as the farts and tarts brigade. Instagram was for *dumb—slutty-mum-bum-models* and narcissistic, tattooed assclowns lost in love with their biceps and their own fabricated, poncey-macho personas and false, bullcrap images.

This new wave of younger kids, all craved and wanted "real" in their world. Success, to them, was not how many idiots liked you on Instagram, Tic-Tok or FB...It was living your best life with true authenticity.

Just like tattoos, Hitler-style-hair-dos, manicured-beards, vapid-Botox stares above droll, squid-lipped-inflated duck-lips and ANY Botox, filler, cosmetic surgery or vain surgical-stupidity that of any sort the older mob used (always showcased on social media along with their virtue-signalling causes) this new movement of modern kids now looked at any form of social media and digital communication as horridly *uncool*.

Even films and TV shows had begun to bore them, due to the uncreative, politically charged, message obsessed drivel that was constantly being pumped out by the studios, streaming channels and their potato headed writing teams and showrunners, trying to pass their muck off as entertaining and original.

Now kids played outdoors until it got dark, or it rained, and then they selectively read books and comics from the past. They started listening to early Blues, Jazz, 20's, through to 70's and 80's music and maybe as far as some of the early 90's. They borrowed music from their grandparents and listened along with them on their old record players, cassette and CD players. They watched old 80's and earlier films on DVDs and even on prehistoric VHS tapes.

The bland, droll, uncreative, crappy drivel of an excuse for music that was being foisted upon them in the present day was now recognised for what it was...absolute, sheer, dead-assed, uncool, demonic vomit.

Kids got into making campfires at night in their backyards and sitting around and talking with each other in person, and none of them had a phone on them to pull-out and take a selfie with so they could show-off what they were doing...they didn't care anymore.

"Smart" devices were now considered totally stupid and lame by kids everywhere. They were socialising with each other properly, like in the "old days", the way people had always communicated before the digital-tech-age had been squeezed-out by big business onto the public like a big dog squatting on a front lawn and squeezing out a massive crap.

Unlike so many ignorant, *uncool* grown-ups who had sat there for the last 25 plus years - 24/7 with their narcissistic faces glued to their stupid phones, kids were now re-developing strong verbal communication skills and learning how to naturally talk verbally with each other in one-to-one settings in-person.

They were now verbally telling jokes, doing funny things, having a proper laugh and instead of texting ROFL, they were actually rolling on the floor laughing in front of each other for real.

Kids were hanging out with each other in the real world, all of the time, having real experiences, like people are supposed to do, without a phone to be seen anywhere in anyone's hands.

They were learning to be real and sincere with each other.

They did not project false, idealistic personas like so many older people were addicted to doing. Kids were riding their bikes over to each other's houses so they could get enough of them together for a Scoot-Skittles game, you needed at least 5 kids to play a decent game...and a dog (or three)

Laughter, shouts, cries, and dogs barking and playing with kids in the street once again filled the air like it once had done a long time ago in a much nicer, easier going timeline in a yesteryear era, long, long before. Something wonderful had been brought back to life again in the world.

It was like humanity's soul had been handed back to it in a rustic, seagrass woven basket.

Something horrible, pretentious and rancid had been purged like explosive diarrhoea, flushed away and sent to where it belonged by this much younger generation.

A morose darkness had been lifted over the future of kids and the way they would go about living their lives as adults.

In more ways than one, kids had taken back control of their own lives, their thoughts and their actions rescued from an extraneous and nefarious barrage of influences, leaving it to just their parents, teachers and elders within their families and communities to influence them.

The happiness and liveliness of kids running around and playing merrily outside had begun to fill suburbs everywhere...Just like a bell or bells ringing, it had a harmonic resonance that was healing and uplifting the world.

Kids were actually starting to feel happier and more fulfilled. They were doing better at school and were interacting with each other and their parents in a more compassionate, decent and respectful way.

Some say, it was connected to the bringing back of the ringing of the bells, it was a knock-on effect of this global movement.

All across the world, in many, many countries, advocate groups had restored, rebuilt and reinstated the governing laws to allow the ringing of bells once again in belltowers everywhere.

The sounds of loud ringing bells were welcomed back by people of all creeds, all denominations and all religions everywhere (except for the Luciferian cults and satanists, who hated them). It seemed the sound of bells ringing was something so soothing and missed by so many people, at some very deep and profound level, and welcomed by so many more who had never heard bells ringing before. For just under two years, there had been a continual ringing of bells everywhere across the world.

Lunchtime bells, six O'clock bells, and Sunday mass bells – just about any occasion, it didn't matter – they rang those bells everywhere and they rang them loudly.
No matter where you were, off in the distance, or nearby, or very close and loudly nearby, bells would ring.

And it felt so **good** when they did ring!

Even in the suburbs, off in the distance, folks could hear the ringing bells.

Any quiet street, on any afterschool weekday, weekend or school holiday, was now also filled with the sounds of kids all madly playing away at scoot-skittles, often in unison with the sounds of the bells ringing.

This warm, hazy, mid-October Sunday afternoon in Seabee Close was no exception. It was one of those spring days where you just felt that winter had finally buggerd-off and once again you were feeling the warmth of an early hint of a beautiful summer lapping around the edges of your shoes, slowly soaking into your bones.

Your spirit filled with a growing contentment.

All the awesome fun and enjoyment of the Christmas School Holidays was not far off—and you just knew it was only around the corner – *you felt it*.

Kids everywhere began smiling on the inside, not so much even realising why they were feeling so stoked, just that they had this overwhelming sense of being filled up with an incredible level of cheer and contentment.

Springtime Healing

Coolangatta, Saturday November 16th, 2024

Sherri watched her buddies, who lived on her street, happily playing away. She was sitting comfortably only a short distance away from the activity.

A raised mound of grass on her front lawn faced onto the cul-de-sac, nestled under the shade of an old coolabah tree that covered almost the entire front yard. It was a perfect and pleasant spot for her to watch-on from.

The warm sunshine had also been soaking into the rich, oily leaves of the eucalyptus variety she was sitting under, cocooning her with the scent and blanketing her with its canopy of shade from the overhanging branches.

The air surrounding her was filled with that calming and soothing eucalyptus smell. Magpies were trilling and singing away. Crickets ticked their lazy, metronomic rhythm of summertime tick-tocking that could almost induce hypnosis, and cicadas blended their shimmying synthesiser ambient sounds into the relaxing summertime-sounds of a classic, atmospheric "mixtape" capturing our carefree, Aussie, childhood lives, making it all so blissfully and overwhelmingly:
"Ahhh, here comes Summer…again…at last!"

A light sea breeze had started to blow in from the cool afternoon ocean, hush-shushing lightly through the leaves of the trees….

The halcyon days of an Aussie summer are quite a specific code of sights, sensations and smells that every Aussie kid worth their weight in a barbequed sausage topped over with tomato sauce and then wrapped in a slice of bread with a splash of fried onions on top; or a serve of fish and chips by the sea for dinner, or surfing on an old snapped-off, half foamie surfboard, old beach houses, caravans, tents and shacks, caravan parks, and summertime, school holiday fun, knows only too well.

Everything had a familiar, healing and pleasant effect on Sherri, and on this particular day, it was just what she needed. Good memories ebbed and flowed into her spirit. She couldn't have been more content just sitting there, watching her neighbourhood friends, a familiar site, seeing all of them busily laughing and joking around as they played in the sunshine.

All of it, the completeness of everything, was doing a great job of cheering her up.

And she so desperately needed this right now, so, so much.

Her leg was still aching under the cast and her back and ribs ached beyond measure too, a lot worse than what she was letting on to everyone.

The cast ran from her upper thigh all the way down to her foot. Her tippy-toes were left sticking-out of the cumbersome mass of plaster that had been her leg for the past two months. She had been working very hard every day wriggling her toes and flexing her leg muscles beneath the cast as best she could.

Although the continual therapy training had started to become a bit of a drag, she valued the good it was doing her and knew she would appreciate hitting the ground running (maybe not quite literally) when the cast finally came off.

At least now, she thought appreciatively, she was able to move around without needing a wheelchair like she had done immediately after the accident.

There was still the awkward embarrassment to deal with when she was in a busy, public place. The few times she had been coerced by her dad to come out for a drive to Pacific Fair and Robina Shops with him, just to get her out of the house, had turned into gruelling marathons in battling self-consciousness and mental and physical endurance.

People would stare, although most of them would try not to. Her whole body would ache with the effort. She felt like an old, tired, worn-out pirate with a peg-leg. The bandaging covering her injured eye, black in colour, only exacerbated the feeling that she did indeed look just like a pirate.

Doc Merrington had told her to go easy on it when getting around, she needed to give the bone time to heal and to knit itself together properly. Paradoxically, she also needed to move as much as possible to limit her muscles from wasting away. It was a juggling act between resting the leg and not thumping it around like a battering ram, yet also keeping it moving and progressively having it bear more weight to stop any complications from developing after the cast came off.

Resting carefully in her lap, as she sat there on the front lawn, was an item which for her held the entire weight of the world.

The small cardboard box that she held ever so gently, contained more pain and recuperation than a hundred plaster casts. She dared not look down at the box, nor in it, because she was trying very hard, at least for today, to be content in this lovely spring moment, and trying to not let herself break down crying again.

The mental and physical drain and pain of crying was getting too much for her. She also wanted her friends playing in the street, who were so kind and caring with helping her– who were the best, the most understanding, and the most absolute good natured buddies a kid could ever want to have, she thought – they were like some kind of magic medicine given to her each day as a gift from God, so that she could slowly begin to heal again.

Even though she didn't want to look down at the box, or open it, she also didn't want to take her hands off it. It was her own, personal, Catch-22 dilemma that she was stuck in.

Sherri needed to keep physical contact with it, especially sitting here on the front lawn, right where she was.

Because this was _their_ spot.

This was where they had always sat together on so many perfect days just like this one. Warm sunny days, full of promise and fun. She needed to be touching the only physical item left of him.

Her mind, her heart and her soul were drifting and shifting through time a little. The painkillers had been causing her to space-out somewhat. Yet she remained aware and fixed like an anchor to the space she was in – for it was here, that she allowed herself to acknowledge, here in this spot that required no changing by her imagination, no mental alterations or additives were needed to be done to anything to this spot here, because "the here" was perfect – only "the now" – the actual place in time itself, was something that needed a slight bit of an imaginative adjustment to get it right.

Here on this grassy spot was their special _"chilling-out-together-space"_, they had so many of these all around the house, but this one, without question, was their absolute favourite "space".

Her heart began to form a feeling in her mind that was almost a solid version of him through time, sitting right next to her as he always did.

He was once again, just like he had always been, sitting close by her side, bumped up against her, leaning his heavy torso against her: A big, cuddly, golden, furry rock with a shiny, wet, black nose.

He was a definite manifestation, and she surprisingly didn't burst out crying at the imagined presence of him sitting there in this time-space, despite how real his presence felt to her.

She thought she could even smell his fur and his dog-breath.

Instead of resisting this partial hallucination, she sailed along with it and let her heart just feel the overwhelming reassurance and sense of love that he gave to her just by being there.

In her mind she reached over and casually draped her arm over his back, lazily resting her hand on his head. She even began to lazily scratch behind his big, velvety ears.

Love was all she felt. Overwhelming love, and it was soaking into her soul and her bones more than the warmth of this spring day ever could. It soothed her and it was helping her to heal her broken body and her broken, grieving heart.

She looked around to see if her mum was there too, she knew she was, somewhere, probably inside helping dad, but for now it was just her and old Zeb – like always.

He sat there in spirit, helping her as he'd always done in life, to be strong, to laugh, to enjoy living and to relish the simple things in this life that each day can bring to us;

a walk on the beach or in the park,

food (of any sort and in any quantity – she laughed a little at his drooling love for food, the anguished look on his face waiting for a scrap to be handed to him from the table,

a cuddle every moment of the day that you can spare was always a must do!

And just simply, constantly being with that someone who you unconditionally love so much beyond words, sitting quietly there by your side…

Just being with you –that's all you need to make this world right…

The simple pleasure of just being cuddled-up next to the person who you love most in life…

…When God made a dog, he didn't just sprinkle a little tiny drop of this essence into their collective K9 souls. He shovelled it in until he'd lost count of how many shovel loads he'd put in there…then he kept going for a few shovels more, just to be sure…

As the sea breeze cooled the front yard, his spirit willed her to be strong and to be brave. A bond between them that was as old as time itself, was healing and uplifting her.

"Man's best friend!" she whispered into the empty space next to her.
"This girl's best friend too!"

Then in a flash came the overpowering crying again, followed by the howling that she couldn't control anymore. Why did she allow her herself to do that?! Huh? – Again!?

Her injured stomach, her ribs and her back all began to hurt so painfully from the unstoppable crying. This was why she took the painkillers, mostly for when this emotional crying storm took a hold of her, frequent as it was, unleashing squalls of sharp pain on her injuries, particularly in her ribs.

Hannah, her best friend, who had been carefully watching her out the corner of her eye while she was playing, ever vigilant, yet allowing Sheri some space, worried she was getting a bit smothered lately, ran quickly over to her. Hannah was a year older than Sherri and was always extremely sensible and pragmatic, a good, positive influence. The first thing she did was to sit down next to Sheri, on the side of her good leg, and give her a hug. She said nothing. She did nothing. She just hugged her and knew this was the best and only thing she could do for her friend right now. Just give her a hug.

All of the other kids came over and sat around Sheri, while a couple of them knew the drill and went calmly and quickly inside to get Sheri's dad. They all knew exactly what to do.

The car accident had tragically taken her mum and Zeb. She still had her friends and her dad. They were the miracle that had been keeping her alive.

Just like spring brings new hope –her friends brought her the new hope she so desperately needed – they were her special form of springtime, after having barely survived a cold and horrible winter.

Time's Greatest Task
Gold Coast Hospital – 10:30 am
Thursday December 5th, 2024

Summer was here quite early in full swing, and the humidity had gone through the roof.

There was that rotten itch *–again*! - under the cast– and she knew no manner of contraption – no super large knitting needle (her last attempt at using one of these to get at an itch that was too far down her leg to scratch with her finger, had almost seen it become irretrievably stuck down the inside of her cast.

Doc Merrington would have made her feel like a toddler – again! —had she not of been able to retrieve it with a pair of cooking tongs – which also nearly become stuck too! – She shuddered to imagine the embarrassment of it all if she had to go back and visit the orthopaedic surgery – ***again*** – to remove a pair of cooking tongs and also a knitting needle.

She could still picture Doc Merrington's smirk and the way he tilted his head slightly when she had last managed to get a wooden stationary ruler trapped inside the cast and insisted, she was "being very careful."

He used a special set of long, thin forceps to remove the offending, wooden 30-cm school ruler...concluding the extraction with a loud "Tssssk!"

But her mood was elevated beyond words because today was the day she was actually getting the damn thing removed ...at last! The indignities of the last few weeks no longer weighed in on her. She was as giddy-as-a-billy-goat today—lightheaded with relief. The cast was coming off. *Finally.*

The X-rays had come back clear and positive. Everything was perfectly healed and good as new again. Her bones, once splintered and seemingly destroyed in places, had knitted themselves back together again with a quiet perseverance.

Like a small cut that stops bleeding when you're not looking at it, her body had been healing steadily beneath the plaster and the bruises.

Her chest no longer ached with every breath, and she could twist, lean, and laugh without that sharp stab under her ribs.

It was almost miraculous how normal she felt.

The truth was that the healing hadn't been just physical. Something deeper had begun to shift, too. The panic attacks had faded into quiet memories. She could now sleep through the night without jolting awake at phantom impacts or imagined screams.

She knew there would be some stiffness, and her leg muscles would take at least another six weeks to gain back their full strength—*but no more cast!*

She still had some scars though —small ones along her temple and hairline, a patch of skin on her left forearm that would never quite look the same again.

There was a long, bumpy scar-line that ran from her lower left rib all the way around and down to her lower back. While the seatbelt she had been wearing had saved her life, the edge of it had had also cut sharply and lacerated her body due to the extreme forces of the impact's inertia.

The long scar looked like a samurai had taken a swipe at her with his katana.

And her eye... that was the other thing. The vision in her right eye was better now—*functional*, at least—but the blurriness would come and go, like an old radio trying to find its frequency. Some days it was sharp and clear. Others, it felt like she was looking at the world through a thin veil of smoke.

The specialists had said it might improve further, or it might not. Either way, she was learning to live with it. Adjusting. Accepting.

As the nurse prepared her cast on the support —a small, whirring device that looked like a children's toy more than a surgical tool was brought over by Doc Merrington —she felt a flutter of nerves in her stomach. It wasn't fear, not really. It was something softer. Like reverence. Like crossing a threshold. The Doc was vanquishing her tormenting oppressor; it would be gone in less than a minute or two.

The cast came off with the smell of body odour, plaster-dust and antiseptic. Her leg, pale and thinner than she had remembered it to be, looked almost foreign to her. But it was *hers*. Her skin. Her healing. Her freedom. She flexed her foot slowly. Then her ankle.

Welcome back, she thought.

Time, that slow and stubborn old companion, had done its work. And so had she.

She didn't feel like her old self. Not exactly.
She felt like someone new.
Someone stronger.
Someone still healing.

But healing and getting a lot tougher, nonetheless.

Emotionally too, she was feeling more adjusted and positive. She was experiencing happiness and learning to see the many positive things in life again.

The Ultimate Mandela Effect
Kirra Beach 9:20-p.m
Tuesday 21st January – 2025

A beautiful, light, refreshing sea breeze was blowing-in off from the ocean, cooling everything down after another blistering-hot summer's day. Across Australia, daytime temperatures at this time of the year could get to 40 degrees Celsius over lunchtime… (Just in the shade alone!)

School was due to go back again after almost two months off over the Christmas holidays.

In a weeks' time, kids from kindergarten to primary and high school, right through to university, would all begin their first days of the new school year in the sweltering hot, summer's weather…a not so perfect way to end a long holiday.

A time of great hardship and stress for Aussie kids everywhere, having to end their carefree, summertime break and head-off back to the grind of school once again.

However, it was also a time of great rejoicing and relief for Aussie parents everywhere. Having endured and suffered these last few weeks of the holiday madness, putting-up with the kids at home all day long, bickering with each other, fighting, messing-up the house above-and-beyond its normal level of "mess", constantly asking to be taken somewhere (always at an expensive cost)

Watching night-time TV out on the back patio, Sherri was starting to feel quite bored. These last remaining weeks of the holidays felt like a delicious chocolate cake that she'd eaten too much of. Now she was hungry for something more nutritious. Although she loved being able to read all day and go for a surf whenever she wanted to, and hang-out with her friends and watch movies, her mind was missing the learning and the structure of a good teacher and the challenges of a classroom.

At nine o'clock at night, the day had almost rid itself of the horrible, overpowering heat and humidity, and everything was starting to cool-off just a little.

Most summer evenings could be relatively mild, peaceful and pleasant. A light sea breeze was acting like a natural air-conditioner on everything, progressively washing away the vast pockets of hot air that sat above the land.

With just the sound of the crickets, the breeze and the distant hushing and rumble of the waves on the beach, Sherri lay there watching a very intense, ABC current affairs report on the escalating border-war between China, India and Pakistan.

She had just started to close her lids and doze off when…

 "Sherri — you there? –Sherri? —Crazy Uncle Frank's on the phone," her dad called out from his study-office.
He stood up, walked out of the room and began looking around for her, "Sherri?" he paused, then kept on talking away on the phone, figuring she'd be on her headphones somewhere where she couldn't hear him.

"Yeah, Yeah, exactly— same here! Just keeps dropping every week! I'm off-loading every share I've got before it's too late, buying-up gold," he walked into the kitchen and switched on the light, "And I'm also topping-up my old Chinese bank account with as much renminbi as I can," He walked over to the kitchen bench. He removed a Tupperware cover from the cheesecake they'd had for desert. "Yep! – Too right you are, there's no way in hell you wanna miss that boat!"

"Sherri?" He looked out the kitchen window and saw the soft glow of the TV screen lighting the patio area and knew exactly where she was. He collected a slice of cheesecake and headed out there.

"It just went 21 Aussie dollars to the renminbi now! That's Russia and half a dozen other countries backing it," he paused, "Yeah, yeah, I know, I heard yesterday—bloody Kiwis! Dancing into C.A.R.F.A like a bunch of Hari-Krishnas dancing into a temple with bells on their feet!

Like lambs to the slaughter if you ask me! —Australia's going to be next I tell you!" he took a bite of the cheesecake as he listened.

"Yeah? —Really?! - You don't reckon?" He studied the cheesecake in his hand, then said, "suppose we'll never break free of those Wall-Street scumbags..."

He paused and took a bite of the cheesecake, "How about you mate, you Ok there in Honkers?" He chewed away as he listened to the reply.

"Bugger, that's no good! When are you getting-out?" another pause, — "Glad to hear it."

He walked over to Sherri, "Ok, well, hurry-up and get back here! ...We'll be here when you do." He paused, "Yep, Ok, yeah, no worries. Give us a call when you get in. Just wait at passenger pick-up and I'll drive around the corner and get you. You're flying into Coolangatta, right?" pause, — "Excellent! – can't bloody stand driving all the way up there to Brisbane Airport ...and paying their rip-off parking fees!"

Sherri had almost fully dozed off when she heard her dad talking away.

"Hey dad, What's up?" She said groggily.

She was snuggly curled-up in the large cushion on one of the old, cane, papasan chairs directly in front of the TV.

Her dad walked over to the satellite dish shaped chair she was laying in and perched himself on the edge of it.

The patio was the perfect temperature, as the lingering heat of the day still hadn't quite gone from the house yet. The mozzies and the other nighttime creepy-crawlies were kept at-bay by the flyscreen enclosure surrounding the patio. The cool breeze, the crickets, the distant sound of the waves and the ABC "Four Corners" current affairs show flickering away on the old, tube-screen TV, gave the patio an extremely cosy feel.

"Here she is mate, got herself the coolest place in the house of course! It's been hot as hell here today," he paused, then looked at Sherri thoughtfully, "She's fine mate. Really, she's fine. Thanks for asking. Yeah, I know...Ok, will do...Talk to yah later then buddy, take care" He handed the phone over to Sherri,

"It's Crazy Uncle Frank," He whispered to her loudly.

"I figured that dad," She whispered loudly back to him, then smiled, "who else is gonna be on the phone with you at this time of night?"

She sat up and gave him a quick hug and a kiss before taking the phone from him. Her dad laughed, got up and went back to his study.

"Hello Crazy Uncle Frank – How're you going there?"

"Good sweetheart! —I'm going fine! ...And what did I say before about calling me Uncle.... makes me feel like such an old fart...I don't mind you calling me crazy though, everybody else does!"

"Ok ...in that case...*Hello Crazy Frank*— is that better?" She chuckled away.

"That's much better! —Are you back at school yet Shez?"

"Nope, still got another two weeks to go ...*so bored!*"

"Hah! You kids don't know how good you've got it. What I wouldn't give to have a nice, long holiday like that!"

Sherri laughed, "You'd get bored Uncle Frank! Just like I am now," she laughed again, "I don't suppose you want to shout me to a trip up there for a week or so's holiday in Honkers. That'd brighten-up my last week and a bit of the holidays!"

He laughed too, "Any other time Shez, I'd be only too happy to," his laugh didn't last very long as a sad and serious tone filled his voice.

 "Hong Kong's not safe anymore sweetie. I wish it wasn't the case, but it's been getting worse every day since the war started in India and since China fired missiles into Pakistan. It's chaos and violence, ethnic gangs and factions, militias and Chinese army all shooting the place up. All hell's broken loose here among the ethnic groups. You got gangs and militias shooting it out with police and PRC soldiers, it's gotten so dangerous. I'm pretty sure that any day now China is gonna declare martial law here, then everything's gonna hit the fan fast. I'm getting the hell out."

"Are you alright? —Will you be alright?" She nervously asked.

"I'm fine for now Shez, really, I'm fine. Don't worry. I'm being very careful and working as fast as I can to get myself, my team of people and equipment out. Some people think it's all a storm in a teacup and it will all calm down soon. I think it's going to last longer, and get a heck of a lot worse, and I'm not hanging-around to find-out. So, I'm working-on getting the hell outa here now!"

"How soon is that Uncle Frank?"

"I've just got some bags to pack and I'm busy organising the sea-freight on some stuff that's too heavy to send by post. Takes time. I don't want to leave anything behind that's got special sentimental value or would cost too much to replace ...and that's nearly everything I own!" he perked-up a little, "Hey, keep your eye-out for some equipment that's on its way to you already."

"Ok, I will. But when exactly are *you* getting here?"

"Probably within the next few days sweetheart," he paused for what seemed like ages.

She knew he was collecting his thoughts. His voice had a distinctive sadness to it whenever he spoke in this manner and tone. "But that's not the only reason why I called you Sherri ...far worse things are starting to happen around the world ...there's something else that's got me particularly worried. More so than every damn country doing everything they can to kick-start a nuclear World War. I really need to explain this to you ...something very strange I believe is going to start happening all over the place ...and...I'm worried that if it does ..."

Frank had been carefully studying what was going on around the world in recent months from his specialised laboratory on Lantau Island. He understood the connections and the overlaps of the multiverses only too well. Using specially advanced equipment and technology that he'd invented, he carefully kept-an-eye on the "evil ones" and what they were doing, what they were up to and setting into play, and what they thought they were getting away with in complete secrecy. Their arrogance and absolute power made them think that no other living soul knew what they were doing. However, Crazy Uncle Frank and his team of colleagues at 'Orange Sand" were watching them the whole time.

Orange-Sand had been carefully taking measurements of the congruence's that would ripple across the world and affect life as we knew it. Uncle Frank had been studying the fabric of Sherri's timeline to calculate and restore a suitable timeline for her...A better one.

They were secretly restoring balance to the world and humanity.

The reintroduction of large bells ringing in almost every country had been by no means an arbitrary, random movement.

Orange-Sand had imbedded key assets in every group and invested vast sums of money and manpower into making the global change.

Everything was beginning to go about resetting itself in patterns of positive, emotional flux. Life was flexing off its muscles to try and ward off the horrible attack that was coming, it was reinserting love, happiness and togetherness anywhere it could and in any form of temporal restoration possible. Reality was bracing itself for a storm in the most extraordinarily and wonderful kind of way.

While she was listening, Sherri happened to look up and over to the kitchen window. She could just make out her dad, he was back in the kitchen again, getting some more cheesecake, "Dad, you've already had four pieces of that tonight!" She yelled, "Save some for me or I'm ringing your binge-eating sponsor this second!"
But the brightness of the TV screen and being so sleepy and tired had made her *think* it was her dad that she was looking at...

But it wasn't... Someone else was standing there in the kitchen.

Her jaw dropped and she froze, gasping in disbelief and fear.

Just when she thought she was getting emotionally better. She was now clearly seeing another person standing there in the kitchen, eating a slice of cheesecake, casual as can be!

It was a woman. She had a pleasant, relaxed expression on her face. She was busily tidying up while looking out the window and smiling at Sherri, just like she had always done before.

Sherri froze...

"You there Sweetheart? Sherri? You, Ok? — Sherri? ...Sherri?" The long pause of silence had frightened Uncle Frank, "Sherri? —say something."

Sherri was in absolute shock. She didn't react in any particular way, instead she resorted to a slightly robotic, emotionless manner of facing a terrifying situation. She whispered very slowly and calmly into the phone,

"Ummm, I'm still here Uncle Frank…But" She drew in a deep breath, then a few sobs escaped from somewhere, "I've just started hallucinating again, just now, here, like I was before, and it's really, really bad this time.' She sobbed a few more times. Her semi-trance-like state had automatically prevented her from bursting into tears. Shock was setting-in quite fast.

"Listen sweetheart, listen very, very carefully: I know what's happening to you there, I really do," He paused, "who do you think it is you can see there?"

He then quickly added, "Is it your mum? Is that who you can see?" before Sherri had time to reply.

"Umm …Yes?! …yeah, that's exactly who I can see …clear-as-the-day …and now you're freaking me out too, even more!" she replied, then took a short breath in, "How the hell did you know that's who I could see?!" she asked, then continued before Uncle Frank had time to answer, "I thought it was dad!—or maybe it is? …is it? … I don't know, I'm freaking out here, I'm so tired … my eyes have started playing horrible tricks on me right now Uncle Frank cos I swear I can see mum standing there in the kitchen …washing dishes and smiling at me like she always did!" Sherri sobbed a few more times, tears were rolling down her cheeks, "This is really hurting me to see her Uncle Frank …I just don't need this again! I've been feeling so much better lately! Why is my mind doing this to me again?! How do I make it stop?!?"
Silence.

—"Uncle Frank? You there? I'm really losing it here… I'm going bonkers! —I don't want to move …I'm seeing ghosts right now!" She began to heavily sob but then felt her anxiety and hypotension start to rise-up faster and completely override her crying, stopping it from getting any worse. This, Sherri knew, would eventually cause her to become completely immobilised, then pass-out.

It had happened to her on several occasions before, and she had discovered from these past episodes, that saying the Lord's Prayer helped to calm her down. It had a soothing effect on her runaway anxiety.

"Our Father, who art in heaven— hallowed be thy name ..." she began saying the prayer.

It had started with the trauma of the accident. Initially, when the paramedics arrived on the scene, Sherri was semi-conscious. They quickly began treating her for neurogenic spinal-shock and brain trauma due to her immobility, disorientation, detachment and numbness throughout her entire body.

Although she did have spinal bruising and head trauma, as well as severe lacerations to her torso, face and eyes and multiple fractures, she had also fallen into an acute, stress reaction "ASR" episode too. These psychological symptoms of her trauma had made the physical symptoms of her trauma seem far more critical than they actually were to the attending paramedics.

Since the accident, Sherri had fallen into several episodes of severe fear and anxiety that resulted in her freezing-up and then passing out. After a series of ambulance rides to the emergency ward, she was finally diagnosed and treated for ASR and had started to see a trauma councillor. The episodes had eventually stopped and she had not had one for almost two months.

Until now...

"Sherri, listen to me sweetheart! Don't shut down, you hear me?! Don't you shut down! ...Stay with me on the phone!"

Too late, she could feel the slow, numb, coma-like feeling beginning to engulf her, protecting her from her runaway thoughts and emotions. It was automated, methodical and it was systematically closing her mind down.

"Sherri?! –Stand up! – Please! ...You hear me? Stand up on your feet young lady--NOW!" Frank bellowed the order through the phone at her.

Some faint sense of understanding in her mind, heard his command and made her get to her feet. She took a deep lungful of air in and felt herself begin to reverse the shutdown process that had begun.

She spoke groggily, "Ok, I'm up now Uncle Frank. Now what?" she was still looking directly at her mum through the patio window. Her mum was drying the dishes now with a cloth and putting them away.

"That really is your mum in there Sherri." He sighed heavily, dreading what Sherri's reaction might be. He was now faced with the pressure of explaining an unbelievable and laboriously complicated concept to a 15-year-old suffering from Post-Traumatic Stress Disorder. How could he explain to her that it wasn't a hallucination she was having?!

"I think I'm gonna hang-up on you now Uncle Frank, before I say something really horrible to you before I faint!" The hallucination of her mum was *still* there, she hadn't left Sherri's vision, she hadn't disappeared as magically as she had appeared, nor had she morphed back into her dad. She just kept on being there. The anxiety began to bubble-up inside her again.

"Don't hang-up! Please don't hang-up Sherri! –Please, just listen, listen to me, this is so, so, so very important!" he implored her, "I'm not making some horrible, crazy sick joke! –Really, I'm not! ...I knew you *would* see your mum; that's the reason why I called, I just didn't think you'd see her this early. I hadn't calculated on it being tonight. Maybe over the next few days, but definitely not tonight!" he took a slow breath in, "I thought it might possibly have happened tomorrow morning. That would have been better for you, you would have had a good night's sleep and time to mentally process what I'm calling to tell you now ..."

"You mean, you knew I was going to hallucinate and see Mum?!?—How did you know for crying-out-loud?!!" Sherri yelled.

"I knew you were going to see your mum Shez...because" he paused and let out an awkward sigh, then said, "Because...there's no easy way to say this,"

He waited a moment longer, "because that's not a hallucination you're seeing. That's really your mum Sherri. That's her...that's my sister ...she's always been there," he quickly added, "...now." A long silence followed, and he kept explaining, "she is alive and well...now" He changed his tone, lowering his voice, "I would never disrespect or hurt you by making-up something as bat-crap crazy as this Sherri. This is not some kind of deluded, phantasmagorical brain-fart I'm having here! This really is no joke. I would not call you and say something like this, if it wasn't true."

"I'm hanging up now *-Crazy-* Uncle Frank*!*" she said as she slowly moved the phone away from her ear so she could see the red hang-up button on the touchscreen. Her finger hovered above it for a few seconds. She began to sob a few more times out of anger and apprehension, feeling bewildered, but she couldn't push-down on the red button and hang-up.

He yelled-out as loud as he could to get her attention, "—PLEASE DON'T HANG UP ON ME! I CAN HELP! ...I WAS CALLING TO HELP YOU! –SOMETHING REALLY STRANGE AND WONDERFUL IS HAPPENING EVERYWHERE AROUND THE WORLD SHERRI!"

She could hear him still. He sounded small as he yelled-out from the phone's earpiece in front of her. She kept listening to his tiny voice. But he sounded, somehow, in some way believable, in some perceptibly weird kind of way. He meant it. She knew that he meant it. Uncle Frank would never hurt her –never!

 His heart was always in the right place. As crazy and eccentric as he was, he wasn't capable of being hurtful. So, what the hell was he on about then?!

Whatever's going on up there in Hong Kong must be pretty crazy and there must be something even more crazier going-on in the world to make him call and say something like this!

She pressed the 'hands-free' speaker icon. He had her attention.

"I'm still here," she said softly, then waited a second, "I'm listening."

He lowered his voice a little, then continued, "Something very, very bizarre and unbelievable is going on all around the world right now Sherri —you've got to believe me, there is something really, really big about to happen!"
"Ok. What? –what's going to happen?" She kept looking at her mum.

"You know how I've studied and worked on the weirdest of weird, Above-Top-Secret science projects for years now, you've heard it all before! You know some of the crazy, whacky secretive stuff I've been involved with, right?! Right? ...Remember?" He waited.

"Yeah, of course I remember all of it." She was listening and she was gaining her composure, but she could still see her mum—*alive*... "I know most of it. You've told me a lot of really crazy, weird and wonderful science-stuff."

"Well, nothing—And I mean absolutely **nothing** gets any crazier than what we have been doing at Orange Sand Sherri, especially what we've been doing at CERN."

She answered steadily, "What my eyes are seeing right now certainly suggests that! - But this is beyond crazy Uncle Frank!! I'm having a hallucination and you're telling me it's not a hallucination and that it's real?!?!" her temper began to rise, "I'm going bananas here, and you're telling me *that's really her?! My mum, your sister, is back from the dead?!*"

"It's not as simple as dead or alive – and NO she is not a zombie either or something like that – you have to understand that we exist in multiple timelines Sherri and nothing, *nothing*...about this concept is simple or easy to explain ...or believe for that matter! How do you think I feel trying to explain it to you now? Please just hear me out!?" He paused to collect his thoughts, then went on, "Remember, not too long ago, you were freaking out over the spelling of BRAGGS apple cider vinegar? You were using it to make your own home-made lemonade. You couldn't wait to tell me about something weird you'd discovered? ...remember? ...you thought at the time you were going bonkers...you thought it was the accident causing your memory to glitch?"

"Yeah, they changed the company name to BRAGG. The 'S' got deleted from the end of the name on their labels –but when I Googled-it to see why they had changed it, all the links I found said that BRAGG was always the way it had been spelt – forever—right from the get-go, ever since the company started! –It was never BRAGGS." then Sherri fell into a long, deep pause, "Ohhhhh my smoked salmon roll! – ***the Mandela Effect!***

Something instantly jackbooted Sherri's mind to wake-up and begin to recollect all the many other freaky 'Mandela Effect' changes she'd noticed over the succession of time following that first discovery.

"You are right over the target now young lady. We are living in an intersectional multiverse, and things are really getting Freaky Friday, only it's every day of the damn week!" Frank explained quickly.

"After discovering that and then noticing the spelling of Tumric was now Turmeric, my friend Hannah showed me that stupid, silver leg that 3CPO had suddenly started to have," She paused, "I must have watched all of the original Star Wars trilogy a million times." she mused, "but I'd never seen that silver leg before!"

"Me too," added Uncle Frank, "I was only 10 when 'A New Hope' first opened in theatres. I must have seen that first Star Wars movie more than a gazillion times over the following years of my life, and yet I *never*, *ever* once remember seeing that stupid, silver lower leg 3CPO now has ...he was always all gold—head to toe! ...I even have some old action figures of him and both legs are gold! Now, you'd think the toy makers would not have missed that detail!?"

'Exactly!" Said Sherri excitedly, although she was still hallucinating.

Her mum stopped looking out the window and went back to tidying away.

Sherri watched her place three desert bowls on the drying rack. Why was there three? Dad didn't use a bowl when he had eaten that other slice.

Just at that moment, her mum left the kitchen and walked off to another room. Sherri stared at the back door anxiously, half expecting her mum to come walking-out onto the back patio and join her. Then she would defiantly scream and pass-out. But nothing followed.

It seemed the hallucination had run its course and finished. Just like that. It was gone. At last!

So, Uncle Frank did maybe know what he was doing. Maybe this conversation he'd started upon was on purpose and he knew it would be just the ticket to close her mind down and stop her from seeing the hallucination? But how did he know she was going to have one in the first place? And how did he know who she would hallucinate seeing? – And the precise time that she would see it?

She was starting to enjoy another, deep 'Crazy Uncle Frank conspiracy conversation" the type that would always open a can-of-worms for her to go off on a journey of inquiry-based learning and research, reading and watching a ton of material, just like every other conversation before had done. These topics were the ones she always loved discussing with him. She could feel herself calming down a whole lot. This was just another Crazy Uncle Frank "Think Piece"

"This is some **HUGE *Mandela Effect*** my mind is having!" she stated with an equally huge amount of relief that could be discernibly heard over the phone.

"You've sort-of figured it out there sweetheart" Frank said calmly.

Sherri sat herself back down into the papasan chair. "Sort of? Have I sort-of lost the plot too? Is that what you're saying?"

"You haven't lost the plot Sherri—that's really your mum." He paused, then spoke more assertively "You need to go and talk to her Shez – Be brave, face your fears and go and talk to her, be with her, give her a hug – just go with the flow of this cosmic and crazy moment – even tell her – or ask her if she's experienced any weirdness for the last 7 months."

"You're still trying to tell me she's really here? *-Seriously?!*"

"She is – it takes too much explaining –too much science, and it's not even my exact speciality field so much as it is your Uncle Aldo's. He's the one who's creating new miracles every day." He paused and huffed out loudly then continued on "I really have to go now Shez –time is running fast – I will explain everything, all the details to you when I get there, but for now, I know you've got this –just embrace the beauty of having your mum back in your life again there, without freaking-out or needing to know why – I've really gotta bail sweety and get back on the ferry over to Lantau Island, it's too hectic here in central Honkers at this hour of the day, but I will try and speak with you very shortly – Okay? – like maybe tomorrow –Yes?"
–He collected his last words, "Please don't freak out – be happy – simply accept this moment for what it is – take care – and remember: there's nothing to be scared of."

"Okay I will try and lean into it." She paused for a moment to wipe her eyes "–you take care up there."

"I'll do my best Shez –remember you're the best, smartest, most awesome teenager in the whole world –now go and have one of the craziest and most beautiful moments you'll ever likely to have in your entire lifetime, and give your mum a big hug for me!" the call got cut off before she could say anything further to him. The line made an odd thrumming loop.

"Mum?" she called-out tentatively into the hallway, barely sticking her head through the patio door for fear of what she might see. Seconds passed for what seemed like minutes.
Nothing. No reply...

Ok, she'd just bought into a whole truckload of Uncle Frank's craziness —again, and her own hallucinations, she conceded annoyingly to herself.

"MUM, you there?" She yelled loudly, just one last time, just to give it a final try before forgetting the whole damn episode and wisely getting herself off to bed.

"In here honey" yelled her mum back, **"Dad and I are looking at some old photos of you as a baby on his computer."**

Sherri kept staring into the flyscreen and the hallway beyond —frozen in place...

The Night That Wasn't Supposed to Be

Her heart skidded the way a bike does on gravel.

She stood stock still, staring at the now-dark, shadowed hallway. The glow from the TV in the patio area, pulsed on her face, and her body was still revved-up with the cocktail of adrenaline and confusion left over from... all of *that which shouldn't possibly be real —but was looking and now sounding to be so.*

She swallowed.

She hadn't moved or taken a step since she heard the voice reply back to her.

Her *mum's* voice.

Casual. Normal. Not ghostly, nor warped or warbled. Just... there.

Her knees wobbled slightly.

Then came the soft murmur of laughter — *her dad's laugh* — unmistakable, followed by her mother's more subtle giggle. They were in there. Together. At the study desk.

Her dad wasn't freaking out —he was just behaving like it was any other normal night from before...before...

Looking at photos.

Photos of *her*.

"Just go in," she whispered to herself. "You're awake. You're still here. Just go in."

She stepped lightly through the flyscreen door, her fingers brushing against the latch to ground herself. The hallway was dim, only a single hallway light buzzing gently overhead.

Her footfalls felt like thunder.

Her breath was a fog siren.

She reached the open study door.

Her dad was seated, hunched slightly forward, tapping the screen, moving the arrow key to flip through the digital photos on his old desktop PC screen. And just behind him, resting her chin casually on his shoulder and smiling at the screen, was her mother.

Wearing the same soft grey jumper Sherri always remembered. The same hairband. The same scent—*that smell*—vanilla almond and cotton sheets in summer...her mum's smell.

They didn't look up.

They were looking at a baby photo of her covered in spaghetti Bolognese, sitting in a highchair, howling away in their old unit, the one they had first lived in at Tugun.

"I told you she used to get her food everywhere," her mum said warmly. "Even in her nostrils."

"You were just relieved she wasn't throwing it on you," her dad chuckled.

"I had to *hose* that highchair down so many times, remember?"

Sherri's mouth opened. Then closed. Then opened again.

She stepped forward gently.

Her mum looked up at last.

"Hi, sweetie," she said, eyes kind. "You, okay? You look like you've seen a ghost."

Sherri let out a short, shaky breath that almost resembled a laugh. She nodded slowly, eyes wide...then she started to cry.

"I'm... I'm okay," she managed. "I just didn't know you were here."

And she rushed over to her and hugged her mum with all the might that she could physically muster and wept her heart out.

Somewhat confused and worried, her mum hugged her back and cradled her and steadied her.

Looking concerned she gently exclaimed, "Hey, hey, hey there, hey now, what's happened?! Why all the tears?"

"Oh..." she took a moment and tried to make her feelings settle down "Oh I'm just feeling a bit emotional and overtired that's all –and I really needed a hug from you." She smiled.

Her dad turned in his chair. "Well, this should cheer you up! I managed to locate the baby photos we'd thought we'd gone and lost when my old hard-drive crashed –finally, after searching around on an old back-up drive," he said proudly. "We just had to take a trip down memory-lane looking through them all. Tomorrow we are going to the printers to get prints made up. Your mum was just reminding me how *you* used to bark at the neighbour's dog and try to get it to play fetch through the fence in this photo here."

Sherri blinked. "I did?"

Her mum smiled, resting a hand gently on Sherri's arm. "You were *obsessed* with dogs from the day you could crawl."

The touch was light, but real.

Sheri felt every molecule of it.

Her eyes stung.

Her brain kept screaming: *This is wrong. This is impossible. She died. She's dead. We buried her.*

And yet... here she was.

Casual. Warm. Present.

As if she'd never left.

As if *the accident* had never happened.

As if the timeline had been... rewritten.

"I'm going to grab a drink," her dad said, pushing back from the desk. "Anyone want a chamomile tea or hot chocolate?"

"No thanks," said her mum.

Sherri shook her head, barely able to move.

And now, suddenly, it was just the two of them.

Her mum turned slightly and patted the empty seat beside her. "Come sit, hon."

Sheri sat slowly, like someone entering a sacred space. Her pulse thundered in her ears.

Her mum leaned back slightly in the chair, arms crossed lightly over her chest, looking at her with soft eyes.

"You're a little bit emotional tonight …you probably should get yourself to bed as soon as you can. It looks like you might be needing a good night's sleep." Thinking she was still grieving Zeb, she added, "Maybe we can look at getting a puppy this week, if it's not too soon, I think we should look around?"

Sheri nodded.

A pause.

"I... I just had a dream earlier when I dozed-off in the papasan," she said carefully. "One of those vivid ones. You know?"

"About me?"

Sherri's eyes flicked to her mother's face.

It was a genuine question. No knowing smile. No hidden agenda.

"Yeah," she said softly. "Sort of."

"Well," her mother said, brushing some hair behind her ear and laughing a little, "I hope I was fabulous, brave and dashing in it, just like I am in real life?"

Sherri smiled faintly. "You always are mum...anytime of the day"

Then her voice trembled. "I've just really missed you lately. I mean... I know that sounds weird. But... I don't know. Just... a feeling."

Her mum leaned over and kissed the side of her head and hugged her.

"I'm not going anywhere, Shez. You've got me here on-call 24/7."

Sheri closed her eyes.

She didn't say anything.

She didn't have to.

Later that night, lying in bed, the moonlight casting patterns through her blinds, Sheri stared up at the ceiling, her hand resting on her heart.

The house was silent, save for the occasional creak of the cooling timber.

She reached over and grabbed her notebook, scribbling something without turning on the light:

The universe doesn't make mistakes. It edits them.

Tonight, it edited my mum back into existence.

An Early Start to a Re-Written Day

The downstairs landline rang once.

Then again.

Then a third time — like it always did when she was trying not to wake anyone else up in the apartment...except Byron.

Byron cracked one bleary eye open, then swung out of bed robotically. He already knew who it was. No one else ever called on the landline...And never at this early hour.

It was 5:00am.

Of course it was.

He animated himself just enough to stagger over to the phone, pick up the receiver and answer groggily.

As he listened, a small release of adrenaline mixed with a large dose of mystical intrigue that was soon rapidly shooting through his system.

Twenty minutes later, he rolled up to Sheri's place, the low whirr of his electric bike humming like a mosquito coming down to land as it approached. He quietly fixed the horseshoe padlock around the letterbox's post, pulled the paper coffee tray from the front basket, and made his way around the side of the house, careful not to wake anyone up.

The flyscreen door on the patio creaked gently open.

She was already waiting there, barefoot, wearing an oversized T-shirt and her dad's old Okanui board shorts. The smell of melted cheese and warm toast drifted over to him like a welcome-home hug.

"I knew you'd be up," she said.

"I wasn't," he replied, frowning with a smile, holding up the coffees. "But you did sound pretty shaken-up with your Twilight-Zone situation. So here I am —wide awake."

She gave a small, grateful smile. "You brought the good kind? Parettizi's Deli?"

"Always! – Adaptogenic Vanilla for you. Long black for me."

He stepped inside the patio, where the warmth of the oven and the smell of the grilled cheese still clung to the air. The old papasan chair had been pushed back into its place, tucked against the wall away from the switched-off TV. The dull din of the ocean could be faintly heard in the distance.

She handed him half of a toasted cheese baguette wrapped in a napkin. The cheese was crispy on the edges, golden and caramelised.

They walked back out to the front yard and sat down on the cul-de-sac's curb, watching the sun slowly come up.

Steam wafted from the cups in the cardboard tray between them.

"I didn't want to wake the others," she said. "Hope there wasn't any complaints?"

"Not a pip –everyone slept through all the initial rings" He looked worriedly at her "The most important thing is, are YOU okay?"

"No." She lowered her nose over the coffee and slowly inhaled it "I used up all my energy trying not to react to the situation last night. I said nothing to either one of them. A million things I could of, should of, would have said, and nothing came out of me except tears and crying! I said nothing to them. I just went with it like I was in a play letting the script walk me around, until I was finally lying in bed."

He waited. "I would have done the same Shez. Probably just stood there gawking and lost for words too." He looked over his shoulder back towards the house, "Is she ...."

"She's still here hasn't vanished" Sheri whispered. "It wasn't just a night-time thing Byro. After I got off the phone to you just now, I heard her up and about in the kitchen, asking Dad if he wants his eggs fried or scrambled."

Byron blinked.

"She asked him if he wanted his eggs fried," Sheri repeated slowly, "or scrambled."

She looked at him, eyes wide and glossy. "She used to always ask that, every morning when she'd go into the kitchen and start making us breakfast. Word for word. And then he'd always say the same thing back to her."

Byron spoke the words. He'd called around often enough to their place in the past on many early morning surf trips, always stopping long enough to have some breakfast with her and her parents before they left. He knew her dad's reply only too well: "Fried. Less hassle washing up."

They both exhaled incredulously.

"She's not a ghost," Sheri whispered. "She's not some time-slip. She's just... here. Like none of it happened. Like the accident never happened. Like Zeb never—"

She stopped.

Byron reached for his coffee but didn't drink. He just wrapped his hands around the warmth.

"Is Zeb...?" He trailed off, looking around, without finishing.

She quickly shook her head, eyes watering up.

"Your leg? Ribs?" staring down at her leg.

"The scars and the aches are all still there –the accident **did** happen."

"I remember your mum dying," he said quietly. "I remember Zeb's collar. The funeral. I remember Principal Ballard holding you up in the hallway after you tried to come back to school too early and couldn't manage it, you were calling out for your mum, before you collapsed. And I remember..." he shook his head slightly, eyes flickering, "...I remember sitting at your kitchen table only two weeks ago while she scolded me for madly scratching away at a mosquito bite, telling me I'd get a scar."

Sheri looked at him. "You remember *both versions*?"

He nodded.

"And I've started to remember my dad being here too," he added, voice tightening. "I remember smelling his aftershave in the hallway last week. His laugh. We were

90

watching TV together only a few nights ago. He cooked dinner on the BBQ the other night, and he tapped the tongs the way he always tapped the tongs three times before flipping anything over."

"Is he back too?"

"Nope, he isn't" Byron said. "That's just it –he absolutely isn't...But the memory of him still being here has become almost as strong as the memory of him running-out on us." He took a sip from the coffee, "One is real –the other isn't –but I still don't have any answers as to why he left us, why he ran-out on us, or where he went to. No answers."

"It gets stronger after they ring the bells." He added slowly. "Whenever they ring the bells, a new, happy memory floats back into my mind."

A long pause.

Sheri tore a piece off the edge of her baguette, then whispered, "Do you think we're dreaming all of these memories –like our subconscious minds have begun taking over and our dreams are now controlling things, telling our waking minds what to think, what to remember, creating new, fabricated realities?"

"No."

"Hallucinating?"

"No."

"Are we dead or something and we don't know it yet?"

Byron raised a condescending eyebrow, tilting his head in her direction.

She almost laughed.

"Maybe," he said with a small smile, "we're waking up to something new."

Sheri placed the cup and baguette down and leaned back, putting her arms behind her for support. "I feel like I'm made of glass right now. Like if something knocks me too hard, I'll crack and my mind and spirit will spill out."

"Then we make sure you don't get knocked, and we make sure you don't crack." Byron said gently.

They ate in silence for a while, the early morning stillness wrapping around them like a blanket. Somewhere, a kookaburra cackled and then went quiet again.

Byron sipped his coffee.

Sheri looked over. "If I ever forget that she was gone..., will you remind me?"

He nodded. "And if I ever forget that one version of my dad still remained here, never ran-out on us and actually did the right thing...will you do the same?"

She bumped her knee against his.

"Deal."

No Morning Coffee for Frank

Mui Wo / Silvermine Bay, Lantau Island –and dawn had just started stretching its arms.

The faint scent of seaweed and diesel hovered over the harbor, clinging to the misty, early morning humidity like a staggering drunk holds onto a lamppost at midnight.

Uncle Frank ambled slowly down the concrete promenade beside the ferry pier, deep in thoughts, hands clasped behind his back, seemingly a man who had absolutely nowhere urgent that he needed to be—which of course was a complete lie...he needed to be everywhere in a hundred different places, all at once.

He was partially singing the lyrics to an old 80's hit song by a band called A Flock of Seagulls: "I Ran", almost correctly, but not quite spot on, repeatedly getting the words absurdly wrong.

Behind him, the timeworn three-decker ferry that ran to Central and back, sat chugging, gently docked and seemingly half-asleep. Locals were already lining up for egg noodles and milk tea at the old harbour-side eateries that lined the north side of the pier. Their timing was always tight in the mornings, either eating and gulping down their meal or getting it bagged-up before rushing-off to catch the ferry just as it was about to leave, on the hour-every hour, and right before the ferry's gangway would start to rise-up. The low hum of wok fires and loud, chattering Cantonese mixed with the rhythmic slosh of the waves beneath the jetty.

Frank's Kung-Fu slippers softly padded along as he strolled toward the little footbridge near the canal, where Silvermine Bay's beach began. He was part of the way there, mentally running through a million things, including last night's conversation with Sherri.

His last shipment to her had left the island the night before: a battered old sea container full of quantum chips, backup drive cubes, and the encrypted chrono-locking matrixes. The circuitry schematics and flux-conductors embedded inside an old 60's Kelvinator fridge, were some of the key pieces to everything Orange Sand had built to save the world...one day — and the very items "The Order" wanted to pry out from his cold, dead hands.

Too bad for them. His hands were warm and he was alive, and the cargo was seaward bound safely on its way to Coolangatta.

 He began whistling the guitar solo from the old 80's song, when he noticed something was... off.

Four men loitered just past the very last eatery, dressed like budget mercenaries in tactical camo-pants and black K-Mart issue polo-neck tops. Tourists never loitered here— and tourists also never dressed in clichéd crap like these guys were wearing, not in this cursedly humid Hong Kong weather, and tourists never hung-about at this early hour of the morning over here in Mui Wo either. Tourists also did not normally have two-way earpieces and did not stand around trying to look ever so cool-and-normal in an awkwardly fake pose. They were talking to each other stiffly in clipped tones, nodding toward Frank.

He took in a deep breath and sighed. "Oh joy," he muttered, patting his pocket like he'd misplaced something. "Just once, I'd like to finish a sunrise stroll without being abducted."

As he turned to walk casually back toward the pier, one of the men peeled off from the group to cut across the walkway, blocking his path. Another moved in and intercepted him from behind. A third stepped out from the side eatery exit, completely boxing him in.

"Doctor Franklin Jules Kendrick," said the forth goon as he closed distance and stood directly in front of Frank. "You're coming with us."

"I'm terribly sorry, ladies," answered Frank, glancing at his wrist with no watch on it. "I'm late for a foot massage with a one-eyed woman who swears she can adjust all my meridians and give me the best happy ending I've ever had before in my life. So that's a BIG, massive...PISS-OFF to you cologne-slathered plonkers! I'm not going anywhere with you guys!"

Two of the men grabbed his arms—not gently.

"Yikes! Consent, fellas! This isn't prom night at Quantico; can we establish a "safe" word here?" Frank jeered, as they spun him around. "And I'm not sure if the happy ending you're planning for me is the same one that my lady masseuse has planned for me...Orrrr is it perhaps? Maybe?" He raised an eyebrow and laughed at them.

He was roughly frogmarched toward the small boat ramp just past the footbridge. A black Zodiac waited there in the shallow water, engine idling, another two steroid-addled, over-muscled goons sat in the boat. The agents shoved him down into the rubber craft, seating him beside a crate stencilled with Chinese characters and some ominous-looking cooling-vents on the side of it.

The goon who sat next to the outboard engine, gave a terse nod to his colleagues, and throttled up the motor. Frank concluded: I'm going wherever it is they are taking me -**six men total**—no martial art moves could ever get me out of this pickle.

"I love this neighbourhood, you know guys," Frank said as the Zodiac roared to life, slicing through the morning chop. "You tossers are really wrecking the vibe here!"

No one responded. They rounded the southern tip of the bay, skimming past a small canal where freshwater trickled out from a hillside stream. The beach faded behind them, as Mui Wo's quiet charm disappeared beneath a rising cloak of mist.

Frank squinted toward Discovery Bay in the distance.

The Zodiac slowed.

Then a *ripple* broke the surface of the water.

A long, low metallic shape breached just enough to expose a bulbous conning tower. Rusted grey. Unmarked. Camouflaged with algae mats and displacement netting. A retro-fitted diesel-electric sub, moored out of sight, invisible to satellites, ferries and other watercraft alike. These old subs were more silent when running submerged than any of the newer, nuclear class of subs could ever hope to be.

"Of course," Frank muttered. "Every megalomaniacal schmuck needs their own rusty sub full of goons and probably an underwater base to go with it." They pulled-up alongside the conning tower. A hatch cracked open with a pressurised hiss.

As they hauled Frank up the ladder, he called-out over his shoulder to the goons, "If anyone's got any of those CBD gummy-bears, now would be the time to give me a handful. I get travel sick riding in old, rusty sardine-tins. I'm likely to barf chunks all over you blokes without some form of weed in my system.

The goons didn't respond. They never did.

But Uncle Frank wasn't worried —not yet.

For emergency situations like this, he always had an "Ace up his sleeve".

Or, as was the case on this particular morning, he had an "Ace up his tooth".

Not a Yellow Submarine

The dull hum of the boat's air filtration-system buzzed faintly, mixing in with the occasional *clunk* of unseen machinery. The crew passing by the small mess quarters, spoke in low grumbles, annoyed that their eating area had now been turned into an interrogation room, door closed.

Frank sat handcuffed to a chair affixed to the floor, his legs crossed as if he were waiting to get himself a haircut.

Across from him, Captain Marlowe of *The Order* paced back and forth like a wind-up fascist action figure in his immaculate uniform and boots. The captain had the build of a rugby player and the putrid smell and charm of a rotting, fly-blown meatloaf, the result of too many bad steroids and just being a general and complete asshole.

Behind him stood two more operatives — identically bland, dullard, military cut-out gorillas whose glassy eyes made you wonder if they still had souls, or if they'd gone and sold them for a well-paid, cushy gig, such as working security detail for an evil, secret cabal?

"Doctor Kendrick," Marlowe drawled, voice slow and precise. "You *are going to* help us over the next few days with bringing our non-Euclidian array online, ensuring it will be working to capacity at CERN. The chrono-pulse we have managed to build, so far –and have almost working correctly, was built upon and modelled from your equations.

However, we've only discovered now that we can't quite finish the project without your further input –being the smart-ass delinquent that you are, you had to go and rip us off by making a joke of the contract you'd signed with CERN, failing to deliver on the actual workable schematics like you were supposed to do, like you had negotiated – like you had agreed upon doing, remember? Yet, you definitely took our very generous payment, didn't you?! –In effect, we paid you handsomely –and you went and completely ripped-us-off!"

Frank raised an eyebrow, lazily gazing ahead, examining the interior wall of the sub's mess room behind where Marlowe was standing. Then he looked down and began studying the floor beneath his feet. He then looked-up and smiled at Marlowe and started to chuckle.

"Buyer Beware! That's what they always say…You stupid twat." He laughed some more at Marlowe "I had a suspicion you shmucks were hiding behind the whole deal and were so obviously up to no good over there – and be dammed if I was gonna be gullible enough to hand over a proper, fully-working formula for constructing an advanced Euclidian interface module. Whatever evil-assed shit you guys were up to, and whatever shenanigans you've already gotten away with by changing-up this reality through all those annoyingly small, piss-ant ways that you've been altering things around with –I wasn't down for advancing your tech any further so you could get a whole lot bigger and better at messing around with the world!"

Frank then closed his eyes and puffed out, "You really did surprise me though, I gotta say, I one-hundred-precent didn't think my high school scribbles would end up being taken so seriously and would wind-up getting built by you idiots. It blew me away as you began to so blatantly test changing things in your evil Saturday morning cartoon show that you shitheads had been secretly hatching-out for real."

He opened his eyes again and looked angrily at Marlowe, "You really are such an ignorant Muppet –you know that?!

You and your gang of imbeciles have NO freaking idea what you're actually doing over there at CERN – do you?!?"

"Oh, but we do Kendrick. We really do." He sneered. "And you *will* comply. You will help us to get better at it. Or you will pay the ultimate price –The Riftwalkers are perfecting their timelines!"

"Oh *God*, not the Riftwalkers again," Frank groaned, rolling his eyes. "You know, if I had a dollar for every time some greasy bootlicking, numb-nutted twat said their name, like it was meant to impress me, or make me shit in my ballerina shoes, I'd be wealthy enough to build myself the same tech you guys have – then I'd be the one altering reality, and I would erase you panty-liners and those demonic buttholes from our existence here –instead of the monopoly man's monocle –or screwing-over the funniest moment in 007's Moonraker, like you twat-knuckles have been doing for laughs!"

One of the guards stepped forward ready to punch him, but Marlowe raised a hand and waved him away. "You think this is a game, don't you Frank? The Fracture Point is already primed. You've lost. You'll do your part, or we will make what happened at your Sanctuary last night, look like a tea-party compared to what we are going to do to your family."

Frank's eyes narrowed, just slightly. "What did you do to the Sanctuary?!"

Marlowe smirked. "You don't know about it yet, do you?" He chuckled. "We found your little, not-so-secret lab –it was not-so well hidden-away and we paid it a visit. Our boys had a very wild party there late last night ...yes, we sure did. We really got to work on it, and now...unfortunately...you're precious little command and research centre IS ALL GONE! Orange Sand's Hong Kong facility has now been neutralized. We destroyed everything!

...Including the dogs too, I might add. All of them are sadly no longer with us."

Frank's heart broke in a split-second with overwhelming anguish and pain.

That was it...

His expression flickered wildly— just a twitch of the jaw. The bastards had killed the dogs! That was a line even demons shouldn't cross.

Marlowe was now laughing back at him, relishing in the moment.

"You should've heard them, Doctor Kendrick. All that howling and yelping. Made the extermination feel... canonical."

Frank blinked once incredulously. "You're bragging about killing dogs now?! You're lower than a snake's nut-sack!" He fought back his fury and tears.

Marlowe smirked. "You bred them to be special. Hyper-sensitives. Empathic channels between man and canine. Trackers of the harmonic pulse. You built your whole little Orange Sand fantasy around them. Did you think we wouldn't notice that? Were you so self-absorbed in your research and too naïve to think that the Riftwalkers wouldn't sense what was going on there and eventually locate it?"

He straightened, gesturing to one of his men who held up a cracked tablet displaying still images — cages, burning outposts, scorch marks in the soil. Broken collars. Dead beaten, bloody and broken bodies of dogs, as well as the lab staff, all of them dead.

Frank's eyes twitched. He didn't say a word.

"They died slowly and painfully, Kendrick, you should know that" Marlowe continued, voice syrupy with sadistic contempt. "Cried for you. Stayed in their pens even as the fires started. That's dumb loyalty for you. Waste of neural evolution if you ask me."

Frank's jaw clenched. He whispered gravely, "You **sick – sick** as they bloody get **BASTARD!** Hell won't be able to hurt you enough times over for what you've done." His eyes now became glassy, tears and his heavy breathing increased, brought on by the rage coursing through his entire being "Oh... you *really*, ***REALLY*** shouldn't have done that." he said softly.

"Oh, don't get all weepy on me. One of them survived, I hear," Marlowe added with a mock curiosity. "The black and white border collie. Left quite a few years ago, when it was still a puppy, with that... that deranged cyclotron gremlin that you're friends with at CERN. The anti-social bozo that no one likes with the body-odour problem. A nutter and a half if ever there was one. What's his name again? Old chubby-guts with the condiment-stains all over his greasy lab-coat and the Goku hairstyle?"

Frank tilted his head, a faint smile blooming — bitter, but sharp, his eyes stared at the floor. The man he was referring to was not just a colleague; he was the wild card in Frank's deck. A very unique spanner to throw into the works if ever he needed to, and most importantly, one of his last surviving, best friends.

Slowly, Frank spoke "His name's Paxton Alderson, and he's one of the smartest human beings on the planet, but you wouldn't know that because stupid scum like you couldn't recognise a truly gifted person even if they were standing right in front of you. Paxton knows what he's doing. He *asked* me for the pick of the litter; he loves dogs beyond words." Frank said quietly. "Said he wanted a really special one...a 'soulful one.' so I gave him *Jasper*."

Marlowe scoffed back at him. "A special dog? – None of them really seemed that special to me Kendrick. They all died in the most un-special of ways, and none of them put up any special kind of fight either."

Frank fought back his rage.

"Jasper's not just a very special dog," he murmured intensely. "He's our failsafe...he's our cosmic backup, in case we lost the others, and that's why I gave him to Aldo."

For a split second, a tremor of fear and unease flickered across Captain Marlowe's eyes. Then it was gone.

"I don't care what he is," Marlowe sneered. "We've sent a team over there to kill him. You're fat, pudgy friend and your special dog, both of them will be dead within a day from now. Just how slowly and painfully they die, depends on how you go about helping us."

Frank met his eyes — calm and steady, "No, they absolutely won't be dead within a day from now, and I'll be there making damn sure of that! –And, I also won't be helping you guys either."

He paused and confidently gibed, "However, you and your merry gang of dickheads jammed into this rusty, old shit-bucket ..." He laughed, "You're all going to be dead within just a minute or two from now."

Click.

His tongue pushed the nano-speck tucked up inside his back, molar tooth.

Click.

A subtle tremor vibrated through his skull — a chirping frequency no one else heard.

The nano-speck instantly expanded into a jelly-bean-sized node which he spat-out into his palm. It synched with his bio-chi making a soft metallic *whrrip*, like folding dimensions in reverse. A rapid twist of his fingers — index to thumb, pinkie to palm, in an exact coded sequence — and the jellybean grew instantly in size again.

Suddenly, he was holding something that shouldn't exist in this timeline.

A black-and-chrome, oblong, musket-shaped pistol, humming with dimensional resonance, its barrel glowing with *impossible* green-red energy that cast dancing shadows on the walls.

The two guards momentarily froze, faltered back, unsure what to do.

Frank instantly fired the weapon.

He shot once directly at the bulkhead wall behind Marlowe — a *blazing green bolt* ripped through the air like a scream, slamming against the metal. With a sonic boom and a *shlurping* crunch of space-time tearing like paper, a swirling *five-foot-wide portal* bloomed in the wall — bright solid fluorescent orange-blue, alive, shrieking with wormhole wind.

Then he simultaneously fired a second shot down directly between his Kung-Fu slippers.

The floor beneath Frank exploded in a spiral of light and plasma. His chair dropped through it like a coin dropping down a slot, and so did he.

Gone in a blink.

The floor portal rapidly began to close up again. One of the guards screamed. He'd instantly grabbed onto a bulkhead rail to stop himself from dropping down into the hole when it opened up only seconds ago. Now he was frantically trying to raise his legs high enough to get them out of the way as the edges of the portal started to rapidly close-up.

He was too slow, and his dangling legs were too low to get his feet clear. The closing portal neatly sliced through his ankles. He shrieked and let go of the railing he was holding onto, dropping with a hard thud onto the now returned steel plated decking that had reformed beneath him. He continued to emit an ear-piercing scream as he wriggled about writhing in pain. Blood was fountaining out from the two meaty stumps at the end of his legs spraying in all directions. Marlowe and the other remaining goon were sprayed from head to toe with blood. Worse was still to come...

The other portal in the wall had begun to pulse and groan...

Marlowe stumbled backward in shock, wiping blood away from his eyes, he quickly began looking around to see where he could run to.

Too late.

The upright portal on the bulkhead wall had only *held itself closed for just enough micro-seconds so that Frank could fall through his portal in the floor*, then the bulkhead wall portal gave way and erupted open — but this time not with radiant light coming in from another, far-off location.

It spewed-in cold, dark seawater from the outside of the hull. It became a big, gaping hole in the wall, just as Frank's portal was closing up.

A solid, ferocious five-foot-wide *column of ocean* thundered in like a divine battering ram. The pressure crushed the nearest guard instantly. Control panels sparked. The room buckled. Marlowe barely had time to look up before the rushing ocean slammed against him, crunching him into the ceiling like a rag doll. He gave-out one final, gurgling scream as his backbone and ribs were all snapped into small pieces, then—

Blackness.

Within seconds, the entire mid-section of the hull was flooded. Then the rear. Then the forward torpedo room. The submarine's lights flickered on and off, then died. It listed hard-over to starboard, alarm sirens still blaring away uselessly to a now fully drowned crew. Somewhere not too far from Discovery Bay, it sank down to the bottom of the sea floor — a tubular, useless hunk of metal now filled with water, ruined secret plans and the sunken egos of dead men who thought they were unstoppable and could one day rule the world.

Franklin Jules Kendrick lay still as a meditating monk, alive and relatively well –breathing air, yet unimpressed as a man who'd seen the world end — a few times over now — and still hadn't had his morning cup of coffee.

His cuffed wrists ached a whole lot, his legs and butt really hurt from free-falling down several feet onto a hard, tiled surface while still seated in a chair. Miraculously though, he didn't receive any breaks, sprains, cracks or cuts in the process...or any urgent need to go visit a proctologist either...the aluminium chair on the other hand, was a complete, crumpled mess. Most of the discomfort he was now feeling, came from the kiddie pool's worth of very cold seawater that had gushed down onto him just as his portal above him was closing up.

He had safely made his way into the bitterly cold, freezing weather of Geneva.

There he lay on the cold floor, toppled over onto his side, drenched thoroughly to the bone, sensing his body temperature rapidly plummeting in the overcast, snowy, winter's afternoon.

To make matters worse, the apartment he was now in, had no heating turned on and the lounge-room window had been left wide open to the outside conditions. A chilly, sub-zero breeze was gently blowing in. The entire living space had the steady temperature of a freezer chest.

The lounge-room floor was now covered in a huge puddle of fresh seawater that had splashed down onto it in the ensuing seconds as the portal in the ceiling above had closed-up. Books, magazines, ornaments and furniture were all strewn about by the brief and instantaneous deluge of water. Half a dozen different sized fish had also made their way into the room and were now all madly flapping around on the floor next to Frank, as well as a pair of military jackboots with bloody, severed stumps protruding out the end of them.

The quiet, peaceful living space had become a chaotic, water-logged mess.

He stiffly climbed to his feet with a loud groan and a hiss. There was just one goal he had in mind presently; Get these damned cuffs off! –A Houdini life-skill that he'd completely overlooked learning how to do in the past. One of those essential tricks that he should've taken a moment or two to master at some point but had always put off doing. He was mentally kicking himself now, because he'd always known it would definitely have come in handy one day... just like today. Regardless, he trudged off to the kitchen to try his luck anyway.

He figured that once he got the damn cuffs off, he might just try having a go at getting that morning cup of coffee he was initially after in the first place, before he'd been so rudely interrupted by a gang of buttheads, even though it was technically now an "afternoon coffee", since it had just gone 5-p.m. in Geneva.

He remorsefully realised that he was thirty minutes too late in his jump back through time. It wasn't far enough back to ring and alert –and maybe even help prevent the attack on the Sanctuary –He was rushing, under pressure, as he tried to quickly calculate the two portals, their timing, his destination as well as the time-zone differences between Geneva and Hong Kong, and then telepathically program all of this into the portal-pistol in less than a few seconds. Under the circumstances, it was sheer luck that he had landed where he wanted to go, and on the very same day he'd jumped on, instead of falling onto a Triceratops's tusk in some Jurassic swamp.

The grief, shock and sorrow of what they'd unstoppably done to his sacred workspace and his dogs back on Lantau was consuming him beyond measure. He needed to focus for the moment on just getting the cuffs off – coffee would come next – then he'd turn on the heating up to full blast, and take a long, hot shower until the tank of hot water ran out...then prepare some food, light the fireplace and eventually allow himself the necessary time he needed to grieve properly while he tided-up the place.

A Very Big Con CERN

The old 1974 Volkswagen L-Bug's 1600 engine protested furiously as it was forced down a gear into second while rapidly approaching the roundabout at 90-km hour.

The trusty McPherson steering struts that were fitted out onto all these Superbugs, did their thing as it held fast into the bend and didn't roll over like earlier Beetle models tended to want to do at speed around a corner.

Each morning as Aldo came thundering off from the main road of Rte de Meyrin, almost crashing into the guard kiosk, causing the guards to scamper in fear and almost taking-out the small boom-gate if it wasn't raised-up, he would then plant his foot down hard on the gas pedal as far as it would go and try and see if he could set himself a new land-speed record for the 150-meter dash down Rte Pauli, until the roundabout at the end would inevitably put a halt to his V-Dub's-velocity. Despite the math in his head that said otherwise, he couldn't seem to break past the 90-kmh barrier.

Ignoring the yellow painted zebra crossings and the technicians who might've been trying to use those crossings to go into the electronics pool over in Building 13 on the right-hand side of the road, he never failed to hit his 90-kmh daily gallop. And the daily complaints and video captures of his crazy fly-bys to CERN's management were just as regular as was Aldo's daily attempts to set a new record for himself.

Jasper sat in the passenger's seat, loving every minute of the roller-coaster ride into work. He felt Aldo's enjoyment and rebellious glee for life as if it were his very own set of emotions.

The egg-beater engine roared away. Jasper leant out the window and barked at anyone they passed by on his side, and Aldo did almost the same thing by hurling verbal abuse at anyone making gestures over on his side or filming him...or just minding their own business cycling along on the side of the road (he hated cyclists).

The "burnt mango" paint job (half faded to papaya in parts) caught the early morning Geneva light like a citrus disco-ball. The roof was dented, the side mirror held on with a zip-tie, and the back seat had long ago been claimed by dog hair, soldering kits, and an unlabelled, modified reiki-resonator that occasionally pulsated with a low, thundering hum of what he called "sub-luminal healing-burps."

Jasper let out a short *woof* from the passenger seat as he leant over hard into the left-hand turn of the roundabout.

"Yeah, yeah. I know. I drive like a madman on pre-workout-formula and disco-dust --but never so bad as to put you in harm's way buddy."

The burnt mango missile screeched through the last few meters of the turn and then straitened awkwardly up as it exited the roundabout. The deceleration was so fast that it caused Jasper to place a paw onto the dashboard to stop himself from toppling forwards from his seat... a trick that he'd cleverly learnt to do ages ago while riding with his crazy human driver.

As they made their way around another hard left turn further in, they zoomed past **Building 124** over on the right-hand side of the small road they were on. With its two absurd architectural decorations protruding from its roof-awnings —it housed the Physics Department Bicycle Service —and of course, not being able to help themselves, they went and put half a bicycle bursting out of the wall in two places like a failed teleportation experiment — The absolute cringe of it constantly made Aldo wince every time he looked at it

He scowled at the entire structure like it owed him money.

"Symbol of everything wrong with modern science," he muttered. "Bikes. Cycling. Carbon-Emissions. Compression Lycra. Diets –Optimism."

A pair of cyclists in full CERN-issued Lycra-kit waved politely as he drove by them.

 "Get a Volkswagen!" he yelled out the window.

Jasper barked in agreement. It was a ritual now. They were always loitering out the front there in the mornings and always seemed to be in need of Aldo's giving them some of his environmental tips.

The cyclists just laughed — like they always did. Everyone at CERN knew Aldo was a complete and absolute nutter.
But he was *their nutter*. And deep down, most of them kind of liked him.

Another, slower left turn was then made into a row of car bays running next to the Synchrocyclotron's building 160 –he coasted down to the very last of the bays on the right side and parked directly in front of a mature, 35-year-old Red Oak tree.

Back when Aldo first started parking here in this exact, same spot in the first years of his work at the Synchrocyclotron, the red oak was barely taller than the Superbug. Just a spindly stick with a plastic support stake and a tag that read *Quercus rubra*.

"Hey there little guy, hang in there." He'd once said to it on a cold winter's day, many, many years ago, while he was closing the car door and looking over at it covered in snow. He then walked past it and gave it a pat on the trunk. Then every morning onwards, it became his ritual to pat the tree and say something encouraging to it.

Many a morning he said nothing to it and just patted the trunk as he quietly stood there with tears running down his face, feeling the weight and desperation of the world slowly eating away at him, crushing him down, hoping the tree would silently say something back to him in its own special way that was encouraging, communicating an uplifting vibe to his spirit and soul in a silent language that he could take to heart and use to heal himself with.

Sometimes it looked quite concerningly sad, sick and decrepit. He worried on occasions if the poor tree would make it. Other days he felt quite concerningly sad, sick and decrepit and wondered if he would make it.

Thirty-five years later, the two of them had outlived five supervisors, three parking signs, and Aldo's faith in humanity. It hadn't gone anywhere, and nor had he.

He still gave it a pat every morning. Out of respect and solidarity.

This tree mattered. This tree stayed. Even when everything else in his world had changed so much.

The red oak in the carpark had been there almost as long as the magnetic shielding inside the Synchrocyclotron building. Aldo always claimed it grew faster than most trees and survived the way it did because it could 'feel the field.'

Jasper just liked it because it dropped the best sticks for a quick throw and fetch session as they walked over to the entrance.

The Synchrocyclotron had been there longer than most of the staff at CERN had been alive. Its walls didn't echo anymore — they just remembered. Aldo liked that. You couldn't fake the weight of the real science that had been collected and soaked into the concrete here."

He let out a grunt as he reached over to the glove-box and began rummaging around inside of it. Always pushing past a nest of wires, old lanyards, batteries, fuses and what might have once been a sandwich, before he could grab his CERN access card. The magnetic strip was half-peeling away, held together with cello tape and some hope in what the future might hold.

As he was opening the door and stepping out of the car, Jasper hurriedly scampered over his lap and bounded out, running over to the tree, sniffing the base and giving it a single approving, quick pee — ritual complete.

Aldo walked past the tree and gave it his daily pat — not out of superstition, but out of something older. Something unspoken.

"Come on, Jas. Let's go pretend I'm a normal person for fifteen minutes."
They crossed the lot. The side entrance to Building 160 clicked open with a reluctant beep. Inside, the air was different — dry, clinical, and humming with the ghosts of antediluvian physicists and the vintage, sub-atomic particles they once worked with.

Aldo took the back stairwell down one level, nodding to a photo line-up of the old, faded portraitures of the original Synchrocyclotron team as he passed by them. Jasper padded close behind, ears twitching at the distant thrum of dormant machinery.

The door to the hidden room wasn't marked, but the smudge of an old shoe scuff just below the concealed handle gave it away. Aldo tapped a short code on a keypad hidden behind a loose wall panel, and the lock gave a soft click.

Inside, Orange Sand's secret morning-meeting was already underway.

"Ah, il nostro mango man," called out Dr. Vittorio Esposito, a wiry Italian with permanent safety goggles perched on his forehead and a pencil behind his ear. "Almost on time — must've hit a new record, eh?"

"Sixty-eight seconds faster than yesterday," Aldo replied, tossing his badge onto the table. "I think the Bug's learning."

"You keep pushing it like that," said Etienne Roux, a tall, sharp-featured French physicist in a turtleneck and long scarf, "and it will achieve time travel — backwards — to the scrapyard."

"Says the lady who drives a vintage, rusty, old Citron," Aldo chortled.

"Well, well, well…" came the smooth British accent of Dr. Harriet "Hairy-Legs" Lindley, her big-booted feet propped on the edge of the table as she cradled a mug that read: **SUPERPOSITION ME ON TOP.**
"Look who's decided to grace us with his fragrant presence. Smells today like a fine blend of midlife crisis, matched with zero shampoo and conditioner."

"Don't be jealous, Hairy-Legs, not everyone can rock a
majestic mane like this one."
Aldo ran a hand through his orange, ginger curls, giving
them a theatrical flick.
"Natural burnt mango hair and a matching burnt mango
car — now *that's* style! Just tell your brand of hair dye it
needs to do better if it wants to rock some of this
illustrious, ginger-swagger."

"I'm more of a dusky aubergine girl myself," she said with
a wink and a chuckle.
"And I've never used hair dye in my life. My carpet
matches my drapes."
She winked again — comically this time — then laughed.

"Of course not! — and I wouldn't have guessed otherwise,"
Aldo chuckled.

A low, well-needed wave of laughter passed between them
all — quick, genuine, unguarded.

While Aldo was seating himself down at the table, Jasper
quickly trotted around, doing the rounds, stopping briefly
to receive a pat and some fawning praise from each of the
physicists. He loved people — and these were his people.

There was something about their hands, their eyes, their
field — as if they carried the residue of something ancient,
noble, and tired. They were all very worried today, and
close to scared — he could smell it in their skin, sense it in
the way they breathed.
Their pulse harmonics were off. His licks and his presence
helped to lower their condition.

His presence recalibrated them. Each touch, each scratch
behind the ear, each murmur of affection — it wasn't just
comfort. It was a resonance alignment. It's what dogs have
always done. It's what all dogs will always do for humans.

He finally curled down at Aldo's feet, emitting a small, contented huff that quietly began to repair the room.

Then Etienne spoke, her jovial tone had instantly shifted over to a heavy solemness. "We've had another ping from Prague. The Order's repositioning—again."

"They're preparing for something bigger," Vittorio added. "We're seeing field distortions near Geneva, Lyon, even as far as Kraków. It's not just probes anymore. They're amping up for something bigger."

"I'd also add that it's been noted how their scouting and frenetic scanning seems to have slowed down to a point of having stopped altogether – They're not looking anymore." Doctor Roux gravely stated. She looked adoringly at Jasper contentedly laying on his side on the floor near to where she was sitting. "Dogs weren't captured by the hijackers who took over this world – they were seeded here later-on by the God-Force as helpers, protectors and soul-stabilizers – when dogs are near, soul fracturing can't occur –they reinforce –they strengthen heart-frequency fields that prevent psychic interference."

She leant down and over and reached-out to give Jasper a rub on his fluffy tummy, then quickly sat back up again and concluded "This is why dogs are being targeted: without question, they are going after dogs in some way – we just haven't figured-out how. But, without them here, human souls become easier to fragment, harvest, and enslave…And worse still, without them, we speculate, this situation could become a permanent one, with no possible way out, an eternal trap for everyone."

She looked at Aldo directly with a sadness in her eyes that almost made him want to cry

"They're going to try and destroy our beautiful best friends and our connection with them – It's my unshakeable suspicion they are going to try and eradicate dogs altogether from humanity's collective existence…somehow."

Aldo looked worriedly down to Jasper.

Doctor "Hairy-Legs" sat forward, sombre and serious now. "Whatever it is, it's accelerating. Sub-luminal shifts are spiking. We picked up a phase-glide event yesterday that matched the Kraków wave signature. Keep your ears to the ground Aldo while you're doing your tests today. Be very careful –as careful you can old chap. They're moving fast… but so are we. We still have a good trick or two up our sleeve that we can throw at them." She said, ending in a slightly upbeat, pluckier tone.

Etienne gave Aldo a nod, changing the subject. "And how's the young girl doing? Frank's lovely niece?"

Aldo nodded slowly. "She's… holding well. The thread held. The rewrite's stable. We just couldn't save her dog too." He looked around the room "Jasper and the bells hit the right harmonics yesterday morning, the non-Euclidian amplifier manifested a mend in the timeline, and my good friend's deceased sister is now alive and well."

Vittorio crossed himself softly. "Thank God for the bells."

"And thank God for the networks that kept them intact," Aldo added gently. "Every council member, every agent, every soul that risked exposure to reinstate them. It wasn't just cultural restoration — it was a harmonics recalibration. It reset the lattice. That's what the Riftwalkers don't understand…yet."

"Well, we also need to thank your special furry friend here and his distinctive howl." Doctor Lindley said her voice softening as she looked lovingly at Jasper, who had now jumped into the spare seat next to Aldo. "That howl — I still can't explain how you triangulated the pitch corridor. It was like... like a perfect harmonic key pressed at the right quantum depth. You didn't just tune him — you found a needle in a dimensional haystack that seems to be saving the day."

"Dogs hear the field," Aldo said simply. "They always have. We managed to build a lab and finally developed the tech that was quiet enough to listen back and understand their souls."

No one spoke for a few moments.

Vittorio stood, walked over and clapped him on the shoulder with surprising tenderness. "Well, *E allora, mio dolce amico dal cuore nobile*, our daily briefing update must be kept short, otherwise we risk drawing attention to our absences." He looked at Aldo and smiled "You've got your work cut out for you today, old friend –as do the rest of us." He waved a finger around jokingly at the other physicists. "Let's all get stuck-into-it, like only we know how to do, shall we?"

Aldo smiled at his colleagues and nodded. His Asperger's got the better of him, leaving him wordless. He loved them, they were his good people –his good friends, and he felt good just being around them. Jasper felt it too. Rising slowly from his seat, Aldo turned to head to the door. Jasper jumped down and trotted over to the door too, getting their first, tail wagging, waiting for Aldo to come over.

"Time to ring the quiet ones today my special sheepherder." he said patting him on the head as he opened the door.

And the two of them were gone.

"Keep your radar finely tuned for any signs of danger," Etienne said after Aldo had left the meeting. "I fear they will try and do something horrible to Paxton first. I don't know what, or how, or when, just my intuition is screaming-out that he's in very big danger – or is it Dr Kendrick? –or both of them?" She looked to Vittorio "Please, as subtly as you can and without raising any alarm with Paxton to their presence, can you have one of our security-teams double their detail over him?"

"I'll make a call to Luc now and get him onto it. Aldo needs to work without being overwhelmed with fear or paranoia, so yes -agreed we mustn't alarm him to more of our security than there already is – I'll tell Luc and his boys to keep themselves discreet and low, but make sure he's absolutely protected at the same time." Vittorio replied.

"The Riftwalkers aren't patient. They've waited long enough to play their ultimate card and now they can sense we are on the verge of closing them down for good." Doctor "Hairy" added in her clipped Manchester accent. "Our gloves just came off people, and I say we hit 'em as hard and as fast as we possibly can –give them one of those good old knuckle-sandwiches my Grandad always spoke about serving-up to the bad guys when they were well overdue for one –right in the old kisser!"

The others nodded repeatedly, smiled and then rose to leave the room.

Doctor Paxton Alderson and Jasper in the Lab of Good Vibrations

"If every soul is only a waveform, still resonating
somewhere in the cosmic field, while life is but a
harmonic vibrancy,
then what is death, really?
Is it some kind of silence? – it can't be!
—or is it the pause between notes, waiting to be
played once again?

I keep asking myself this… over and over again…
if everything is a vibration,
perhaps love is the ultimate frequency that never
fades.
Perhaps, because of love, we never really die.
Perhaps we only change our harmonics

—our own specific waveform simply begins to
fluctuate slightly.

And if the living world could sing together with
love as one —If we could all create beautiful, exact
harmonies and sounds,
could we sing those who have passed back to life?
Is there, somewhere, a special resonance
waiting to be played that could reset all of us?"

—Doctor Paxton Alderson, May 25, 2024

Singing Bowls of Sadness

He strolled through the bottom of a large arch that formed a giant-sized letter A.

Five more of these red, steel girders arranged in this shape completed the structural supports that ran along the outside of the synchrocyclotron building, giving it a distinctive look that was pleasing to his eye.

Jasper bounded towards their old tree in front of them and found a decent sized stick, then brought it back to his master.

"We might drive around and park-up there today buddy. I haven't got the time to walk there." He said, patting Jasper's head. "Just a couple of throws. That'll have to do for now." He hurled the stick with all his might. Jasper shot off after it — a blur of pure, in-the-moment dog joy.

They eventually climbed into the L-Bug and reversed out of the bay they were in, then took it slowly around the adjacent right turn at the end, driving past the long row of bikes parked next to the old building.

Keeping the bug slow, he turned left and headed all the way down the back road towards a tree-lined, grassy knoll forming a long, T-section embankment at the very end.

He slowly veered left into a bay directly in front of a twelve-foot-high, non-descript, tin shed tucked into the grassy embankment. Beside the shed to one side, ran a set of time-worn concrete steps all the way up to the back. Five meters over on the opposite side of the shed was a series of diagonally sloping tin covers. This slight angle prevented any snow build-up during the winter months.

The old shed was unmarked, unregistered, and untraceable in any of the official CERN schema.

Its purpose? Unknown. Its contents? Assumed irrelevant, but most likely functionally necessary in some non-scientific, mundane way. Most who actually took a long enough look at it, guessed sewerage, water pumps, or electrical utilities. Yet, no one ever really gave it any thought after seeing it there.

And that was exactly how Aldo wanted it.

That's exactly the way Aldo liked it and why he loved it. Simple, basic camouflage and concealment at its best.

Built mostly at night and in the wee early hours of the morning, he and his small, breakaway team of Orange Sand members had designed and engineered his special lab some fifty meters underground. Using compact, next-generation equipment, they tunnelled and installed an incredibly strong, mag-lev platform to ferry all the phenomenally heavy items down and up on the eight meter by four meter platform –entirely hidden under the old, rusty, tin covers.

All of the bells and highly sensitive items of equipment were taken down to his lab using this powerful elevator, including the behemoth sized, 6.5-tonne "La Gardéeuse".

A monstrous, bronze bell, 2.5 metres in diameter. Acquired by Aldo two decades earlier during a liquidation-sale at a monastery in the Haute-Provence.

Other collectors fought for chalices and faded tapestries. Aldo came only for this majestic bell.

It pulsated with something ancient. Something *real*. His measuring devices told him "This was the one he needed!"

Favours were called in. Papers forged. A reinforced flatbed truck rolled out in silence under a moonless sky.

By the time it reached Geneva at 3:00 AM, customs officers had already been paid to glance the other way.

The offloading was done with reverence — like a funeral procession — rolling past back gates and service roads rarely used by CERN staff.
And then, in the predawn stillness, *La Gardéeuse* descended down into the earth.

Lowered by an advanced, super-powerful, electromagnetic winch-crane on the back of the truck, guided by gloved hands and held breaths, it was placed gently onto the elevator platform, then vanished, sinking slowly down into Aldo's hidden cathedral of sound.

Upon successful completion of his lab in absolute, undetected, clandestine fashion, the secret good-guy scientists at CERN had managed to score themselves a massive win over the secret bad-guy scientists who were also there too. The bad guys had been likewise operating in their own, secret bad-guy labs that they'd secretly gone and built on the sly…But Aldo's lab was a game changer among game changers.

As soon as the bells were all mounted into place inside their new home, he began to ring them. Although unheard aboveground by human ears, every demon and evil spirit within a one-kilometre radius packed their bags and headed for the hills…so to speak…demons HATE any type of bell ringing of any sort – especially a six tonne, bronze giant!

The "Chalice of Re-Awakening" — that's what Aldo called this hybrid system lab. Part baroque cathedral, part sonic collider, part dog-bed. It was his masterpiece of acoustic alchemy. Wave-particle physics and old-school steampunk had hooked-up and had an off-the-records, wild and precocious kid.

Jasper's howls, when channelled through the tone matrix and harmonized with the bronze ring of *La Gardéeuse* and the ghost-chords of the ancient Tartarian pipe organ, formed what Aldo termed the "Resonant Teardrop" — a ripple not just of sound and light, but of reality itself.

A frequency beyond detection. A vibration beyond corruption.

The Riftwalkers couldn't digest it — they couldn't even *see* where it was situated. Its resonance rendered it invisible to their tracking tech, reducing them down to the equivalent of a blind person in a dense mist, trying to claw away at a bad smell with a gaff-hook.

It was more than camouflage.

It was soul-coded immunity.

They climbed out of the Bug and padded across the cracked bitumen toward the concrete steps. The tin shed loomed plain and expressionless, tucked into the embankment like the old, forgotten utility shack that it was supposed to be.

The front door was always closed now, even though Aldo often used to leave it ajar from time to time — a little psychological bait for any of the nosy-parkers poking around.

Behind that lower front door? A decoy room — small, musty, and convincingly dull. Two mid-sized water tanks churned and cycled endlessly, their circuits humming, with outdated circuit boards blinking away pointlessly on the wall.

The audio illusion of vital plumbing work going-on, was surprisingly effective. A few labels in French and Swiss, some forged maintenance paperwork, and a faint mildew scent finished the job. A perfect ruse for the nearby sticky-beaks and passers-by.

Nowadays, he had no need to leave it open anymore, like he did when he first built the lab, seemingly popping up overnight like it did. Building 172, just next door, had long since become a true storage closet —the original staff vacated years ago, now a bland, locked, irrelevant building, just like one of many on the site. No one gave either structure a second glance anymore. And that's how Aldo liked it.

Jasper gave a quiet woof and looked up at him expectantly.

"Alright, mon ami," Aldo muttered, glancing around one last time. "Let's go ring the bells of war."

They went up the concrete steps at the side of the shed and through the small gate at the top that led to the proper door situated around the back corner.

This door was more robust, discreet, yet fortified in a nonchalant style. He reached beneath the fake fuse box beside the door, triggered the hidden biometric latch, and the unassuming entrance door shhhhhhh-ed open with a low mechanical slide.

Cool, dry air spilled upward from the darkness below. With a final glance toward the distant CERN buildings above, Aldo and Jasper stepped into the shadows — and the door whispered shut behind them.

The passage sloped gently at first, then steepened into a spiralling descent of raw stone and reinforced steel. Faint, violet-blue, LED lights illuminated the steps just enough to see where they were going. The walls were embedded with a layered insulation — magnetic shielding, acoustic dampening, and something Aldo only referred to as "soul padding."

Jasper's claws clicked lightly on the metal grates as they went.

Halfway down, sat the elevator platform's landing area, in readiness for them — a matte-black, hard-rubber, thickly layered, huge rectangular slab, big enough to carry an elephant or two and strong enough to lower an entire cathedral bell or organ without a tremble. Aldo tapped away at the copper pad beside it and whispered, *"La Gardéeuse."*

The elevator hummed to life, safety rails efficiently rose-up around the sides and the platform began to descend.

As the dim light faded above, and the warmth of the surface receded, Aldo's face took on a quiet glow caused by the fairy lights that covered the safety railing — anticipation, defiance, maybe even a touch of reverence.

Below, the old machines that had been married to the new ones, were waiting patiently. The chalice was warming up.

And the music — the true music — was about to begin.

Aldo's lab was madness and brilliance wrapped in copper wires and the spiritual echoes of a cathedral.

Fifty meters below the surface, carved out like a subterranean sanctum, the chamber stretched wider than most imagined possible beneath CERN. It pulsed with life — not just from the machines, but from the eerie harmony of the space itself. The walls were lined with a strange dampening material that warped light slightly, bending shadows in unpredictable ways, as if the lab itself didn't fully agree with standard, Euclidean geometry.

At the heart of it all stood a towering console — a Frankenstein's dream of science fiction and sacred ritual. Curved panels of brushed aluminium stood shoulder to shoulder with polished brass knobs, vacuum tubes, glowing glyphs, and sleek next-gen holographic touchscreens. It looked like a starship flight deck built by Nikola Tesla and a Tibetan monk on a mushroom bender. Oscilloscopes blinked. Holograms hovered. Even a few humming reel-to-reels clicked away in the background, archiving and recording things no human ear could parse.

Just left of the central cluster, tucked between a suspended plasma array and an old rack of steampunk voltage meters, sat an antique, baroque organ-keyboard, its wood lovingly restored, its ivory keys burnished from decades of prayerful performance. Thick, coiled cables now linked it to the rest of Aldo's matrix — so that sacred sound and science could play as one. Looming above, in the dim curve of the ceiling, a bank of massive cathedral organ pipes rose like bronze tusks — scavenged from old Tartarian ruins across Europe, repurposed into sonic weapons of resonance. Their silent majesty stood in contrast to the pulsing equipment below — a temple within a machine.

Suspended from the high dome hung La Gardéeuse, the majestic six-tonne bronze bell, flanked by two smaller siblings acquired from different centuries — each tuned, mounted, and connected to a resonance harmonizer. Around the perimeter stood clusters of Tibetan singing bowls, crystal chimes, quartz rods, and bell trees, all wired in subtle mesh to superconductive coils. Every one of them had a voice — and Aldo knew how to make them sing.

Jasper's platform sat just left of centre — a raised, copper-plated dais, with spirals of Tesla coils rising behind it and fine copper filaments running underneath forming an ancient circuit board partly designed by druids. Above him, an intricate spider-web of waveguides. In front of him, a vintage 1950's chrome microphone, lovingly restored — the kind Sinatra might've crooned into — now wired-up to a bank of quantum bio-resonance readers.

Aldo stood tall at his throne of dials and theory, hands poised, coat flapping slightly from the lab's recycled air flow. His eyes sparkled with mischief.

"Alright, buddy," he said, flipping open the red plexiglass cover of an absurdly oversized, cartoon-style throw-switch, labelled simply: *ON*.

"You ready to start work?"

Jasper gave a small, eager bark.

With a grin, Aldo threw the switch down hard.
The lab *hummed*. The universe *listened*.

Around seven hours later, they had already performed three successful runs since the morning. The bowls — tuned with impossible precision — were beginning to resonate not just in harmonic frequency, but in something deeper. Something *time-rooted*. The synchronicity between the bowls, the Tartarian organ, and La Gardéeuse's low, thunderous pulse had created a stabilised frequency Aldo could only describe in metaphysical terms.

This final, late afternoon run — the fourth — was their most daring one yet.

The goal: to *restore life*. Not metaphorically. Literally…to restore life –again.

Twenty-three monks from a remote monastery in the Bhutanese Himalayas, slaughtered weeks earlier by the Riftwalkers. Aldo had acquired every shred of their acoustic DNA: the bowls they used, the trumpets, the conch shells, the great bronze gongs — even the resonant architecture of the temple's inner sanctum, encoded via old acoustic chamber scans.

It had taken weeks to prepare the sequence. Jasper had been perfectly attuned all morning — his howls rippling through the harmonic matrix with clarity and strength. Each tone matched a resonance field. Each bowl, when struck and amplified, created a vibratory scaffolding upon which spirit and memory could climb back onto.

A shimmering, Golden-Ratio arc of blue-white resonance began to form between the largest bowls. The air around them pulsed softly, bending with sacred vibration. Jasper's howl sustained the harmonic peak, his voice woven into the tones like a living filament of light.

Above the array, a holographic mandala spun slowly — not mere ornament, but a frequency map. Aldo had transcribed the ancient sand mandala from the Bhutanese monastery into a complex array of Hertz waveforms, each concentric ring corresponding to a precise resonant calibration. This was more than art. It was resurrection. The bowls, the bell, the Rouen organ, and Jasper himself — all were now synchronizing with the encoded soul-print of the lost monks. And for a moment, impossibly, the alignment began to hold. They were on their way home again.

As the final notes began to rise, Aldo adjusted the modulation dials, heart pounding. The waveform on the central display was locking into a golden helix. A shimmering arc of blue-white resonance began to form between the largest bowls.

Jasper howled once more — a piercing, majestic song-tone — and then he suddenly *yelped loudly*.

Aldo froze.

The dog crumpled to the floor like a marionette with cut strings.

"JASPER!"

He slammed the main kill switch. The resonance collapsed instantly into silence. Even the organ let out a residual moan.

Aldo scrambled across the platform to where Jasper lay on his copper-filament pad, limp and still, one paw curled unnaturally under his chest. His eyes were closed, breath faint.

"No, no, no — *mon garçon*, stay with me—"

He cradled Jasper's head gently, his heart hammering louder than the bells had ever rung. He scanned the vitals — nothing immediate. No pulse irregularities. But something had hit him. Something *else*. Something *hard* and *brutal*.

He didn't know it yet, but across the world, something pure and irreplaceable had just been ripped apart, destroyed — savaged by forces so cruel and sadistic they defied all human understanding. So many innocent lives had just been taken in the night, their light extinguished without warning, and without a single shred of mercy...many of those souls had been psychically and ethereally connected to their furry brother who was now lying unconscious in Aldo's arms.

And somewhere just as equally far away, the bells of that lost monastery would now remain forever silent. Their sacred prayers, bell ringing and chanting would continue to remain nothing more than the faint echoes of the past.

Jasper slowly began to regain consciousness. His whimpers belayed the degree to which he was shaken, scared and mentally and emotionally wounded. He nuzzled Aldo like a nervous, newborn puppy. Aldo wept. His beautiful best friend was hurt, and he didn't know why or how.

Half an hour later, he had carefully carried Jasper in his arms all the way up on the elevator platform and then down the steps and into the car. Placing him gently on the back seat and covering him with a warm blanket. He seemed to be Okay for now, but whatever it was had left him entirely weak and possibly in need of a visit to the Vet if he didn't improve.

Off they drove west, the L-Bug roaring along Rte de Meyrin, back to Aldo's apartment.

He planned to stoke the cast-iron-stove heater in the lounge room and get it roaring away first thing, just as soon as he got in the door, then he would set Jasper down in front of it.

And Just Like That...

They sat together on the edge of the curb, coffee cups in hand, the early morning air cool and thick with silence. Sherri hadn't said much since the sun came up, and Byron was unusually quiet too — as if some unspoken heaviness had just suddenly settled over their neighbourhood, an unseen, ashen kind of invisible snow of sorts.

Her mother was back. Whole. Laughing in the kitchen just before dawn like nothing had happened.

But there was something else going on. Something enormous. Something heavy and dark,

And neither of them could shake the strange hollowness that clung to the corners of their minds...An empty space was now there that shouldn't be there.

Birds chirped. The breeze picked up. Cars rolled slowly out from garages and driveways. The world was moving on, but it was limping in some imperceptible way.

They both stared at the old bamboo garden pole sticking out from the lawn nearby — the makeshift dog-flag from their Scoot-Skittles matches. It was still there, fluttering faintly. The hand-painted paw pads, worn but distinct, watched back at them like the eyes of a long-gone, faded ghost staring into their souls.

Sherri blinked. "Byron... what animal is that again? On the flag?"

Byron squinted. "I... dunno. It's some kind of animal paw, though. Right? A tiger?"

"Yeah." She ran a thumb along the cup's edge. "We've always played Skittles with that up, but I just realised... I don't remember why we painted that on there? And also, how did we get the Scoot part of the name either?"

He frowned. "Scoot. Yeah. Was that someone's nickname, maybe? Or because you can use a scooter or something...? I can't bloody remember now...it's gone."

They both paused...frozen.

A chill passed through them like a soft exhale from a deeper place.

Far across the globe — an empty dog bowl sat untouched beneath a kitchen table in Saskatchewan. The middle-aged lady looked down at it wondering why a large metal bowl was there, why had she put that thing down there on the floor in the first place? - And why did her heart and soul suddenly ache so badly today? Why did she feel like all she wanted to do was to curl up in a ball and cry her heart out?

In Berlin, a child was crying at the edge of a park, holding a chewed-up tennis ball with no memory of why he was throwing it, or holding it, and why it was all wet with slobbery liquid.

In Kyoto, a Buddhist priest lit incense without understanding why the temple had an empty leash rack near the entry steps. He just felt overwhelming love for the empty space inside one of the unknown harnesses laying on the ground – something was remaining there, a spiritual energy he could sense that was so full of unconditional love, and yet, it just wasn't there anymore either. Gone.

And in Nairobi, a blind man patted the side of his leg as he stepped out into the street, waiting for a companion who had never existed. Who was it he relied on so much to get him through the day and through all those long, cold nights? – His imagination was playing tricks on him he figured…or was it? Had there been someone there once that he loved so much, beyond any words in his language that he could find to describe how strong that love he felt was? Or was he just getting a little old and a bit over emotional today? He was on his own, and yet he could faintly feel the heart and spirit of a best friend and a guardian, somewhere, not too far away. Who was that?!

All over the world, small relics remained — old, worn and weathered leashes, half-buried bones, paw prints and tufts of fur that were dissipating from where those things had worn into the habits of households, sofas, clothing and car seats. They were becoming orphaned memories, untethered and drifting away from reality and also away from the minds they once belonged to.

The word "dog" and any understanding or memory of the species was now missing.

And all across the world, hearts began to ache without knowing why— not sharply, but with a slow, deep, soul-breaking sorrow.

As if someone dearly, impossibly loved had just died suddenly.
But no one could say who it was, or why.
There was no tangible way to describe the way everyone felt today.

Minds almost entirely forgot –Yet hearts broke with an unknowing anguish as the soul of humanity cried out with a confused harrowing grief…The world seemed a desperately crushing, hollow place to be in today.

Back in Coolangatta, Jake rolled up on his skateboard, tossing a casual wave. "Yo, we heading down the road today? There's a crew from PBC setting up a Skittles game in the SCU carpark."

Byron looked up. "Yeah? Could be good."

Sherri, still dazed, asked, "Did you hear about my mum?"

Jake shrugged. "What about her?"

"She... she came back last night. From the—" she paused, unsure how to say it. "From being gone."

Jake looked confused. "What do yah mean, being gone?– Where'd she go to exactly?"

That quiet, eerie chill hit again. The strange blankness. Byron scratched his temple.

The less you thought about it – the more the absent memories started to fade from the mind.

"Oh, she didn't go anywhere special, forget about it. She just drove down to Ballina to see my Aunty – almost had an accident on the way home." Sherri wanted to see if it would trigger any memories in Jake... Nothing.

"Okay, is she alright?" He asked back robotically.

"She's perfectly fine now. It was a close shave with a two-carriage truck. Just about collided into the side of her while she was merging out onto the M1." Sherri replied as a bait to see if anything further could be spotted in his facial expression to indicate he remembered something about the original accident...Nothing did. Jake's face just stared blankly, reflecting a mind that had no remnant scraps anymore of that version.

That's when she remembered, with a fresh, striking clarity, everything about this new, second, alternate accident –A drunk driver had veered off the road and gone up onto the pedestrian footpath striking her from behind. Almost with no warning, the car rammed into her while she was walking to the park. She hadn't a clue why she was walking to the park in the first place. Had it not of been for the first responders in a nearby house providing vital first aid, she would not have survived. In her mind, there was no longer a clear memory of the accident involving her mum and her colliding with the truck as they were driving home from Balina…Not in this timeline. She still felt it, she remembered it and yet could now only just vaguely recall it. Had she skipped over from some other, slightly different multiverse?

She'd lost her mum in that other multiversal timeline, she wasn't ever going to forget that, but she suddenly realised she was forgetting, something more. What else had happened? There had been more to it, she felt there was more loss, more heartbreak than what she was remembering of the original accident, and also this second version too. Was there somebody else involved in both accidents? Who was it? Could it be possible she was completely forgetting about someone?

"Let's get going hey?" Byron said enthusiastically, breaking the weird vibe they were falling into.

They grabbed their boards, bikes and scooters and set off. The path to the carpark was familiar, but something about it felt… observed. Like they were walking into a memory that was still being written.

By the time they reached the SCU carpark, Marvin and Jacinta were already there, setting up bottles and cones. Hannah was sitting cross-legged on the curb, sketching away on a little drawing pad she had resting in her lap.

She'd drawn the other kids and had started to sketch the milk bottle with the dog-flag, when she suddenly froze and eerily gazed at it. She started crying. Noticing her crying and then looking to see what was causing her to cry, they all suddenly saw it together – all of them at once. They properly saw it with their full awareness.

The flag hadn't changed. It had resisted going. Same bamboo stick. Same stitched canvas. Same funny paw print they'd painted onto it with black paint.

But now the paw shimmered faintly, like it was brushed in memory instead of paint.

The bamboo stick and the flag attached to it, stuck out from the same, old, 3-litre milk bottle. The very same one that Jacinta had hurled at Jake on that Saturday afternoon eons ago when they invented the game. Jake had used an old can of spray paint to mark it, as he had grown a special, sentimental attachment to it and saw it as the "seed" of the game. Over time, that particular bottle was used again and again (they almost religiously didn't change the water in it – only topping it up when it got spilled over).

 This particular bottle had become a sentimental favourite for all of the group to use also –it was their one and only game bottle. They cherished it and took good care of it...it was their lucky bottle, the only one they ever used for their...

Jake blurted it out loudly, "Dog Base!" Everyone stopped. Nobody said a word.

Marvin's eyes welled with a sudden rush of tears. "Who... who was Scoot? Was he someone I knew? Where did he go? Did he die or something?"

No one could answer.

They all just stood there, looking at the flag as though it was a relic dug out of some long-buried temple. Reverence mixed with sorrow. A collective heartache for something or someone they couldn't name. A low, phantom howl echoed faintly on the breeze — not quite real. But felt.

And for the first time, they knew: something had been torn away from them. And they all missed that something more than their hearts could bear.

But the longer they looked at the flag, the paw print and the bamboo stick in the old, plastic milk bottle that was half-filled with water, the more a powerful light began to shine through in their minds. A smiling face was looking back at them from the emptiness. A tail was wagging and there were two eyes so full of love and happiness staring through the Universal ether directly into their hearts and souls....

Dog! –Dog! –Dog...they were faintly beginning to remember a word...The word had lived-on through them. It was now made from canvas, old black paint forming a paw print, a bamboo stick and a scratched-up, painted-on, plastic 3-litre milk bottle.

It stood there silently yelling at them in an unspoken cosmic language that their hearts were rapidly translating and re-unpacking and reinserting into their memories.

Then, slowly, all together as one, they whispered the word in an astonished realisation and reverence:

"**Dog**" –The word *dog* had power. The word –*dog*- had life to it...Happiness and laughter bubbled up from it...Love was personified in the word they were now remembering. The bottle and the flag gave them that remembrance.

Jake had saved that old bottle because he saw it as the seed of the game.

Now the bottle had become the seed that would save humanity and rescue our best friends too.

Murder and Theft

Eurasia, Late Stone Age

– Upper Palaeolithic Period
– 38,752 years BC
...and 9 hours beforehand.

...Somewhere west of present day *Kaktolga Кактолга* near the Ergun River border region of China and Russia...

The flowing water of the Ergun River was bloated and heavy at this time of the year. A far away glacier-melt was taking place thousands of kilometres upstream and had filled the river to capacity, causing it to burst at its banks in many places.

Plants and wildlife flourished in this warm, fertile, humid and well irrigated region as the season slowly rolled into summer.

A chance encounter a few months ago had brought the two of them together –although greater forces of goodness and love had played a greater hand in the actual process, more than just chance alone did.

The young boy was carrying a dozen Vaal-rabbits back to his tribe's camp area. He'd butchered and cooked-up one of them on a makeshift fire earlier, devouring most of it to assuage his lunchtime hunger. What little was left, he'd kept close on-hand to nibble away on as he trudged back home over the muddy ground.

That's when they crossed paths, stopped and stared straight into each other's eyes.

He had no fear of them. They'd never attacked or come close to posing any kind of threat to anyone in his clan.

In fact, their nearby presence, as well as an increase in their numbers, was proving to be a safe and reassuring development as they seemed to be helping to keep the more ferocious and feared predators at bay, especially during the nights.

Both species had begun to smell each other and had grown acquainted with their nearby presence. Their scents had already introduced themselves and made friends.

He was fond of them, often watching them pass by at a distance in common areas during the day. He thought they were very beautiful creatures, and he found himself instinctively drawn towards them without any fear.

The wolf was on her own. Cautious, but not scared. Her nose raised, she sniffed in his direction. The cooked meat of the Vaal-rabbit was an enticingly, delectable smell. Meat being cooked was something new to her pack and they had only recently begun to catch the smell of it wafting on the breeze, always drawing them closer to the humans when they caught a whiff of it.

Now, with her tail wagging and head dipping, she was drawn to move closer and smell and sniff more. She was salivating, yet something more drew her nearer to this creature that impulsively she ought to have feared and kept at a good distance away from, but didn't.

He drew-down the cooked rabbit from his shoulder-sling and began to tear-off a piece of meat. Lowering himself to a crouch, arm outstretched, he began to gently wave it around. In a low, hushed, and loving tone, he coaxed the animal to come closer.

She looked at the piece of meat he was holding; it smelt inviting but there was something more to it, she also felt drawn to his spirit, his face, his smell too and she wagged her tail even more as she slowly padded closer.

The distance between them closed from 5 meters down to 3. Then 2...she paused and sat on her haunches. He coaxed and cooed and waved the meat, extending his arm straight out as far as it would go. Slowly she stood and moved again.

She padded closer.

He held his breath, heart thudding like a drum. His arm trembled from holding it out for so long, but he didn't dare move. The wind was silent. Even the river seemed to hush in anticipation.

Then, with one final slow step, she reached forward and gently took the meat from his hand. Their eyes met again. A strange and ancient recognition passed between them — a connection not forged in words or history, but in something older: love and trust.

He reached forward and touched her fur.

It was softer than he imagined. It smelt like...home. Warm and soothing, as if life itself was buzzing within each hair. She didn't flinch. She looked at him with caring eyes.

He smelt her dog smell. And ran his hands softly down her coat, becoming the first human to do this.

She began to lick the greasy fat from his hand and his face. He laughed with joy and happiness. And as she licked away, she became the first dog to lick a human hand and face and imprint on our smell, as well as our hearts and our souls forever onwards.

And in that divine moment, angels sang — not with trumpets, but with the hushed harmony of true, unconditional love, honouring the birth of something special and sacred into our world and our lives.

A beautiful, hidden fabric of the universe had begun to draw tight, as if a golden thread had just been stitched together by boy and wolf into one shared, eternal pathway for all of humanity to follow along.

Almost every day, around the same time, they would meet each other in the same spot where they would excitedly greet, pat and cuddle. He always had something to feed her. There were always more laughs, licks, tail-wagging and belly-rubs the more times they met.

It might've lasted forever and grown...as this union would become the bridge on which more humans and wolves would have bonded and became best friends... it did start to happen ...

But then the air shattered.

It didn't crack or explode — it was ripped. Torn like cloth.

A high-pitched, *metallic shriek* tore across the sky, like a violin string being wrenched loose from the bones of time. The grass flattened. The river recoiled.

The boy fell backward.

And something fell *through* the sky. Then another one, and another — not flying, not teleporting — but *tearing* and clawing their way down through the air.

Like ashen, shadowy liquorice drenched in crude oil, the Riftwalkers emerged with angular limbs, writhing joints, and hollows where their eyes should've been. They didn't walk; they *twitched*. They *skipped* across space with a seething hatred and horror. Their entrance smelled of burnt hair, sulphur and rotting meat.

Usually, nine out of ten of their attempts to rip through a time-field had failed. This one had succeeded. By mistake.

They hadn't meant to arrive here…exactly…

But they saw the wolf. They saw the boy. And something inside them snarled with malicious hunger and opportunistic relish as it would assuredly fit in with their plans non-the-less.

One of them bellowed — a wet, rattling roar like a butcher's saw in a basilica.

The timber wolf growled and took a protective stance before the boy, her hackles raised, tail stiff, a defiant spirit burning in her hazel eyes.

She would not run. Her canine sprit didn't know why, but she was protecting a human.

She *would not* let them harm this person whom she loved so much.

But the Riftwalkers did not hesitate.

They lunged.

And though she fought — she fought with a ferocity that transcended pure love and devotion— there were too many of them, too fast, too cruel. Her yelps rang out in pain and courage. The boy screamed her name, though he hadn't given her one yet.

Then silence.

She was limp.

Broken...dead.

They tossed her into the raging river like garbage.

The boy ran, blind with tears, heart torn to pieces, chased by fear and unmitigated grief.

He couldn't know it — but the human race had just been robbed...and ruined.

Something sacred had just been destroyed.

The Riftwalkers could no longer maintain coherence within the local spacetime field and began to collapse inward, vacuumed back into the jagged folds of the non-Euclidean manifold they had so violently ruptured through. As their crude, occult-tech wormhole destabilised, several were lost—smashed apart at the subatomic level, their forms decohering into raw quantum noise as they were scattered across the jagged quasicrystalline lattice of their own malformed dimensional breach.

Yet, the task they'd initially set out to do was now complete.

They were ready to launch their spiritual takeover and enslavement of humanity, and as far as they were aware, nothing was going to stop them now.

A Small Fire of Hope

The old apartment was warm now—too warm, maybe—but Frank liked it that way. The cast-iron stove roared with life in the corner, its glass door glowing orange, carbonising and devouring into ash the last trace of the feet he'd removed from the pair of boots and tossed in there. He didn't want to think about anything too much right now as he slid the iron poker back into place, watching the flickering flames dancing behind the grate. The boots—well, they'd been quietly disposed of in the recycling bin out back, doused with bleach, sole side up, just old, worn-out footwear no longer needed anymore.

The pleasant, homely smell of lemon-pepper fish now filled the room, mingling with the faint scent of smouldering wood and the citrus edge of cleaning spray. The pasta boiled gently on the stovetop, vegetables simmering in garlic beside it.

Frank moved through the apartment space with a kind of reverent orderliness. He'd busily cleaned away everything, dried and tidied it all back up to its original condition. Switching on an old, retro lamp beside the front door, he finally allowed himself to relax a little. The old-world glow of the old-fashioned bulb, cast a golden halo over the cast-iron fireplace stove, the 85-inch TV screen, the sofa, the rug (now completely dry) and the armchairs, as it illuminated the living space against the deep darkness of the cold winter's night outside.

Then came the sound of keys jingling.

The lock turned. A pause. Then the door creaked open, and Aldo stepped in slowly —absolutely tired, sad and worn-out, but not alone.

Jasper.

He hobbled forward very slowly, tail wagging like a metronome struggling to find tempo. But the moment he saw Frank, he broke into an excited sprint, legs all springy, tail wagging wildly, and for a short while he was a puppy again.

Frank dropped down and sat cross-legged. "Jasparrrrr! -- You legend!"

The two snuzzled—old best friends, reunited beyond time and logistical odds. Jasper licked the side of Frank's face before collapsing into him from exhaustion, breathing heavily, his weight and warmth something Frank hadn't realised just how much he'd missed.

Aldo was smiling as he made his way into the lounge. "Hey! look at you! Good to see you again man! This is a well needed surprise!" He glanced back at the doorway and scratched his head. "I guess I must have left the front door completely unlocked again, like I usually do when I'm racing off to work in the mornings." He was laughing as he walked over and jovially gave Frank a hearty handshake and a pat on the arm.

"Don't worry, it was well and truly locked-up properly, but you did leave the main window over there wide-as-can-be open." Frank gestured, "It was like a cold storage room in here when I got in! It's taken me a good few hours to warm and dry the place up."

Aldo looked at the window and laughed, "That's right, I was temporarily airing the place out before leaving – I always forget to close something!" He went and sat down in one of the sofa chairs near the fireplace to warm his hands. "You're timing's perfect though, however, we've had a rough afternoon, so some good company is just the perfect remedy for that. When exactly did you fly in?"

"Hmmmm, well, you see, I didn't so much fly in. More the case of me dropping down into here only a couple of hours ago now." Frank pointed to the ceiling and then the chrono-pistol resting on the coffee table. "It's been a very crazy, upsetting and hectic day I gotta say. Had myself a rather stressful and rushed early morning start, which led to some very hasty and unplanned travel arrangements, far worse than the hassles of catching a plane –let me tell you. It was more a case of me simply having no other options than to drop into here when I did."

Aldo nodded, immediately understanding exactly how Frank had arrived with no further explanation needed.

"I know what a cheap skate you can be, but has the cost of plane tickets really gone up that much recently? You do realise, it's probably way safer to travel by air than it is to portal jump – right?" He laughed a little.

"Trust me, a nice warm, cushy first-class seat would have been my first and only option in getting here today, compared to the hastened escape I needed to take, but it was one of those mornings where I just couldn't seem to catch a break –I didn't even get to drink my morning coffee!" He rubbed the side of his face "Lucky for me I was beta-testing the dimensionally folded concealment parameters..." He gestured to the portal-gun again "of that device, tucked inside my back molar, for a rainy-day moment and wouldn't you know it, that raining day was this morning. I defiantly wouldn't be here now if I hadn't of decided to shrink it down and test it out yesterday – and your place wouldn't be so lovely and warm, and dinner wouldn't be almost ready either."

"Well, glad you made it safely here in one piece." Aldo breathed in "Smells good too whatever you're cooking away in there. You should've been a chef!" He pointed to Jasper resting in Frank's lap. "He sure seems happy to see you, but he's definitely bushed-out. Something hit him hard this afternoon. I just don't know what it was. He had me extremely worried there for a while, but he seems a thousand times better now –especially since he's seen you!"

Frank was gently stroking Jasper's fluffy mane. "He does seem to be completely fragged-out. Not a trace of his usual, Border-Collie, hyperactive self. When did this happen?" Frank asked, his voice deeply concerned. Partially joining dots as they began appearing in his mind.

Aldo sighed and pulled off his coat. "Around four – right in the middle of an almost successful harmonic, life restoring re-alignment session. He just suddenly collapsed in the lab – passed-out ...it was like something smashed into him, but from the inside out."

Frank's expression darkened. He looked towards the fireplace, staring into it with a brooding anger. "I think that lines-up succinctly with something horrible that happened earlier..."

Aldo raised an eyebrow. "And what was that?"

Frank began to slowly explain to him the morning's events and what Marlowe had told him aboard the sub about the attack on the Sanctuary the night before. He looked at the old clock on the wall and continued, "That hit on the Sanctuary would have been just when you were in the final stages of your harmonic session – it lines up with the time zone over in Hong Kong!"

Frank then hesitated, angry and annoyed, then blurted out. "When I was escaping, I was so bloody frantic and overwhelmed and upset that I messed up on my time-zone calculations. I was telepathically programming the portal-gun to jump me back in time to here. My aim was to physically get here and to also have travelled back enough hours in time to be able to call and warn the Sanctuary. Only when I arrived here, did I realise I was half-an hour too late. I messed-up on my time-zone calculations." He pointed to an empty box of tissues on the coffee table. "I've done all the crying I think I can spare for one day. I'm not going to mentally punish and beat myself up anymore. At least that bastard Marlow is now fish food and the Order has lost a sub and an entire crew of goons."

"Oh man! That breaks my heart on so many levels. I'm so, so sorry Frank – It's all starting to get so terribly disgusting and horrendous out there – they certainly are busy launching some kind of next-level campaign of some kind then, aren't they?!"

Frank could only nod back as he pulled out his phone, a worried look had flooded his face. "Hold-on buddy. Let me check something first."

He called Sherri.

"Uncle Frank?" Her voice was soft, trembling. "Are you okay? Where are you?"

"I'm okay sweetie, I'm safe, and I'm here with Uncle Aldo in Geneva now. I got out of Hong Kong in a hurry and without any scratches. How about you Shez? You sound a bit on edge, what's going on there?"

There was silence on the other end. Then: "We remembered, Uncle Frank. Me, Byron, all of us. This morning...we didn't remember at first. But then...later on

in the morning, something about the old Scoot-Skittles
stuff, the flag... it all came flooding back to us. The dogs!
The dogs have ALL gone.”

Frank had started to ask the question, but then he realised
he already knew the answer.

“What do you mean you didn't remember? What did you
forget?” As he asked the question, he was consciously
aware that a section of his own mind had no memory
anymore whatsoever of what dogs were —he just didn't
remember dogs – at all...and yet there was Jasper laying
curled-up, head resting in his lap...A dog.

Frank closed his eyes, mental and emotional pain flooded
him. “They've ALL GONE! ALL OF THEM - gone! –
They've been deleted – But you guys remembered them
there Shez? Right? How?”

“I wish I didn't,” she whispered. “Because it hurts so badly
to remember – it causes so much pain missing them.” She
paused. “I'd forgotten Zeb Uncle Frank! – He just wasn't
there at all, at first, then it all came back.” She sobbed a
little, paused, then regained her resolve and continued.

“My friends and I, we'd completely forgotten they ever
existed – they just weren't there anymore in our minds or
in the world – anywhere – disappeared - gone -but we
each felt something terrible and it flooded back into our
memories when we were about to play a game of scoot-
skittles.” She stopped to briefly think, rubbed her head,
frowned, and then went on “It was the old flag with the
paw print on it that caused us to remember. Something
about the game was too strong to let us forget – it's so
weird, it's like we can now see two different versions of life
that are somehow running along at the same time, only
we're stuck in the horrible, rubbish version of the two!”

Frank looked down at Jasper, sleeping. "Sherri... Jasper's still here."

There was a pause. Then she said slowly and quietly, "Then he's maybe the last dog on Earth now Uncle Frank."

Dire, emergency thoughts and plans came flooding into Frank's mind –urgency beyond measure filled his veins.

"I gotta go sweetie – I'm sorry - I'll call you back very shortly – I gotta talk with Uncle Aldo some more. --You guys hang-tight there, don't go freaking out, just sit tight, hang-low and keep an eye out for my equipment, it should get there any day now. We're gonna need that! Alright?

"Okay, talk to you soon."

Frank ended the call slowly, setting the phone down on the coffee table.

Aldo was watching him closely. "Frank...?"

"They've erased dogs from our world's timeline, Aldo. All of them. Gone..."

And then Aldo felt it too. His mind percolated-up the erasure and the absence of "dog" from his memories. Yet, simultaneously, another part of his mind had been preserved and equally remembered them. His special laboratory had also protected his mind, and Jasper's existence, and as a result it was preserving his memories and acting like a reversing agent on the erasure. Jasper was reforming reality just by simply being there in the world.

If there is memory – then there's a way back.

Aldo's brow furrowed. "Jasper… he didn't just collapse!
He felt something monumental. Something
massive…That's what slammed into him!"

Frank nodded. "Yeah. And also, the attack on the
Sanctuary happened at the same time too—he would have
also felt that slam into him on the etheric band."

Aldo, thinking things through, spoke very slowly "When
they killed everyone at the Sanctuary – staff and dogs.
Burnt it all to the ground. It wasn't just about destruction.
They were timing it to coincide with another event,
weren't they? But what exactly?"

Frank's voice was quiet, contemplative as he repeated.
"They were definitely timing it with something else –
squashing-out all of the variables in their path…It was
something even bigger – A master stroke of evil…But,
how, where and what did the bastards actually do to pull-
it-off?"

Aldo's eyes widened. "The genesis wolf. The very first wolf
and the very first person. That's what they were after!
That's what they've been searching for all along. All those
parametric quantum sweeps we've been continually
detecting. They were formulating a proximal time
convergence. They located a nexus point in time to go
back to and destroy the bond!"

Frank blinked. "You're referring to… the original bond
between man and dog?"

"Yes! –Exactly! That's what the bastards have done!
They've erased it!" Aldo said. "Right about the same time
they hit the sanctuary. Jasper would have felt ALL of it! It
ALL came crashing through the ether into him- all at
once. That's what hit him so hard from the inside out.
Even though we were protected and shielded by my lab's

insulation fields, enough for him to survive a timeline change that should have erased him altogether, he still felt the kick of it trying to rip him out of existence, as well as the psychic cries of his brothers and sisters being murdered.”

Aldo stepped over to the fire, he needed the extra warmth. A cold, dark chill had consumed him. As he stood with his back to it, he looked down at Jasper sleeping cradled in Frank’s lap. “Our guy here really is special – he survived being erased. The walls. The dampening fields. It must have protected him from the Riftwalker’s reset!”

Frank nodded. “And probably also all the harmonics inside of there would have disrupted the E8 fabric of their reset. Those bells and the Tartarian organs would have broken-up their wave-field...Jasper shouldn’t be here anymore Aldo, and yet here he is.”

Aldo’s eyes burned. “Then that means we’re holding onto possibly the very last chance of saving the world.”

Frank brushed his hand over Jasper’s coat. “He’s maybe our last hope.”

Although he and Aldo hadn’t thought it through any further, over on the other side of the world, in Kirra Beach, Frank’s niece and her friends were also going to contribute in their own, very special way to saving the world too...

Brothers in Arms

It seemed like a hundred lifetimes ago to him now. A skinny, pimply faced teenager wandering up unannounced to the front gate of Fort de Nogent.

He'd presented himself at the gate carrying no ID papers, nothing, just his unshaven, raggedy, unwashed self. A true urchin of the streets.

Young, reckless, homeless, a common car thief looking for redemption and escape from the law. The Legion had offered him the clean slate that he was so desperately in need of.

They let him in through the gate and gave him a number, like they did with everyone.

After a lengthy vetting process involving medical, psyche and fitness evaluations, he was formally accepted and sent to the 4th Foreign Regiment (4e RE). This was the Legion's basic training centre in the small town of Castelnaudary, south of France.

At 17-years of age, signing himself away to serve in the Legion for 5 years felt like an entire lifetime's commitment to take on as a teenager. But for the first time in his life, he had a true home and something that felt like a real family he could be part of.

He'd come a long way in his military career since he stood at that front gate all those years ago. Over the decades that followed, he stayed-on, reenlisting and earning his promotional stripes across some of the world's most volatile flashpoints. He'd served in Djibouti, France's long-standing strategic outpost in East Africa, and deployed to Rwanda during the fraught days of

Operation Turquoise—a mission draped in humanitarian intent but shadowed by controversy and media speculation. In the Balkans, he'd endured the brutal winters of Bosnia, escorting aid convoys under UNPROFOR and later IFOR, watching peace unravel at the end of a barrel, then be restored again, at the end of a barrel. He'd patrolled the dense jungles of the Central African Republic, slogged-it-out through desert operations in Chad during Operation Épervier, and witnessed firsthand how fragile civil order and humanity became when the world's citizenry turned their backs on the plight of another land and its people, ignoring them completely.

He rose through the Legion's brutal meritocracy the only way anyone ever did—through quiet, steady competence, unflinching loyalty, and the kind of battlefield bravery and intuition that couldn't be taught from a Boot-Camp or training-room manual. From foot patrols in the sweltering Djibouti sun to leading night-time extractions in Sarajevo, he earned every single stripe and medal they gave to him. By the time they had promoted him up to Chief Warrant Officer, no one questioned it—he'd already become the man others looked-up to and relied upon when things started to get a little crazy out in the field.

Twenty years of service in the Legion had carved him into something more than a soldier. He was a witness to many world events, a keeper of hard truths, a loner as well as a decent, ethical man who knew how to walk the thin, grey, semitransparent line one had to walk along in life as an old veteran. In order to thread his way through an intensely bipolar world split between cultural chaos and control, Luc had navigated each step of the way safely.

He was quite happy now these days. No emptiness, no regrets. He didn't suffer with an ex-soldier's case of not knowing what to do with himself. He'd found his second home and he loved it. He'd found an occupation after leaving the Legionaries and he loved this new job —both his new home and his new job were good and decent ones and provided him with a strong, continuing sense of place, pride and purpose. Orange Sand were his "Good Guys" as he always liked calling them, and the peaceful city of Geneva had become his new, perfect niche to settle into during this later chapter of his life.

They were good, decent people and he took pride in working for them. He could trust them. He could tell they were all "good souls" as he really had developed a strong sense for telling who was a "good soul" over the years, and most definitely who wasn't. He was at peace knowing he was on the side of good and they were together as a team doing something positive and working toward protecting what mattered in the world.

He always liked doing security detail watching over Doc Aldo – he was the nicest and funniest of guys – not an academic snob or arrogant in any way at all. Whenever his boss, Doctor Vittorio assigned him to watch over Doc Aldo, he was always happy to do so. They would often have the best of chats about so many amazing things and inevitably Doc Aldo would have him laughing away in stitches about something funny he'd said.

He immensely admired Aldo...although he'd have to admit, the British Doctor, the one from Manchester who always wore the knee-high boots, with her cheeky, sharp tongue, cool feisty demeanour and that take-the-piss attitude —Dr. Harriet Lindley, or *"Hairy-Legs"* as they all liked to call her—she had a way of staying on his mind a little longer than was professionally appropriate. He wasn't sure what it was about her exactly—maybe her laugh, maybe her fiery spirit—or those long legs, which were fantastic, and despite the nickname they'd given to her, appeared smooth – to his sharp, well-trained eyes, he couldn't detect a single hair on them, but something about her made him feel like there was still something left unfinished in his life.

He'd seen too much, experienced so much in life so far, but he was still yet to see a beautiful bride come walking down the aisle towards him on his very own wedding day, and he was still to see and experience his own, newly born child come into the world too. His soul was longing for something special to add into the world, a few extra, more beautiful, loving moments and heart-moving experiences, instead of subtracting them away from the world most of the time.

The large campervan they were discreetly hidden away in, sat tucked beneath a snow-covered linden tree in a small, vacant space adjacent to Aldo's apartment, windows all blacked out. Inside, a small diesel heater did a splendid job of warming the space, while dim screens cast a pale green light over the quiet, focused faces of Luc and his men. The air smelled faintly of coffee, gun oil, and the metallic tang of cooled electronics.

Chief Warrant Officer Luc Renard watched the thermal feed without blinking. Onscreen, a figure moved about inside Aldo's apartment — cleaning, lighting the stove, tending to the fire, like he actually lived there. They'd only just noticed him an hour ago. He knew Aldo had no other family besides his elderly mother. They were just about to burst in, secure him and start asking questions, just in case he was an assailant. Then they noticed he was cleaning, mopping, showering, cooking and tidying the place. Luc just had no idea who the hell the guy was and how on Earth he'd gotten in there in the first place. They'd been watching the apartment closely all day since early morning, as soon as Doc Vittorio had put them onto the task.

"I better check with the away team and Vittorio."

Luc pressed the coded-two-way receiver mic on his throat. "How is Aldo travelling?"

A second voice crackled in from the mobile car that had been following Aldo. "Car just left CERN heading down Rte de Meyrin. ETA—less than 10 minutes. No tails – no hostiles – all clear – although he's driving quite erratic and speeding."

Luc laughed and replied "So what's new there?" He clicked his throat mic again.

"Command, this is Ghost Fox. We've got a stranger in the nest. Appears non-hostile. Male, early sixties. Operating like he owns the place. Not on the current list. Checking status with primary."

He switched channels, voice quieter now.

"Doctor Vittorio, I have a visual confirmed on an unknown male inside Subject A's apartment. We are not certain how he entered. No outside approach. No forced entry. He just appeared inside an hour ago. He's been very busy cleaning, he took some rubbish outside to the trash, and he's not acting in any way suspiciously, just cooking and tidying the place, took a shower, mopped the floor, and lit the fireplace. We noticed he was sitting in the living room and appeared to be crying for a while, now he's turning on all the lights."

A short pause.

"Describe him to me please," Vittorio said.

"Lean build. Caucasian. Mid-sixties. Beard. Long white-grey hippy length hair.

Another pause, longer this time.

"That's Frank," Vittorio finally said, his tone easing up a little.

Luc's eyebrows lifted. "Doctor Franklin Kendrick? He looks different from the file photos. You didn't say he'd be there."

"Because I didn't know he was going to be there. And you have his crew-cut, shaven Army file photos there. No Woodstock hippy ones. No communication was made. If he's there now… something's changed…something's up…They may need help."

Vittorio said in a grave tone, "Keep your head on a sharp swivel there Luc– like I briefed you before, they are in all likelihood facing a high degree of danger."

Luc let that sink-in for a beat. Then toggled back to team comms.

"Eyes sharp. Subject-A is arriving soon."

The old Volkswagen L-Bug chugged into view, shuddering as it hit a pothole and bounced up the curb. Headlights blinked, then died. The driver's door swung open.

Luc leaned forward slightly, gazing intently at the monitor screen.

"Visual on Aldo. He's not alone in the car."

The passenger door popped.

And that's when they all saw **Jasper.**

The black-and-white blur hit the ground, moving slowly alongside Aldo as if it was the most natural thing in the world.

Luc blinked hard.

"What the hell is that?"

Méliès, his second in command, leaned in, squinting. "Looks like a…" He stopped mid-sentence, brow creased.

"Probably one of the doc's crazy, genetic experiments," he jokingly muttered.

Luc tapped the mic again, never taking his eyes off the feed.

"Doctor Vittorio, we've got Doc Aldo and he's with an unknown animal. Repeat, subject has brought with him in the car an unknown species…size of a bobcat –but it's not feline…it's a solid, furry, panda-like coat, quadruped of some kind."

Then Sergeant Ardennes sitting beside Luc blurted it out "That's a DOG!"

A sharp inhale crackled over the comm.

"…Confirmed?" Vittorio's voice was different now — sharper, heavier, like someone hearing a name they thought they'd never heard before, but remembered they had.

"Clear as day. Medium build. Walking slowly beside the doc. Border-Collie. It's Jasper. I forgot what they were for a second or two and what they looked like – I just a blanked-out –what the hell is that all about?! What's

going on? I feel weird seeing one now for some reason?”
Luc clicked off the mic and sat back in his chair.

But even as he said it, something sat wrong in his gut —
not fear, not suspicion. **A kind of awe.** A feeling he
hadn't had in decades. Not since that sky turned neon-
orange in Rwanda, when the jungle went silent and
something older than man passed overhead silently.

He looked back at the screen, narrowed his eyes. Softly, to
no one in particular, he muttered,

“Mon Dieu... qu'est-ce que tu es, toi?”

Some of his team made the sign of the cross.

The Seeds of Retribution

By late evening, they'd eaten the last of the fish —
gratefully consumed by Aldo and Jasper, who had by now
slowly regained his K-9 appetite. He licked his bowl clean
and then nudged Aldo's foot gently before curling back
into his chosen spot by the fireplace, sighing as he melted
into the rug.

Frank sipped his coffee mixed with a ton of coco. "We'll
need a safe space to build it. The decisive-invalidater can't
be prepped in any ordinary lab—not with the Order agents
likely scanning and tracking away with their energy
sweeps."

"My lab, due to the levels of stealth enhancement I've built
into it, is our only option then really," Aldo said, wiping
his hands. "I'll retrofit it with more dampening shroud
and containment lattice in the morning. We'll make it a
Hyper Quiet Zone."

Frank stood and stretched. "I really need a decent night's
sleep, but another half hour of calculating my devices
schematics will put my mind to rest before dozing off. I
say we call it a day at this stage, try not to stress and
overthink things too much. Tomorrow, we make a fresh
start early in the morning, but not before we've had a
decent breakfast."

"Agreed." said Aldo, "I will teleport over to help with the
build at your sister's place in Kirra, later in the morning,
but not before I've sorted the lab out for you. It should be
fun going over there to help with building your
unorthodox and eccentric wormhole generator, while you
put together your special gift for our Riftwalker pals.

Then, maybe you can meet us later-on in the day to see how things are going?"

"Sounds like a decent plan old chap. But how do we get from A to B? I only have 3 shots left on my portal gun and it takes me a month to charge it up for just one shot. I need at least 2 for my special delivery I've got planned to the Riftwalkers flophouse."

Aldo stood up, "Similar to your unique gun there, I have a special and unique bit of tech that I've also developed for any possible, sudden exit and entry travel off the books. It's my in-case-of-an-emergency, or running into any unforeseen danger contingency device, and also for one of those rainy days where I might just want to go on an El-cheapo holiday somewhere warm, and not bother with a visa or a passport.

He walked over to a nearby bookshelf. From one of the higher mantles of the shelf, he retrieved a dull silver spray can down from it—oddly mechanical in its design, a relic of some forgotten, yesteryear tech. He gave the can a small shake.

"You're going to spray yourself with mosquito repellent?" Frank asked jokingly.

"More like step through an intelligent, interdimensional cloud in a can," Aldo replied, Giving the can a once over inspection. "It's linked to my conscious intent. One burst, and I can step through the spray-mist it creates and be wherever I need to be."

"Have you tested it before?"

"No, no, no, not exactly on myself, but I have successfully teleported a walnut. So, in theory, I'm 99.5% certain it will work like a charm with a living body."

"You're a madman," Frank grinned.

"Takes one to know one."

They both laughed, a moment of levity amidst the weight of all that they'd been talking about previously.

Frank looked over at the bookshelf behind where Aldo was standing. In a large frame on the middle shelf was an old family photo. He pointed and asked, "How's your mum doing these days?"

Aldo sighed, "Well, apart from stubbornly refusing to move out of our old family home in Nantes and into a state-of-the-art retirement village here in Geneva, she's holding up okay I guess, but I worry for her all the time there in that old place, all by herself."

"Did you ever find out who the mystery chap in the striped shirt standing next to your grandfather in the photo was? Your mum always spoke about him being the most amazing person, yet, we have never really gotten to the bottom of who he was."

"All she has ever said was that he saved their lives. He was a part of their resistance team and was a part of our family for a short while too. Saved my grandmother and grandfather's lives, my mother and father's too …saved everyone.

I remember my mum stubbornly standing in the doorway of her old restaurant, looking down the street that one very last time before closing it up for good. She'd gotten just too old to keep running it. She was holding onto the old OPEN / CLOSED sign. My grandparents had long passed away, I asked her what she was thinking, and she replied, "Still hoping Sergio might suddenly walk down the street after all these years and see me here, and my restaurant, and stop in, sit down, and I could make him his favourite dish, and we could talk again and laugh." Then she started crying. – Something out of this world happened during those war years, during that guy's stay at my family's home…Mum always said she believes it's why her and Dad encouraged me so much to become a scientist."

Frank smiled warmly, "She's such a lovely old dear your mum, I'd say she just doesn't want to leave the memories behind in that cosy, old family home of yours. It really is so lovely there in Nantes. She always said to me, every time I met her, that you were going to play your role in saving the world…she said it was something that runs in your family."

Aldo looked over to Jasper and smiled. "Well, it certainly is something that runs in my old dog here." He stepped over and crouched down by Jasper, ran his hand over the dog's fur one last time before bed. "Rest easy, old boy. You've earned it."

Frank turned to the schematics he'd been busily scribbling away on at the coffee table. Scrap sheets of paper covered almost the entire table. He rolled up his sleeves and got to work. He was going to make a more powerful decisive-invalidater bomb than before. This one would have an unstoppable timer-delay so he could leave it there as his own, very special, surprise calling-card for the Riftwalkers, right in the middle of their nest. It was time to wipe the bastards out.

By 11:30-pm, he was too tired to go on but had completed the working schematic design he needed and a good plan for a stealth-suit that would capitalise on Aldo's special dampening field that he'd used to paint his lab's walls with.

He walked over and gave Jasper a cuddle, then grabbed a blanket and laid down on the large 3-seat sofa, falling sound asleep almost immediately.

Jasper got up and padded over. He paused, then hopped-up onto the sofa and nestled in snugly beside Frank.

Man and dog were now sleeping comfortably together...again...

Love and peace filled the ether, a small jitter-bug's glow shone-out into what was now a dark abyss rapidly blanketing the world.

Memory Always Finds its Way Home

Geneva, Switzerland, 2340 hours,
Rue de la Fontaine, Champel –

The clink of a wine bottle echoed faintly as Dr. Vittorio Esposito slid the final bolt into place behind them. The old cellar beneath his Champel townhouse was humid, stone-lined, and aromatic with age. Rows of Bordeaux and dusty bottles of Amarone flanked the room like silent sentinels. A section of wall rippled—molecular bricks shimmering away—as the concealed panel dematerialized, revealing a sleek, softly lit chamber lined with cheeses, old data drives, vintage wine bottles and analogue screens.

This was where Orange Sand now gathered—again—but with a few new faces from the wider, secret circle of the organisation.

"Thank you for coming," Vittorio said, voice low but urgent. "The timeline has fractured. We're operating blind now. But memory—" he tapped his temple—"memory knows its way back."

Helena Madsen, serene and hawk-eyed, folded her arms as she surveyed the room. Marcus Iqbal, already fiddling with his pocket field-mapper, nodded. Simone Giraud, hands tucked into her scarf, offered a single breath: "Something shifted. I could feel it before you even called…Something is really off, my usual depression just plummeted to a new low, like never before."

Dr. Lindley leaned back in her chair, arms crossed, boots muddy. "You guys have been out of the loop a little." she said, motioning to the newcomers. "We need more good minds like you on this, urgently. Let's see if we can get you all up to speed. And just so you know, I'm feeling the same way too. My dark mood has gone an extra multiplier darker. Something horrible has happened and I don't know what it is. I'm trying to figure out a way to dance back from the darkness myself."

Etienne Roux gave her a look. "Aren't we all?"

Vittorio walked to the centre console, wiping condensation from an old flat screen. "I think this might help you. I've pulled surviving fragments. These shouldn't exist anymore, and some very recent CCTV footage I want you to see."

He pressed a key.

Grainy lab footage played—Jasper, younger, tail wagging, standing calmly in Aldo's lab amid resonance bell tests. He stared into the lens of the camera almost as if he were staring into the future, peering into the minds of the team watching the old VHS tape, then he turned and howled. The frequency meter next to him spiked sharply. Then again—another howl, a spike. Pure harmonics, like music from another epoch.

Simone gasped. "I know that sound…I know that animal!"

"Wait," Marcus whispered. "Dogs… They aren't in my mind anymore; it's like they've been erased. Yet, I remember them now seeing that video. Not their absence —but the silence of my memories – an eerie nothingness that has followed me from the past…it's a deathly silence."

The second video flickered on—CCTV, captured not more than an hour ago by the security team outside Aldo's apartment. Jasper hopping from Aldo's car. Head alert, tail lifted. That same look of mission.

They all exclaimed: "DOGS! – And that's Jasper!"

Etienne exhaled. "He was always the key. We just didn't understand that he *was*."

Vittorio nodded gravely. "He's not just a dog. He's a resonance stabiliser. The howl harmonises timelines—draws threads back into coherence. We believe the Riftwalkers succeeded in at least one goal: the full deletion of all canine influence from shared consciousness. Jasper is a relic. A holdout. Possibly the last dog on Earth."

There was a silence— a weighty sacredness was suspended in the miasma of their shared thoughts.

Dr. Lindley broke it, voice gravelled but sharp. "I've been working on a sequence for a while now. Something to throw back at the Riftwalkers. Something that merges time-coded sound pulses with multi-bell harmonics. A kind of 'time signature song'—that restores life that has been wrongfully stolen, but I can't seem to crack it. Not yet. The sequence continually eludes me like a recipe I'm trying to cook, but I just can't seem to get the flavour right."

Helena spoke softly. "Like a coded, mnemonic symphony?"

"Exactly," Lindley replied. "But I need *all* the bells. Not just some. All. Resonating together...around the world, while I run the sequence. And I need *him*. Jasper. In the room when we trigger it."

Simone turned to her. "Why?"

"Because it's not just tech," Lindley said. "It's *soul-field memory*. His howl tunes it. It's like pressing the universe's reset button with a sound it's been waiting to hear again since the beginning of time."

"That could flip the timeline back to its original status." Vittorio whispered.

Marcus frowned. "And if we fail?"

"Then the deletion holds," Vittorio said. "And we lose the lattice forever."

There was another silence.

Vittorio continued, "Then the Riftwalkers will consume humanity's collective souls, one by one, and we become nothing more than a greyscale, paddock of bland husks of depleted life-forms, trapped here forever – no turning back to the light and to love and to true freedom if we fail."

Finally, Helena leaned in. "Then we don't fail."

Simone nodded, eyes glassy. "I remember my childhood dog now. Tamba. She had a lopsided tail and used to lick rain off the windows. I hadn't thought of her in years. I couldn't – didn't - remember her at all today...until just now."

"The memory was buried," Etienne said. "But not gone. That's why we called you three in here. You've all been in magnetically sealed laboratories for this last twenty four hours —your minds and memories weren't entirely burnt-out by proximity to this new timeline. You're fresh enough to remember."

Vittorio turned to the console again, about to place a secure call to Luc.

He clicked the microphone. And then—

Static **hissed** on the wall's two-way communication channel

"Hold on a moment boss," came Luc's voice replying back through the transmission, calm but tight. "We've got company just arrived. Looks like **hostiles.** An old, Bedford van. Just parked up outside Aldo's apartment. Armed. Paramilitary cut-outs exiting the van. Moving slowly and cautiously. Clearly not aware of our presence here."

Vittorio clicked the mic "Luc—". He then released it

"We're engaging now," Luc cut in. "Protecting our assets. Will update shortly. Out."

The room held its breath.

Lindley stood. "That's it then. No more delay. We work fast. We get the bells. We get the dog. And we save what's left of the world.

The two-way hissed again not more than a few minutes later. "Site secure and safe. Hostiles neutralised. Beginning clean-up."

"Good job Luc." Vittorio flicked-off the comms switch.

As soon as he had finished speaking with Luc, Vittorio turned to Doctor "Hairy Legs" Lindley – "When Luc's finished cleaning-up there – I want him to personally watch over you as you go to work in your lab figuring-out that formula – the Riftwalkers will be looking for any possible "antidotes" as they are echoed-out by anyone experimenting with quantum-colour and sound-oscillations – so I need you to be fully protected – When you're ready, the two of you can go and Join Aldo in his lab to make a plan. I'm sending Aldo there for safety as soon as he wakes up in the morning – he's safe for now so let him have a good night's rest – And I also need to find out what Frank's up to."

Doctor Lindley smiled and nodded, despite staring down into the darkest abyss facing humanity, she would soon be seeing the head of security again, and in close proximity. Hope was shining a small, slightly selfish, ray down in her direction she thought.

Building a Better Past

The tilt-truck carrying the large-sized sea-container on the back, beeped and beeped its way down the very long and broad driveway. Using rear mounted cameras, the old driver was able to navigate his way accurately to within a foot of the super-large garage door at the bottom of the drive. Byron insisted on helping the driver, waving his arms awkwardly while trying to act like this was a totally normal delivery to this house and he'd done this a hundred times before. A light drizzle of rain was pattering down on the 10-meter high, colour-bond, tin roofing that generously covered the driveway along its entire length right down to the garage itself.

The previous owner of the property had been a yachting enthusiast and had spared no expense, creating a covered boat-trailer and workshop area beside the house, built absurdly high to allow for masts, cranes, and deliveries.

The only use Sheri's parents ever had for this facility since they'd moved into the property over 15 years ago now, was for parking their 2 cars, laundry clotheslines and for storing most of their unneeded belongings away in the ginormous shed.

Sheri's dad had created a rough semblance of a workshop in there with some rudimentary mechanical tools for his DIY car repairs, woodworking gear and a modest array of power tools and gardening gear. There was also the obligatory beer fridge, pedestal fan and an old, scroungy sofa and a TV for when he just wanted to get some quality "man cave" time away from the world too.

Standing with her mum next to her, Sheri watched the truck come to a stop. The two of them looked on with interest as the hydraulic lifting cradle began to shuffle and lift the sea-container backwards off the truck. The driver then began to deftly snail the rig forwards returning the lifting beam back onto the truck into its cradle position. He climbed out of the cab, jumped down and began shuffling through the paperwork he needed to have signed, then he climbed back up, revved up the engine and ascended up and out of the driveway.

"How full do you think Uncle Frank has packed that thing Shez?" Her mum asked with a laugh.

"I'd say every square inch of it is jammed full mum. When we open those doors, it's gonna be like one of those gag peanut tins I used to have when I was seven, remember? As soon as you open the lid, the foam snake springs out." She replied excitedly.

Just at the moment, over on the side of the driveway, Aldo suddenly appeared, stepping out through a puff of glowing, tinselly mist, a silver spray can holstered on his belt like an interdimensional cowboy, with Jasper trotting loyally beside him. He spread his arms wide with a laughing smile.

"Good to see you have safely received your Fringe Science Care Package from the Frank Kendrick's Weird World of Crazy Inventions Foundation."

Jasper woofed.

Sherri and her mum erupted into laughter, happy, surprised shrieks and incredulously loud hellos as they hugged and welcomed both Aldo and Jasper.

Her mum sobbed a little as she began patting Jasper, then looked up and said with astonishment "They've gone – but they haven't?! This guy's still here? Is my mind going dotty?!"

"No mum, you're just like everyone else in the world today, but Jasper being here, it is resetting your mind for you." She looked at Aldo. "And Uncle Aldo and Uncle Frank and my friends and I, we are gonna make everything go right again. We're gonna fix this mum."

Aldo nodded repeatedly – wishing he had the same confidence and enthusiasm as Sheri did.

With the closed doors of the seatainer facing into the open garage, Aldo undid them by unfastening the long steel bars that held them closed and levered them open on their hinges. The two doors creaked open as he one by one walked both of them outwards.

Inside, the container was packed wall-to-wall with Frank's equipment — plasma coils, chrono-nodes, dark matter alignment tubes, a Doppler-harmonic stabiliser, three Italian coffee machines (of varying degrees of eccentricity), and, in the very back, the sacred Kelvinator fridge. Chipped, scratched and dented but packed with potential.

Byron opened the old fridge. "Smells like cold pizza, fried wontons and a museum display."

Aldo clapped his hands. "Perfect. Frank's special Meccano set in a really big box, all ready to go! I say we build a wormhole, shall we?"

The garage transformed into a lab of mad invention. Wires snaked along rafters. Jasper supervised from an old beanbag. Aldo, donned in his lab technician's coat and high-vis-socks, adjusted thermal regulators and flicked at gauges while muttering about quantum harmonics.

Sherri and Byron worked side by side, fitting stabilisers to the fridge's side panels, threading micro-filaments and cables through a multi-level coil matrix.

"Hand me the flux-reduction shifter," Sherri said.

Byron passed it to her, their hands brushing.

They paused.

Aldo, noticing, chuckled softly to himself and didn't say a word.

As the afternoon rolled on, Byron wiped sweat from his brow. "You ever think, like, maybe this was all meant to happen? Us doing this?"

Sherri gave him a sideways look. "Building a fridge that can punch through spacetime?"

"I mean..." he grinned, "yeah."

She smiled. "Maybe."

Aldo sat back on an old stool. "You know, I always thought I'd settle down someday. Have a couple of little ones. Raise them on a diet of weird science and classical jazz."

Sherri looked at him. "You still can Uncle Aldo – You're not too over the hill yet...But you're starting to get there a little...but still have a ways to go yet."

Aldo laughed and shrugged. "Gotta meet the right lady first. Someone who doesn't mind a crazy guy who's slightly eccentric and prefers a teleportation spray can over first-class air travel, and is joined at the hip to a highly opinionated dog...Oh, yeah, and she's gotta dig radiant gingers too."

Jasper woofed a few times again. Sherri pulled a face and held her hand to her ear and said, "I think he's saying: Who in the World doesn't love gingers?!"

They all laughed. For a moment, it felt like things were going to be okay…They were going to save the day.

But across the world in Geneva, Frank stood alone in Aldo's lab, his fingers gliding over the newly shaped shell of the Decisive-Invalidator — a small, grim device the size of a coffee plunger.

He was going to plant it in the Riftwalker's nest, deep in their subterranean realm. As he stood in the quiet stillness of the lab, the device felt heavier in his hand than it was.

He hadn't told Sherri. He didn't want her worrying. He hadn't told Aldo he'd be leaving so soon. He didn't want *any* of them to worry.

Only Aldo knew the score and the odds, but he didn't know Frank wasn't going to call in and see him first before leaving to go on this mission.

 Frank slid the final component into the Decisive-Invalidator's casing. It gave a soft *click*.

He picked up his chrono-portal gun. Only three jumps left.

He looked at the schematics. He looked at the clock. He fired the chrono-gun.

Then he stepped into the shimmering gate, disappearing in a ripple of light and silence.

Back in Kirra, the final power core was being installed beneath the fridge.

Sherri tightened the last bolt. Byron passed her the Allen key with a grin.

“Now we just need Frank.”

They didn’t know it – not yet — Frank had already gone.

He was now crouched in the most literal version of being in the belly of the beast…and it really, really stank in there.

Frank squatted in the foul gloom, half-submerged in what passed for atmosphere inside the Riftwalker’s nest. The walls pulsed—veined with twitching nerves, slick with mucous that breathed. A glutinous hiss echoed from the flesh-lined corridors, and something distant slopped wetly through the sludge.

The stench was beyond rot: it was the memory of every decayed thing, distilled into a choking musk that soaked into his skin and soul alike. Ink-like, bioluminescent sacs throbbed dimly, casting shadows of the unspeakable evil that resided there.

He gripped the chrono-blade he’d brought along with him as his preferred weapon of choice. Not yet. Not yet. Only if he needed to.

Frank was the virus buried in the gut of a nightmare, and he had some infecting to do.

Through the Kelvinator Glass

The following morning, after having sprayed himself back to his lab to fetch some equipment and then back to Kirra again, Aldo arrived at Sherri's with a few extra, vital parts under his arm and an even bigger smile on his face. He stepped out of the foggy spray cloud left behind by his interdimensional can of mist, coughing theatrically.

"Note to self: maybe scent the next can of cosmic-spray a lemon or lavender scent…Not stale-rusty-fart."

Sherri opened the garage and waved him in. She jokingly coughed a few times too. "It does have a farty, egg smell to it. Or is that just your excuse to let-rip each time you do a jump?" They both chuckled as Aldo shook his head in denial.

"I swear, it's the mist – not me." He exclaimed laughing away.

Sherri pointed to the fridge and its surrounds, "We've got about half of it connected. The Kelvinator's holding up like a true, old champion."

Byron was already underneath the fridge on a creeper trolley, tightening brackets and threading more of the micro-cables through a nest of housing coils.

"Did you see Uncle Frank?" She asked.

"I'm guessing he ducked out to gather some gear from somewhere before he drops in here –although, I'm a bit worried as he's probably going to be running low on jumps –unless he's figured-out a new way to recharge his chrono-gun faster than normal, he's gonna need me to chip-in with a few jumps before he...." Aldo cautiously trailed off.

"Before he what?" Sherri picked up on the thread.

"Goes to blow-up the Riftwalkers nest –or should I say: invalidates their existence within multiple Euclidean spacetimes." He could now see the look of worry instantly begin to enter Sherri's expression "—But! Before you go and have a red-cordial-esque episode of worry – Your Uncle has it all safely figured out – and he has made the most remarkable invisible suit that I've ever seen before. It basically makes him non-existent." Aldo paused just long enough to see her slightly lower her expression of shock, then continued, "He just pops-into their nest undetected, plants his invalidator, then he pops back out again and safely makes his way back to here. The invalidator dissolves the Riftwalkers, leaving us unhindered to then go back in time and mend the tear without any trouble whatsoever."

Sherri nodded, she was seeing the merits, "They'll be gone for good. We get to fix the rift in time. And they, and all their sycophantic, human lackeys, are no longer here to mess things up so badly ever again." She puffed-out some hair away from her brow "I like it! – And I have the most unwavering faith in Uncle Frank to knock those bastards out of the ballpark." She smiled and pointed to the embryonic looking Kelvinator fridge nestled in a bed of wires and coiling tubes. "Let's get cracking away on our end of the plan here, shall we Doctor Paxton?".

He laughed, "Indeed young lady! Let's get cracking-away with saving the world!"

The three of them worked in an intuitive pace. Aldo calibrated the harmonic modulator. Sherri tuned the helix sequencer with a borrowed old-school oscilloscope. Byron handled the chassis stabilisers. They moved around each other with an industrial ease, tossing tools, catching hurled snacks, cracking jokes, listening to old, classic songs being played over the radio on 94.1 FM blaring away from a super-old, vintage tube-radio as they sang along and laughed, more than they had expected they would under the given circumstances.

"Feels like we're building a time-travelling, 50's barbecue grill," Byron quipped, lifting one of the main, quasi-crystal arc regulators.

"It *will* definitely char-grill your atoms to carbon, if it's misaligned," Aldo said cheerfully.

Jasper barked once. Then padded over to sit beside Sherri as she screwed in the photon-aligner ring. She gave him a head rub and a hug. He loved hugs. Some dogs didn't so much, they just tolerated hugs, but Jasper cherished them like they were soul-food.

"You know," she said softly, "I think he knows what we're doing here."

"He *always* knows," said Aldo. "He's been through more timelines than I have."

They worked through lunch, eating toasties from a sandwich press plugged into a spare fusion relay. As dusk approached, the final panel clicked into place. The Kelvinator shimmered faintly now — no longer just an old fridge, but a gateway to other worlds and timelines.

Inside the garage, fairy lights flickered from the rafters, casting strange patterns over the polished dome of the wormhole chamber. Byron stood next to Sherri, holding a spool of insulated filament. He didn't say anything for a moment.

Then, "I'm glad it's us, you know?" He paused, "You and me – whatever might happen, good or bad, I'm with you..."

She looked at him and smiled. "Yeah. Me too."

They held hands properly for the first time, nothing more, just simply holding hands and looking into each other's eyes and smiling, and the universe started to heal itself a little bit more.

The Resonance Tape

Marseille, Thursday 7th March 1985.

The Peugeot had a worn leather interior and a single cassette stuck in the deck. Luc stole the car because it looked fast. He kept the cassette-tape because the song playing made him feel something he'd never felt before—hope.

Welcome to Your Life

Geneva Thursday 18th January 2025

The Kombi rumbled gently beneath them as Luc guided it one-handed through Geneva's slumbering streets. Beyond the treetops, the lake shimmered with a sparkling effervescence as if it were a mouth full of moon-candy-crackle being visually represented. The lake and the city lights blinked away at them, a thousand sleepy fireflies bidding goodnight to all.

In the passenger seat, Lindley had kicked off her boots and curled her feet up on the dash. Her gorgeous silhouette glowed in the amber flicker of the passing streetlamps. The air between them was charged with a rare and happy stillness.

He'd driven in his own car to come and collect her, after he and his team had managed to swiftly dispatch the small handful of thugs sent to kill Doc Aldo.

"Did Aldo or Frank know what was going on outside?" She tentatively queried.

"No, actually, no one knew what was going on outside…including the amateur-hour bozos they'd sent to hit Aldo." He drew in slowly, then said calmly, "they quietly, in rapid succession, were neutralised while remaining oblivious to our presence there –right up to the last man, sitting in the van listening to Hindi-punk on his earbuds."

"And the van?"

"Expired occupants were reinserted. The van was then relocated to a scrap metal yard across town and then compacted and squished down into a one-ton metal brick –– not more than an hour later."

"Yeeesh! What about all that gooey residue and leakage?"

"Compacter gets hosed-out and bleached, same with the one-ton, metal brick. Rodents and the weather take care of the rest while it sits out in the scrap yard."

Luc reached for the tape deck, holding up an old cassette with worn edges.

"I need some old-time 80's music right about now." He blew the dust off the cassette.

"Let me guess," she said, arching a brow. "Dire Straits. *Brothers in Arms*."

He chuckled. "Wow! So close! So very, very close, but no cigar for the lady. You've got the same year though, well-done! It's 1985 – But this is more of a classic Eighties synth-pop band. Still made it to the top of the charts though."

With a satisfying *clunk*, the cassette clicked into place.

A pippy synth rift instantly mixed into an echoing guitar rift trilling away to a steam-hissing high-hat, ambient vocals and a descending synth line merging into a layered, echoing drum and bass beat that combined with a gentle counter beat. A heavier drumbeat emerged, more hooky synthesiser arrangements followed—then it all eased back and softened-up to allow for the main vocals to come in...

Welcome to your life... there's no turning back...

Luc glanced sideways. "I stole the car this tape was in," he said, matter of fact.

She laughed loudly. "Seriously?!"

"Deadly serious. Drove it across France and parked it near the Foreign Legion recruitment office. Slept overnight in it. Then the following morning, I just walked in and left the car where it was parked. Presented myself to the gatehouse and signed up that same day."

Lindley looked at him with wide, amused eyes. "You were such a rebel without a cause, weren't you?! And yet, you found your cause, and you kept the tape?"

He nodded; eyes fixed on the road. "Only personal item I took in there with me. First time I ever heard a voice telling me to become someone better."

Lindley's gaze flickered—not at Luc, but at the atmosphere between them.

"Luc... that pitch... the interval between the synth and the chords—listen," she said, her voice hushed.

He turned toward her, curious.

"That chord voicing—they're not playing basic triads. There's Lydian color in there, almost modal. You hear it? The sharp 4, the suspended 9—it keeps the resolution floating just out of reach. The melody doesn't land. It *hovers*. And here—wait..."

She pointed towards the tape-deck as the song shifted.

"That's it. *Right there.* The synth line is subtly doubling the guitar note in a repeating pattern of three, yet we feel it in six. Not in unison—but layered with a minuscule phase variance...there's also another sustained synth note being carried underneath the guitar chords as well as the variated synth chords!"

Luc squinted. "You can hear *all of that* in a piece of music?!"

"Oh yeah, like an architect can clearly see a building's design structure just by looking at it —I can clearly hear the design structure in just about any arrangement of music or sound waves." She tapped the dash, "Right there, they're playing the same chord note as a counter variance?"

"Like a mirroring note that's almost synchronised in with the beat, but doesn't quite make it?" He was trying to follow her.

"Yes" she whispered, "It's not quite *aligned*. The synth is ever so slightly delayed. You get this subtle amplitude modulation—just enough for the brain to notice a pulse. It creates a **beat frequency** in the upper mids. Hear that shimmer? It's not just a plain reverb. It's a purposeful, sustained interference."

Luc gave a slow nod. "The same as a wave superposition?"

"Exactly! Constructive and destructive interference—collapsing in and out of coherence." She looked at him and smiled, "You're actually quite scientifically clued-in for a rebel, aren't you?"

He laughed a little then added "Doc Aldo has been teaching me a bit of the basics of particle physics over the years. I can just sort of follow it and make out the fundamental basics when you guys start prattling on about it."

Luc then smiled amusingly and gestured toward the tape-deck. "Am I to understand that the 80's band Tears for Fears has just given you a scientific breakthrough?!"

"That's what I've been chasing all this time in my resonance composition. It's how the resonance forms between bell three and six. It's not just tone—it's timing. Micro-oscillation. You can't program that into an electronic sequencer, nor could I get an AI to figure it out either; it must *drift with a human's heart and intuition, and actual spirit.* Just an imprecise, natural hair's width."

The beat shuffled forward—12/8 time, instead of the rigid pop 4/4. It swung. It *breathed.*

She inhaled sharply. "This bridge here...there's a subtle cross rhythm and then you can hear the polyrhythm...it delays the resolution. It implies a different pulse. Holds the dominant. Suspends it."

She laughed, "This song's composition is beyond brilliant in terms of wave particle physics! It holds onto resolution and delays interference!"

Luc furrowed his brow. "Like memory... refusing to resolve? Refusing to be messed with?"

She smiled. "Yes! Like a counterrhythm does. That *tension*—that separates the beat...that's how our harmonic map fractures. There's a cabasa accenting the spaces in between the high-hat notes further empathising the counterrhythm of the song. The Riftwalkers couldn't delete something like that. It's embedded in the unresolved space that surrounds us."

Turning her ear to the speaker mounted just under the glovebox, she closed her eyes, "Can you hear how the synth is doubling again by playing underneath the vocal melody of the main chorus?" She asked just as ***everybody wants to rule the world*** was being sung.

Luc listened carefully. "I just can, yes —I've never noticed that before, but now that you've pointed it out, I can hear it...yeah, I actually can."

"That's like a memory being buried beneath a reality which has been phased-shifted under dimensional spacetime."

"So, this song..." he trailed.

"...is a quantum, time-stamped signature," she finished. "A sonic anomaly encoded in the mainstream charts of 1985. Probably by accident—but it slipped through. And now? It's the *key*."

Luc blinked, looking at the tape deck with a new reverence.

"I was seventeen," he murmured. "Stealing cars and being a turd was all I knew how to do, it was my life. This song started playing automatically in the stereo of a swanky Renault I'd just hot-wired. I couldn't stop listening to it. Kept hitting rewind and listening to it over and over again. It broke something open inside of me.

I realised how much I wanted to be a good person and how much I really wanted to fight the bad guys in the world.”

“You’ve had the tape ever since?”

“I thought I’d lost it. Found it again in the glovebox, right before all this started.”

She stared out the window for a moment. “Then maybe the tape found *you*.”

The chorus rose again:
Say that you’ll never, never, never need it...

She turned toward him, her expression softened. “Luc... you know what this means?”

He nodded, his eyes still on the road. “It means you’re going to make that soundwave antidote that you’ve been wanting to make all this time.”

She reached out, her fingers brushing against his on the gearshift. “Yes, and it also means that we’re exactly where we’re supposed to be at this moment.”

The Kombi rolled on beneath the canopy of stars—two lives, one song, and a quiet harmony threading between the latices of the world that would, in all likelihood, save the day.

The chorus lifted again:
Holding hands while the walls come tumbling down...

Luc’s hand tightened subtly on the wheel. The Kombi rumbled toward a quiet bend in the road lined with winter-bare trees and soft golden lamps. Without a word, he eased onto the shoulder of the road.

The tires crunched softly over the gravel and snow. He pulled the handbrake towards himself with a series of clicks, then he turned the key. The engine stilled.

For a long second, the only sound was the faint whir of the cassette and the music.

Luc turned toward her. "I'm not really good at... slow."

Lindley didn't say anything. Her eyes were already on his.

He leaned in—no hesitation, no doubt—and kissed her.

It was warm and steady, a kiss that both of them had been waiting longer than the better part of a year to arrive at in the mailroom of their hearts. Not rushed, clumsy or hungry. Just a soulful, *real* kiss. Two proper soul mates acknowledging they were now officially together at long last.

When they parted, she let out a breath she hadn't known she was holding.

"So..." she said softly, brushing a lock of hair from his brow, "the quiet, serious type turns out to be a rebel and a romantic."

Luc gave a half-smile. "Don't tell the others."

She nodded, mock solemn. "Your secret's safe with me."

Outside, the lake lay still, and the world held its breath for them.

"I think you better take me home young man." She jokingly demanded.

He started up the rumbling VW engine and began to drive away slowly.

"Yes, my lady, as you wish."

"And upon doing so, I think you better spend the night with me when we arrive there."

"Yes, my lady, as you wish."

They both laughed as Roland Orzabal's guitar solo played away mixing in with a layered cake of 80's synth-tech melodies, rich chords, textures…and those lyrics:

All for freedom and for pleasure

Nothing ever lasts forever

Everybody wants to rule the World…

All For One

The light above the garage flickered as Sherri ducked under the half-raised roller door. The workbench glowed with soldering irons, wires, and loose circuit boards—Byron already hunched over a twisted copper coil, tongue poking out from the side of his mouth, was in quiet focus.

"You sure this'll fire and reload safely?" she asked, tossing a bag of batteries down on the bench.

Byron didn't look up. "Safely? No… But it should rip through a global space-time field and disintegrate every known law of physics, along with whatever it hits…Maybe."

Sherri cracked a smile. "Good to see you're keeping it real and keeping your expectations humble."

He'd been tinkering with DIY lasers for years, but now with access to some of Uncle Frank's next-gen equipment, he was doing something much more serious—building a defensive laser-blaster weapon they could use against the Riftwalkers *if* they showed up.

The old radio on the shelf was loudly playing Gold Coast's 94.1 FMs adds for its local sponsors. Rhonda was doing the timeless House of Sayam Thai Restaurant add. Then came the music for the news update. A nasal American voice began delivering the headlines:

"In breaking news, tensions continue to escalate between Russian, Chinese and Japanese forces following a disputed incident in the Kuril Islands. The U.S. Sixth Fleet has been placed on high alert in the Pacific and China has mobilised its fleet…"

Sherri looked at Byron and said, "Now that's the sort of **um-biance** I don't really care for much."

They both smiled and laughed.

Another newsreader chimed in, this time with an Australian accent:

"The Dow dropped 800 points before a temporary freeze halted trading on opening today. Analysts are calling it 'the first tremor.'"

Byron walked over and turned the volume down. "They don't really even get it, do they? They probably aren't aware that what they're reporting on now is actually the start of the end of the world. It's the closing-down sale news for this way of life that we've come to know. He walked back over and sat down at the bench, continuing to solder away.

Sherri exhaled. "Yeah. But at least we do…And we're doing something about it."

She reached over and patted him on the shoulder. "And we're going to fix this. We are going to win this because we are the winning team! remember?"

Leaning even closer to him, she whispered softly "You and me, and the others, we are one very awesome powerhouse to contend with."

Then she quickly leaned in and kissed him on the cheek.

He blinked, surprised—but didn't pull away.

They both momentarily stared into each other's eyes and smiled with an expression that only two young teenagers who are madly in love with each other have the capability of expressing.

More kissing might have predictably followed, but then…

A knock at the side gate…

"Garage goblins! Open up!" Hannah's voice sang out—chipper, bright, unmistakable.

Sherri laughed and jogged over to open the gate.

Hannah entered first, her towel poncho fluttering dramatically like a cape, with Jake right behind—lanky and full of energy carrying a jumbo bottle of Pepsi —and Jacinta trailing with a large, brown pizza box with a foil-wrapped garlic bread balancing on top.

"We brought morale and some diner," Jacinta said dryly.

"And sarcasm for desert," Jake added, flinging a half-eaten Mentos at Byron.

Byron caught it without looking. "You're welcome to help out here, the telemetry needs wiring, but one wrong move and you'll fry your retinas."

"I don't need retinas," Jake shrugged. "I need *answers…like what's going on here?!*"

They stepped into the garage and froze in place.

A hush fell over them as they began to take it all in.

The garage no longer looked like any normal garage they'd ever seen before. Tangled coils snaked along the roof beams. Iridescent capacitor banks hummed low against the far wall. Strange blueprints lined the pegboard behind the workbench. Wires trailed from overhead pulleys into a central, half-dismantled *Kelvinator fridge*, now mounted on a platform with a walk-ramp in front of it and surrounded by LED-lit coils padded side to side with more wiring and heavy insulation.

Everything buzzed and hummed and whirred.

The fridge door stood ajar, lined with more cables that shimmered slightly from the fairy lights hitting them.

It had a Christmas display's elegance to how wonderfully lit up it all was.

"What...what is all this?!" Hannah whispered.

"You've gone and built some kind of fancy nuclear bomb, haven't you?" Jake offered.

Sherri grinned. "Worse even! It's a ***time machine...***"

Their eyes widened...

Aldo appeared, breaking the spell, carrying a tray of paper cups, napkins, ice blocks and some paper plates.

"You kids want the full breakdown while you eat?" he said, setting the tray down on an old crate.

"Please," Jacinta replied, blinking at the Kelvinator like it might blink back at her. It somehow looked *alive.*

Aldo motioned them to gather near the fridge. He tapped the side gently.

"This," he said, "used to keep meatloaf and ice-cream sandwiches cold. Now, it bends spacetime."

"Wait—seriously?" Jake said. "Like Doctor Who?"

"Like Einstein," Aldo corrected. "But with a bit of help from Uncle Frank's designs."

He pointed to a cluster of humming coils on the floor. "This is the capacitor array that stabilises the temporal boundary layer. And *this*—" he opened the fridge door a bit wider, "—this is the event threshold. Step through here, and you're inside a controlled wormhole. It takes you back. Way back...or way forwards too."

"To when?" Hannah asked.

"To *where*," Aldo said. "We're still working on the when part."

Jacinta looked pale. "And Sherri's going into that?"

"She is," Aldo said. "Something has fractured the very threadwork of time. If we can establish a 'First Pat'—the original emotional and quantum connection between humans and dogs—we may be able to re-ignite the moment and instantly heal the break."

Jake blinked. "That sounds... not impossible."

"And it's not," Sherri said.

There was silence for a moment.

Then Hannah stepped forward. "If she goes, *we all go*."

Sherri turned to her, eyes shining.

"You sure?"

Hannah placed a hand on her shoulder. "I was there when you lost Zeb, remember? I sat beside you all night. I'm not letting you go into a rift in the universe alone. You've always had our backs. We've got yours."

Jake and Jacinta nodded.

"No questions asked, we're going too." said Jacinta.

"Except, one thing…" Jake added, "can we bring snacks through the wormhole?"

Aldo laughed. "That depends on how many boxes of Arnet's Shapes you can carry on you."

The kids all laughed, and for a moment, the enormity of what they were doing eased under the warmth of their friendship.

Then Aldo grew serious again. "This isn't a school science fair. You're talking about possibly facing some serious danger – But I can protect you and I can keep you safe all of the way. I need to steer the ship so-to-speak from here where I can watch and control the flow-state. Just as long as you understand it could get a bit sketchy and if it does, I'm shutting everything down and bringing you guys back in an instant."

"We understand," Sherri said, steady and calm.

Both Aldo and Sheri then began to explain everything that had happened to the others. They detailed the Riftwalkers and who they were. The attacks and the tumbling decline in circumstances the World was now about to have. It was a hostile, stealth takeover of humanity and they were possibly the last and only ones who could stop it.

Aldo explained how his colleagues in Geneva were going to run a projected, wave-anomaly antidote using a formula engineered to help restore things. The projected waveform would be transmitted out by his colleague from Aldo's secret, underground lab and Jasper would be there also to help synchronise and restore the rift in time with his howls. All the bells around the World would start ringing at the same time too. They were going to make a galvanised counterattack on the Riftwalkers.

Byron flipped a switch, and the machine gave a low hum," Watch this!"

The opened, interior section of the fridge radiated a liquid membrane like it was a bathtub full of glowing water standing upright end-to-end. Colours swayed and danced on the surface.

Hannah stepped beside Sherri, shoulder to shoulder, watching in awe.

"Wherever this fridge thing takes you Shez, and whatever you have to face, I'm going to be there with you too."

And that was that.

They were in this together. They'd made their pact to all go as one, and one for all.

Aldo frowned, "I still need more time to quadrangulate the precise moment."

He fussed with his tablet, "Maybe less than an hour. So, enjoy your pizza and Pepsi and start to get yourselves ready in the meantime guys."

Byron held up his plasma-laser 'That also gives me time to make a holster for this."

Jake raised his voice "Hey! Do I get one of those too?!"

"No buddy – you don't - I'm the Sherrif this time! Besides, it would take me way too long to make another one of these."

Sherri jokingly brought over a flyswatter to Jake and tapped it lightly onto each of his shoulders, "Arise Sir Swatsalot" she handed him the swatter "use this with honour and valour."

Everyone laughed, and for just a heartbeat, everything felt like it might still be okay in the World.

Outside, the wind began to gust, forcefully rising to a slight gale.

Somewhere in the sky, an ugly ripple shimmered like a heatwave above bitumen—unseen by all but felt by the angels watching over the area.

And much further out to sea, a low rumble of thunder could be heard.

Sometimes things start to fall apart much faster than we think...

The Blade of Silence

Frank crouched low in the darkness, his breath shallow beneath the humming shell of the invisible suit. The Riftwalker nest stretched out before him as far as the eye could see —a maze of towering spires and writhing biostructures pulsing with a sickly, violet light. The air crackled faintly, alive with electromagnetic static and the scent of ozone and rot.

He was already past the first line of surveillance nodes. The nest's architecture had shifted again—like it was slightly aware of him. It couldn't quite make heads or tails of his presence and was reacting vaguely. Unsure of who or what exactly Frank might be, or if its actual senses were in need of adjusting.

Organic walls pulsed with small flexes of oozing muscle. Breathing.

He adjusted the frequency dampener on his left glove, silencing the faint whine the Decisive Invalidator emitted when he moved. It was no bigger than a coffee plunger, but dense with complexity—a singularity-wrapped containment matrix with braided tachyon filaments. One misstep, one surge of charge too early, and it would disappear not just the nest—but potentially a square kilometre of the real world above.

He realised the nest was not where he'd calculated it to be. It was a complicated, hidden anomaly where its actual geolocation was, yet his unique gauntlet's tracking device had still managed to locate it. Once Frank had vectored-in the portal gun and made the jump, he then realised a major city was positioned directly above where he was. He couldn't afford any mental distraction unpacking what the ramifications and connections were to this.

Don't think. Pace yourself. Plant the device. Get out.

Frank slid forward, barely disturbing the squishy ground. A Riftwalker passed by on a suspended walkway above, its long head twitching unnaturally to the side—as if sniffing the ether.

He froze.

The suit's anti-sensory mesh held.

It moved on.

Beneath the central dome—where the walls met in a spiralled weft of bone and metal—was the heart chamber. A throne-like edifice of grotesque flesh and circuitry. Pulsing cables fed into it like arteries. That's where he had to go. That was where the Invalidator had to be placed. Right in the nerve-centre. The brain and the heart of this hive-species existence.

He crept closer. There were five Riftwalkers now. Twitchy. Alert.

He reached the edge of the chamber, heart pounding.

Then the suit flickered.

Just for half a second.

But enough.

One of them turned its head.

Frank didn't hesitate.

In one fluid motion, he stashed the Invalidator beneath the massive structure supporting the brain and pressed the activation node. It began to pulse—a steady, golden rhythm. Armed and alive, yet undetectable to their senses.

An ungodly scream erupted.

One of the Riftwalkers had briefly seen him.

Frank withdrew his pythium wrist blade from its forearm sheath with a metallic snap.

The creature lunged in his general direction where it had last glimpsed him—insect-like arms scything forward.

Frank twisted low, slashing upward. The blade found a gap in its plating. Black ichor sprayed. Another Riftwalker screeched in reply.

They were converging. Although they couldn't see him, they knew he was there somewhere, somehow –And worse still…They very quickly had worked-out who exactly who he was!

He bolted.

A narrow tunnel behind the chamber—a service passage woven from coiled biotech and strange scaffolding gave him an escape route. He sprinted away down this passage, the blade still hot in his grip.

One last look over his shoulder—

The Invalidator sat blinking under the throne, pulsing louder now.

The Riftwalkers howled, enraged. Yet they were not aware of what had been stashed in that space. Frank had also imbued it with an invisibility field to their sensory spectrum.

He now ran over gooey, spongey floors.

The countdown had begun.

The Conductor

Vittorio's cellar was partly a modest conference room, and partly a small, well-equipped lab with an additional high-tech, dedicated command room added on. The command section glowed like a thousand tiny suns, each screen showing a fragment of the world — cathedrals, deserts, storm-lashed rooftops, jungle outposts where small bells hung from bamboo scaffolds — every one of them wired into the same invisible pulse. Thick cables ran in vines across the stone floor, merging into a patchwork mainframe that hummed with something more than just electricity. It was alive with screen after screen, some huge, some small, flickering with maps, telemetry, people and raw data — an electronic epitaph to Vittorio's mind and his expansive, global spirit. This was his visual intent: to see everything all at once, to keep Orange Sand's operations in harmony and flowing smoothly across the planet.

He sat hunched at his desk, headset clamped over his silver hair, mouthpiece angled close, eyes darting from screen to screen. He looked less like a physicist now and more like an old, wartime field-radio operator who'd survived and outlasted a long campaign.

On the table beside him, a mug of cold espresso trembled from some low, subterranean rumbles — probably thunder off in the distance, or possibly something deeper, somewhere far below his home...

"Alright, all Orange Sand units," he said, voice steady through the mic. "Status check — all sectors. Let's tune the world, shall we?" Tiny, radio voices answered from everywhere: Cairo. Kyoto. Valparaíso. Alice Springs. Yangzhou. Yau Ma Tei. The Wirral. A massive, secret conglomerate of people world-wide voiced-in. From a gigantic, majestic bell tower in Bruges, to a small, humble temple nestled in the Cambodian jungle...hundreds of random locations here, there and everywhere.

Each voice came through with static, vigour and human spirit — engineers, monks, physicists, composers, high school students, journalists, mechanics, musicians, farmers, priests, ALL of them, everyday people from all walks of life, from all over the place, and ALL of them speaking in a miasma of different languages and dialects. Yet, they ALL had the one same thing in common: They *all were* ready.
They *all* knew the heavy score the world was now facing — And they all knew the enemy was at the gate. They were humanity's last symphony, and they were about to start playing.

"All nodes stand by for harmonic alignment," Vittorio sang out strong and proud.

Suddenly, he froze as a new signal flickered across his console — raw, distorted, pulsing through in an unorthodox way via an abstract channel that shouldn't even exist.

"Impossible..." he whispered.

The room seemingly went quiet as his mind raced. Calculations and patchwork theory cascaded as he madly tried to figure-out how Frank was doing it. The hum of the global network took a back seat for a quick moment. Vittorio leaned forward, listening to the chaotic burst of static and that crazy, unique voice coming through which could only be Frank's, bellowing away, rough, defiant, and positively alive.

Vittorio exhaled an incredulous happy laugh, in-part disbelief, and in-part pride for his old mate's accomplishment.

Despite being half buried in distortion as it emanated out from the Riftwalker's nest, Frank could be heard loud and clear.

"Hey Chief! How's it looking your end?"

Vittorio smiled from ear to ear, "We're on the edge of starting ALL the bells up buddy...And what insane escapade are you undertaking there Doctor Franklin Jules Kendrick?!"

"Well, being the sociable butterfly that I am," he said, coughing through interference, "I flew in here to deliver a little gift for our old pals. One of my special devices you were once so very worried about me making a while back."

Vittorio's heart kicked. "You made **another decisive invalidator**?!"

"Oh yeah! I sure as heck did! Bigger this time even- and better! I'm installing it right now, under their core node. If it works, they'll lose their hive's interdimensional nerve stem and they'll all disappear...forever...in non-Euclidian nowhere-land. And, *IF* it doesn't..." He paused, voice tightening. "Well, let's not dwell on the negatives, eh?"

Vittorio leaned closer to the mic. "Frank, you crazy nutter... I pray you can pull this off old friend and make it back safe."

"Well, that's why I called you collect. If I don't, please make sure my family, Sherri and my sister – and even Aldo too, are all taken care of please, can you? See they are looked after and always kept safe?"

"Of course, Frank! – But let's not think this way –you're going to be okay mi fratello!"

"I literally gotta run now old friend."

"I'm praying for you to succeed Frank – I know you can do it and make it back here safe!"

"I'll do my best Vitto," Frank said, a grin audible even through the static. "See you on the flip side of the waveform my older brother from a polo-parmigiana mumma."

Despite the gravity of *everything*…Vittorio laughed loudly, tears forming at the edges of his eyes.

The channel crackled once, twice — then went dead.

Vittorio sat back in his chair; the room was suddenly too quiet now. The low hum of the servers felt like a pulse without a body.

It had only been forty seconds. He quickly regained his focus.

In front of him was his special orchestra of a thousand or so dedicated people. And then he briefly thought: every orchestra and band needs its breakaway riff artist — the player who breaks time, bends the tempo, seemingly screws things up and yet in so doing, somehow builds a uniqueness into the music that ends-up saving the song as a whole.

Frank was that breakaway riff artist.

The one who refused to stay on the sheet of music everyone else was playing along to but nevertheless always struck the note that no one else could find and inadvertently helped to forge a one-of-a-kind masterpiece.

He was the unorthodox glitch in the human pattern, the discord that revealed the deeper harmony of what it means to be a crazy fruit loop in a world made up of sensible bran flakes. And like every impossible solo artist, like every square peg in a round hole, his chaos was what completed and rounded-out the composition of life and human existence.

A good-hearted delinquent who would burn the rulebook just to keep the lights from going out.

A true mate who would always have his buddies backs and give them all he could, even if it meant laying his life on the line. Even if it meant his reputation and good standing, he'd give it all and not give a damn.

"Alright, maestro Frank," Vittorio murmured quietly into the silence as he made the sign of the cross. "Play your part, my friend... and may God speed."

He then flipped another set of switches; the hum of a thousand bells came online again as the earth itself began to breathe again. On the central screen appeared Dr Lindley in Aldo's lab, busily adjusting resonance sequences on her wall of antique and modern synthesisers. Luc paced behind her, rifle slung over his shoulder, ready for anything.

Another screen flickered to the left of the main screen, it was Jasper, pacing restlessly, sensing what no human could. He was about to settle down, sit on his hind legs and begin doing his thing on the soundwave pad.

"Hairy-Legs! Good to see you!" Vittorio called. "Are you ready there? Is the masterpiece all set to go?"

"You betcha it is, Governor!" she shouted back at him with a huge smile, Jasper gave a sharp *woof*.

Vittorio pinched the bridge of his nose, eyes flicking back to the displays. "Hold your bells steady everyone," he said softly into the mic. "Wait for the signal. We go when the waveform aligns."

Outside, the world was tearing itself apart — riots, armies mobilising, the sky turning strange — yet beneath Geneva, the old Italian man remained utterly calm.

"Hold steady," he repeated. "The waveform is almost aligned."

For a long moment, only the static answered — the static, and the faint melody already beginning to dissolve chaos and drive away evil from the surface of the world.

The global orchestra was about to start up, and it was about to kick the bad guys in the guts — and it was going to be one HUGE and HARD kick!

Please Leave the Fridge Door Open

The garage pulsed with quiet energy.
Light bled from the coils running along the rafters — blue, green, and gold — the same colours that shimmered on the horizon sometimes when the bells began to ring across the world.

The old Kelvinator stood at the centre like a shrine, its white enamel skin covered in cables, stabilisers, and handmade insulation plates. A narrow walk-ramp led to the open door, cold vapour spilling down its steps.

At the old workbench, Aldo adjusted the dials of his compact console — a mess of repurposed instruments and hand-soldered wires. Each meter flickered to a rhythm only he could hear. He modulated sliders and buttons. The man looked less like a scientist and more like a sound-studio engineer tuning-up an invisible rock band.

"Phase holding," Aldo murmured. "Temporal field steady. Let's keep it sweet, kids."

Byron, Sherri, Hannah, Marvin, Jacinta and Jake stood before the humming doorway, faces lit by the refrigerator's spectral glow. A cadmium orange shine, warm to behold, gently bathed their faces. Nobody spoke. Even the air seemed to be listening carefully to what was going on around them.

"Where does it go exactly?" Hannah asked quietly.

Aldo smiled — weary but kind. "Back," he said. "To where it all began. Remember — the portal listens to your intent. Step through together, as one, and with the same intent to see that wolf, or it'll take you different ways."

From somewhere deep inside the circuitry, a low harmonic began to hum — faint at first, then swelling like a living pulse. The Kelvinator trembled. The coils above brightened until they were almost white.

Aldo's hand hovered over the master control, every movement delicate, measured, as though coaxing the instrument rather than commanding it. "Alright gang, let's play our note in this vast, cosmic Jazz band."

He tapped the switch.

The world contracted into light.

Cold air rushed through the garage, carrying the metallic scent of snow. Frost webbed the concrete beneath their feet. The hum rose in pitch until it broke open — not with a bang, but with a *resonant, deep-bass laughter sound: HAH-HAH-HAH-HAH!*

"Go!" Aldo shouted over the sound.

Byron took Sherri's hand. Jake and Hannah followed. Together, they stepped up the ramp and into the bright, swirling mouth of the portal.

For a heartbeat, the world looked like a sheet of vibrating glass.
Then the fridge light snapped and flickered off, leaving Aldo alone in the echoing, humming sounds of the garage — his fingers still moving across the controls like a concert pianist finishing the last phrase of a song.

When Gate Crashers Get Out of Hand…

– *Geneva, 20 minutes ago*

Aldo's old lab was never meant to be beautiful,
yet tonight it looked like a stunning cathedral of copper
and light.

If he were actually in it, on this occasion, he would have
given it a solid nod in admiration, but tonight in his
absence, he'd handed the reins over to his trusted
colleague and good friend Doctor Harriet Lindley. And in
good faith and respect, she was giving it the same
affectionate nod that he would have given it. She really
loved his crazy lab too.

Panels hummed.
Consoles glowed.
Wiring ran like veins through the walls, pulsing with
promise.
The floor vibrated softly under the rising frequencies of
the global bell network, each chime syncing through
quantum tunnelling and arriving here as a shimmering
thread of wonderous sound.

Harriet Lindley stood over the central harmonic console,
fingertips hovering above her keys like a pianist about to
strike a final, perfect chord.
Her jaw was set, her eyes focused.
She could feel it — the entire world was leaning forward.

Luc Renard paced behind her, boots silent on the
concrete, his rifle slung lazily over his shoulder with the
familiar certainty of a man who had carried a weapon that
way longer than most people had worked a 9-to-5 job
through to retirement.

He didn't say a word, but his posture was all tension and animal instinct.

Jasper sat on his custom copper sound-pad, the old microphone hanging above him like a halo.
Each harmonic surge made his fur lift-up slightly, like static drawn toward a storm.

Luc couldn't help but smile when he looked at the fluffy, black and white dog form and the old 50's microphone. "Eat your heart out Sinatra!" he said mostly to himself.

Lindley heard him and broke into a smile. That's what dogs do...they make us smile no matter what the circumstances we're in are.

She checked the global relay grid again. "The bells in Bhutan just came online," she whispered, relieved.

Luc gave a grunt. "And that's good?"

"That's *excellent*," she said. "When the last cluster activates, we'll have the full restorative lattice."

Right on cue, Vittorio's voice crackled through the speaker:

"All the world bells confirmed active now. Initiating total resonance."

And then —

The world rang. Hearts and souls everywhere were lifted up as...

The bells in Paris
and Mumbai
and Kyoto

and Buenos Aires and Boston and around the corner a
little in East Perth
and Reykjavik
and Lusaka, Qingdao, Budapest
and the monastery ruins in Bhutan—

--Thousands of locations everywhere in the World,
wherever there was a bell of some kind, they all started to
ring...

they all chimed
in a single, rising, impossible chorus of worldly,
wonderous sound.

The lab filled with a sound older than language.

Jasper threw his head back and howled. It made his entire
being feel the same way it did when he was rubbed on his
back just in front of his tail.

Luc felt the hairs on his arms stand straight. He felt love
in such an indescribable purity yet instinctively knew to
be ready for the worst.
His hand drifted automatically toward his rifle's grip as he
lowered it down off his shoulder.

Lindley exhaled.
"Aldo, we're stabilising. Send the wave."

Static burst through the speakers — Aldo juggling away in
the garage on the other side of the World in Kirra,
shouting something about portal torsion and backflow.

Then:

Everything went wrong at once.

The lab lights flickered.
The copper pads snapped with blue arcs.
The oscillation screens skittered into nonsense.
Jasper yelped and braced himself, claws scraping. He growled as his hackles raised.

Luc narrowed his eyes.
He could *feel* it — an approaching violence, a wrongness, a pressure in the air like a storm reaching through the walls.

Lindley checked the readouts. "Something's coupling into us — not from Aldo, not from Vittorio. This is external..."

The temperature dropped.

The overhead lights stretched — not flickering but literally *stretching* sideways as if reality was being turned into a rubber-band being pulled.

Jasper snarled, low and ancient, the kind of sound an animal makes when it recognises an enemy it has never seen but has always feared.

Luc lifted his rifle. He flicked the safety off.

A distortion opened two metres away — a bending of the air like heat haze in reverse.
A dark seam split the space.

Lindley whispered, "Oh God... no..."

Two shapes tore their way out of the fracture. Roaring with screeching rage...

Riftwalkers.

They hit the floor snarling, their limbs wrong, their movements stuttering between frames like corrupted footage.

Their skin shimmered with the oily, negative-light ripple of creatures pulled violently through the Bell Harmonic Field.

The first Riftwalker turned to face Jasper, it was about to charge at him. Jasper rumbled with a deep violent snarl. He faced directly into the Riftwalker and stalked forward reverberating with a roar that was so full of violent, K9 menace and rage.

Strangely, the Riftwalker froze. Normally not fearful of anything, the creature recoiled back in a motion that resembled fear and hesitation. It flicked its head from side to side as it faced Jasper, then turned away to face Luc and Harriet.

The Riftwalker decided to lunge at them instead — Luc didn't hesitate.

He fired ten rounds into its head and chest.
The creature jerked backwards, not bleeding, but *disintegrating from the inside out*, collapsing into a vanishing point that screamed like metal scraping against glass before it winked out.

The second Riftwalker screeched and bounded directly for Lindley.

Luc stepped in front of her, fired again, twenty rounds — precise, brutal, perfect.

The second Riftwalker folded in on itself, imploding into a pinpoint of darkness before snapping out of existence with a final, shivering scream.

Silence.

A long, trembling silence.

Luc lowered his rifle and changed out the magazine for a fresh one.
Jasper growled softly, padding over to sniff the scorched concrete where the things had vanished, then peed on the carbon residue left behind.

Lindley forced herself to swallow.
"That... shouldn't have been possible. They should've been trapped in the collapse."

Luc flicked a glance around the room, soldier instincts still firing.
"No breaches left. Equipment intact. You, okay?"

"I'm fine," she said, though her hands shook.
"Everything's... somehow still running."

Luc walked a slow perimeter check, rifle ready.
He didn't see the small, metallic sphere that had rolled under a secondary console — a cold, glossy object the size of a cricket ball, faintly pulsing with negative light.

A Warbilizer.
A negative-band emitter.
A Riftwalker contaminant device.

It sat humming quietly, unnoticed, beginning its subtle sabotage.

Lindley rebooted the array.

Jasper settled back on his copper pad, uneasy.

Luc finally nodded.
"Let's bring it all back online."

They started the system again.

The harmonics rose.

The bells answered.

The wormhole synchronised.

And behind them —
beneath them —
unseen and awakening —
the Warbilizer blinked once,
twice,
and began to spread its toxic distortion!

In-Between Time Travel

The jump didn't feel like motion; it felt like being *remembered* by something that had forgotten who you were.

You felt welcomed back into a home again after never existing before. Something loving and caring was kindly ushering you in and persuading you to sit down, relax and take a seat onto one of the most comfiest sofas you've ever sat down on before in your life.

It was a home that you never knew you had, but you loved it just the same and remembered everything about it.

One moment the kids were stepping through the Kelvinator's liquid membrane that was the portal's threshold and then they were inside the Kelvinator's spiral of bubbling, jelly light— the next, they were falling at what felt like Mach speed through a corridor of frozen colour and fleeting sensations that felt like feathers and soft down brushing over their skin. Warm and cool puffs of air that were soothing and yet rough at the same time.

There were smells of beauty and splendour that felt oddly good and oddly bad at the same time, peculiar, faint tunes that weren't really instrumental yet were familiar sounds of music both pleasant and dimly scary.

Comfort and fear mixed together here in an uneasy way, in such an impossible way that it could never be replicated back in the fixed, real world outside.

Time wasn't linear.

Time inside the wormhole did not flow; it ossified into a tetrahedral crystal; each face a trapped slice of divergent chronology.

It hung in ribbons, dancing in plasmic DNA strands of past and future outcomes braided through a vibrant void that shimmered light spectrums of half sunlight reflecting off oil patches drifting on water.

Fragments of other worlds drifted past them: a steamy rainforest canopy with gibbons yelping; a city of glass with airborne traffic; a vast, sandy desert; monoliths washed in moonlight; bungalows in morning haze; and a tiny sundrenched hut at midday — all beautiful and tranquil vistas blending into one.

A sweet, condensed sugar cube of the majestic expansiveness of our true existence... light, love, wonder, and endless possibilities. An essence of what everything must have been like...before, before.

They bathed in a beautiful radiance, yet beneath that radiance lingered a faint, impossible smudge — the soft suggestion of something ancient and malign brushing its dirty claws across reality long, long ago, and even now — leaving everything forever, quietly altered, bent not just toward harm but toward a slow, irreversible ruin. It felt like a theft so old and so complete that no one alive remembered what had been stolen — only the hollow absence of where it had once lived, a loss so subtle it slipped past the world unnoticed until all that remained was the ruin it had left behind.

And yet, even in the shadow of all that had been taken away, something small and stubborn still glimmered — a fragile brightness persisting in the fractures, a quiet reminder that not all light, nor all of creation's old song, had been stolen away.

The human heart was the battery. Our souls? The radio that would never quit playing that song.

Then came the smack and splatter of shadows...darkness and the growls of hatred...upwelled up ahead.

Figures formed in the swirling, twisting glare further down the tunnel—tall, angular, moving with impossible fluidity. This was their domain. This was where they mostly moved around in. They didn't wobble or teeter here, they glided.

It made Byron feel the way he did in the passenger seat of a car when approaching a group of roadworkers up ahead on a highway. There was always the one worker holding up a large STOP sign on a stick.

This was supposed to be a smooth, linear jump. There wasn't supposed to be any delays nor stops – and there definitely wasn't meant to be any...

Riftwalkers!

Half-real, half-ether, their bodies were stains of light vacuuming fractures in space itself, folding and unfolding as they advanced like floating jellyfish.

"Keep moving!" Sherri shouted, pulling Hannah and Jake forward with her conscious will and whatever physical form her body was currently in as they glided through the non-Euclidean airspace of the wormhole.

Aldo, back at his control station, swore loudly like a trucker – he never swore normally and never used harsh language – but in this moment, as he spotted their horrible blotches suddenly appear on his display panel... he swore like he had never sworn before. He then began to madly punch at keypads and throw switches while doing rapid calculations in an overwhelmingly stressed mind. Looking to his left, he spotted a spare, fermion marker-buoy he had been using to test pathways along the projected wormhole routes. He quickly grabbed the canister, flipped a button and pushed down hard on it until a small, digital display started counting-down from 20-seconds, then he tossed it into the wormhole.

The Riftwalkers glided closer, warping the light around them. Their voices were like reversed thunder that had meaning yet was linguistically unintelligible.
Byron spun, levelling his plasma gun at them, the pulse coils buzzing away as they rapidly began charging up.
He fired.

The shot ripped through the corridor, a streak of electric blue hitting and cutting one of the Riftwalkers in half and causing the others to cascade off in different directions. The impact created an explosion of glass shards of time—fragments of faces, memories, small stars.

The others roared with ungodly sounds of rage.
That's when another one instantly created a spear of oozing light and tossed it. The crackling spear moved through the space with a ghostly velocity and a weird, intelligent accuracy as it single-mindedly kept recorrecting its trajectory several times to close in on Byron. The bolt hurtled straight towards him. The thin, photonic spear shot into his side, bursting out from the back of his torso. It continued off into the endless distance beyond, along with a few streamers of Bryon's blood.

He screamed out in pain and gasped, tumbling forwards through the space he was hurtling through.
The wound burned with dirty, voltaic static.
Sherri screamed his name and caught up to him as the Riftwalkers regathered slowly.

Byron forced a smile, blood and light mixing on his shirt. "Go! I'm fine… it's just… time travel indigestion."

Then, somewhere beyond them, Aldo's voice echoed through the collapsing tunnel:

"Hold together! You're almost there—ride the pulse! I've just sent the assholes some butt-hurt – You guys need to keep on track!" He urged them through the neural link he'd created earlier to maintain communication with them.

A voluminous slap of bass roared out from the quantum tunnel behind the Riftwalkers. It was a lightning-fast flick of energy. A snap of light and then an orange-soda spherical mega-balloon of molten particles grew rapidly outwards, expanding and consuming all the remaining Riftwalkers before it popped like a bubble-gum balloon smacking outwards in shards and slapping everything along with it before contracting back into nothingness. And the Riftwalkers were gone.

Aldo recalibrated the parametric pathway the kids were on and began adjusting the reverse spin-state of the quantum channel. He was bringing them in for a soft landing onto some solid ground.

It now felt like they were beginning to slow down. Gravity was tickling at their feet and was returning their trays to an upright position, so to speak.

The loving and kind, indescribable something that had invited them into its home was now gently showing them to the door.

Sensations became normal again. Up was up, Down was down and the ground was where it ought to be again.

Sherri hauled Byron up; the wolf was already howling ahead, its voice locking onto the bell harmonics bleeding in through from the real, interdimensional world beyond. The tunnel twisted down in size, light bending like a whirling, winding ribbon pulled taut—
and then it snapped and closed in a clap, clap, clap, thud, thud, clack sound of a typical wormhole closing up.

And then they were left standing there, almost alone, in...

Eurasia, Late Stone Age

- Upper Palaeolithic Period
-38,752 years BC, and 10 hours beforehand...

Up ahead was a wolf.

Several feet away from it, the newly arrived group of kids
stood —
disoriented, stressed, shaking with adrenaline,
but still together.
Still a team.

Jake had rolled up his T-shirt and was pressing it hard
into Byron's side, his hands were steady despite the fear in
his eyes. Blood seeped between his fingers, but it wasn't
the arterial gush they'd feared — by some merciful sliver
of vectoring luck, the spear had gone cleanly through
missing anything fatal.

Byron clenched his jaw, pale but conscious.
He winced and muttered, "Mate, you're causing more pain
than the spear did –I'm filing a complaint with HR and I
want to speak to a manager."

Jake shot him a quick grin back.
"I'm sorry, Karen – we don't have any managers here just
now, but I can assure you your pain is keeping you
alive...And if you don't mind doing a quick survey –how
would you rate your customer experience so far on a scale
of one to five, with five being wonderful"

"Minus fifty – you guys' suck!" Byron coughed out.

Sherri ignored their exchange — she was already stepping
forward.

Focused.
Centred.
Heightened.

She reached into her jacket and pulled out a plastic, zip-lock bag of diced lamb fillet she'd brought along with her. Grabbing a small piece from the bag, she tossed it toward the wolf.

It landed softly in the grass close to where it was.

The wolf sniffed.
Stepped in.
Ate.
Lifted its golden eyes —straight into hers. Something mixed in the ether and the cosmos as their eyes connected, an uptick in the Universal vibration.

Sherri removed another cube of lamb meat from the bag and slowly waved her arm around, inviting, steady, sure.

Behind her, Hannah held the dog flag high.
Aldo had promised them it would stabilize the matrix, strengthen the tether, "guide" the spirits of this ancient moment back into proper alignment.

But something felt off.

A wormhole should have opened by now.
Bell harmonics blasting.
The wave antidote pouring in from Doc Lindley and Jasper in Aldo's lab.
A safe corridor of sound and light to return back into.

But the air remained still. Quiet.

Wrong.

Sherri felt her stomach tighten.
“Where is it?” she breathed. “What’s the hold up?”

The wolf took another step closer—

And that’s when the Universe completely fractured…

Frank and the Reset

The air over the sodden, dead ridge shivered like a mirage.

Frank clung to the slime covered rock face as another shockwave tore through reality — a harmonic convulsion rolling outward from the bell lattice around the world as it came online was sending the Riftwalker's Nest into conniptions. Dust lifted in spirals; the bones of ruined structures hummed like dying tuning forks; the entire valley floor he was now in, rippled as if something beneath it was waking up in pain.

"Not good… not good…" Frank muttered, forcing breath through clenched teeth.

The Decisive Invalidator — tucked beneath a section of the Nest's heart and nervous system, where he'd stashed it minutes ago — pinged through the quantum relay in his earpiece. Faint. Out of sync. A hair off.

Just like everything else was suddenly "off".

He tapped the side of the device strapped to his forearm — trying to pull a clean signal through.

Static.

Then Lindley's voice, cut to ribbons, came through:

"—ank! —e've got drift— feedback— hurry—"

Then nothing but the rising whine of the collapsing harmonic grid.

Frank scanned the ridge.

The Riftwalker nest — was now erupting into disarray — it pulsed under the soil beneath his feet. A wrongness throbbed from it: a living negativity, a pit of old gravity and malnourished time. The bells were scraping and clawing at it, peeling at its edges, making it convulse like a wounded animal about to vomit.

The turbulence of the entire structure hit Frank again, this time so violently he dropped to one knee.

His breath stuttered.

Cold sweat broke across his back.

He shoved himself upright.

"No. No, no, no. I am not dying here, not like this."

His fingers flew over the chrono-pistol strapped to his waist.

Readings... wrong.
Timer... wrong.
Trajectory... wrong.

He had programmed the jump back without considering the effect of the bells on the Nest and he scolded himself for not having picked up on it earlier before.

"Two jumps left you ding-wit and you almost bungled one up!"

The Nest was beginning to go crazy.

Not just that, he also realised by the time his Invalidator detonated it would be too late. The controlling hive-mind— already enraged by the global bell harmonics washing through it — would have been riled-up enough to start an emergency evacuation process out into multiple, safe timelines, spawning the Hive off into numerous, new locations. Weak as each one of these newly spawned, smaller hives would be, having broken themselves apart from the strength and solidarity of the Mega-Hive, they would survive the Bell Harmonics. They could still rebuild their nests, re-grow in numbers and consolidate into a greater, unified whole later on.

The Invalidator would only be removing a section of them if it didn't go off sooner.

"Damn it," he hissed, slamming his palm against the rock.

He closed his eyes.

Then it hit him — cold, sharp clarity:

I have to go back!
Back to where it's stashed.
Reset the Invalidator for *sooner* — before the bells finish pushing the nest into a complete frenzy of self-preservation.

Another harmonic wave rolled through the valley.
The nest screeched beneath the earth — a sound without lungs, without throat, without mercy.

Frank launched into motion.

He sprinted across the broken ground — lungs tearing, boots sliding, rocks dropping away beneath him as he vaulted from one section to the next. His body protested every step, but he pushed harder. He could feel the nest paying its full attention on him now — like a thousand unseen eyes swivelling toward him through the soil.

A fissure cracked open at his heel.
He leapt over it.

Another ripple buckled the ground beneath him.
He slid sideways — caught himself — kept going.

He spotted the stash point up ahead in the corridor he'd
only just bolted from a few minutes beforehand: the now
collapsed metallic shelf where he'd hidden the Invalidator
core was bending under the strain of Lindley's sequence
and the World's bells all ringing at once.

Running with Olympic speed, he reached the nook it was
tucked into.

His shoulder bounced into the central core, sending a jolt
through his spine. He clawed into the narrow space
between the structure until his fingers brushed the
invalidator.

He yanked it free.

The ground roared beneath him again — a sound like a
mountain inhaling.

Frank didn't allow himself to think.

He twisted open the cannister, fingers trembling, and
began to reset the detonation sequence. The timer digits
stuttered, glitching between numbers as the interference
grew worse.

"Come on... come ON..."

The device flickered.
Then snapped into clarity.

**Detonation time accepted.
Chronal offset: IMMEDIATE.**

Frank exhaled shakily.

And then he felt it.

The nest.

Pressing through the soil.

Reaching toward him.

Hunting. Seeking. Expanding…

The gelatinous walls around him began to shuffle. Something under the earth screamed — a wet, metallic screech that stabbed straight into his bones.

Frank slammed the Invalidator back into place.

“Alright, you bunch of ugly freaks,” he breathed. “You want me? Come take me.”

He fired his chrono-pistol. A blast of blue plasma opened a portal before him.

He hit the activation stud on his arm gauntlet, and the invalidator began to emit a howling whine as it screamed up the acceleration of its tachyon powered coils.

Emerald static began to dance around the spot where the invalidator was tucked away. Only seconds now until it went FEA (Full Euclidean Abstract) and vacuumed everything away within a 9-km spherical convex range into a zero-point nothingness. It would soon become the Universe's largest Hoover vacuum.

A flash of pale blue swallowed him as he stepped through
the portal —
and Frank disappeared, hurled backward through his own
rewound timeline
toward the moment he never should have left.

The nest roared in fury behind him as reality folded in
from the bell harmonics.

Yet still no detonation of the invalidator...

Pressure in the Glass

Vittorio had always loved this room —
his quiet bunker beneath Champel,
where the screens hummed and the world felt readable.

Tonight, it felt like a coffin.

Every bell across the planet had come online within sixty
seconds of each other —
and the effect was breathtaking.

Towers in Europe hummed.
Temple bells in Bhutan resonated.
Churches in South America shuddered with luminous
overtones.
Even the rust-covered fishing bells in small, little tiny,
coastal towns —
long forgotten —
chimed as if remembering their purpose in life.

The entire world was ringing.

His monitors flickered with the synchrony graphs:

HARMONIC UNISON: 99.87%
GLOBAL LATTICE: ACTIVE
RESTORATION WAVE: OPTIMAL

He allowed himself the smallest smile.

Then the readings dipped. They dipped even more...

Then plunged.

Then *fell off the bottom of the screen.*

The lights above him pulsed sickly.
A low, nauseating hum spread through the concrete walls.
The air felt heavier.
Sickly sweeter.
Wrong...Just wrong.

Vittorio pressed his fingertips to his temples.

Humans weren't supposed to feel harmonic
contamination.
Not physically.

Yet his stomach lurched like he'd swallowed seawater.

Another pulse hit him —
a deep oscillation with the taste of metal and rot.

His breath hitched.

He steadied himself on the console.

"This shouldn't be happening..."

One by one, his screens blinked into corrupted signals.

Tokyo bell—
ERROR.
Cardiff bell—
DISSONANT.
Buenos Aires—
PHASE SLIP DETECTED.
Kyoto—
UNSTABLE.

Then the worst notification of all:

**"NEGATIVE BAND SIGNATURE DETECTED —
SOURCE UNKNOWN."**

Vittorio froze.

Negative band?

No.

Impossible!

Every negative-band emitter the Riftwalkers had ever
planted around the world had been hunted down and
neutralised —
every single one —
thanks to the team at the Orange Sand facility in
Meekatharra, Western Australia.

He could still picture the red dust, the shimmering heat,
the circular structure where the psi-lab sat buried beneath
three tonnes of shielding.

It was there the para-dimensional sniffer team —
half remote viewers, half military intuitives,
trained to slip their senses one notch sideways into the
thin, dangerous membranes between probability layers —
They found the last of the Riftwalker contamination
devices. No more had been detected.

And the projection amplifier, that massive steel cylinder
humming with four impossible frequencies at once, would
alert them whenever a new one was placed somewhere,
until not a single Riftwalker emitter remained.

They had cleared the world.

They had done it.

So, the reading on his screen now...
this pulsing, rising, *alive* negative-band signature...should
not exist!

Unless—

Unless the Riftwalkers had smuggled one in during a harmonic breach.

Unless it had been planted in the one place nobody had ever thought to check —

Inside Aldo's resonance lab itself.

Vittorio's skin prickled.

The Warbilizer was no longer hypothetical.

It was awake.

It was in the system.

And through it, the hive-mind had just opened its eyes.

And if so, then every bell on Earth was now singing into corruption.

Every chime.
Every tone.
Every harmonic relay.

Was now a *poisoned, toxic lattice.*

His heart hammered against his ribs.
He slammed the comm switch.

"Lindley? Aldo?
We have contamination in the global grid — I repeat, contamination. Your harmonics are—"

The audio warped mid-sentence.
His own voice bent sideways in his ears.

The control room lights strobed.

His screens pixelated and smeared.

Humans across the world — operators, technicians,
monks, bell keepers —
began clutching tables, chairs, rails.
He saw them through the surveillance feeds,
all getting dizzy, sweating, fainting as the negative-band
interference rippled outward.

A global wave of nausea.

A kind of psychic vertigo.

Something was *pushing back.*

Something mean, nasty and intelligent.

Something angry.

Something in the Riftwalker hive-mind had sensed the
disturbance in its nest —
and now, through the Warbilizer,
it was answering back.

The Riftwalkers had Frank. Now Orange Sand had an AI
Warbilizer.

A surge hit the bunker.
Vittorio slid sideways across the polished floor, knocking
over a stool.

For a moment his vision fractured into black, grey, and
white.

When it snapped back, six words burned on every
monitor:

**HIVE-MIND REACTING -BECOMING META-
PHYSICAL
HIVE-MIND REACTING -BECOMING META-
PHYSICAL
HIVE-MIND REACTING -BECOMING META-
PHYSICAL**

Vittorio's breath left him in a sharp exhale.

He whispered:

"Dear God. They know. They're counteracting."

His hands shook as he reached for the comm.

**"Lindley — whatever's destabilising your lab —
you have seconds to find it. You have to shut it
down! Or every bell we've activated becomes a
weapon *against* us."**

The bunker trembled again.

Vittorio staggered, crashing into the console.

For the first time in years, he felt the sensation of fear
crawl up his spine.

The Riftwalker nest was aware.
It was evolving to the attack.
It was pushing back with force.

And in Doc Aldo's lab in Geneva, under a table, hidden
and unnoticed,
a small metallic sphere pulsed gently —
like an egg about to hatch.

The Warbilizer.

Its bio-crystalline pulse rolled outward —
stronger, darker, hungrier.

Vittorio wiped sweat from his brow.

**"Lindley... Luc... for God's sake... find the source.
Before the world breaks itself in half."**

The Warbilizer Pulse

Back in Aldo's lab, Lindley jolted as every monitor went white.

Luc grabbed her, pulling her back before a panel that had begun to surge with heat started to spark and sizzle.

Jasper howled, retreating onto the floor as the Warbilizer — hidden beneath the console — pulsed again, stronger.

The dog knew the enemy hadn't left properly. It was still here. His eyes narrowed and his growling became louder. Hunting instincts kicked in.

The entire lab shook.
Negative-band distortion flooded every instrument.

Screens flickered with nausea-inducing interference. Tartarian organs sounded sick and ghastly. Harmonics warped into dizzy, low oscillations that made the air vibrate with dread.

Humans across the world — monks, bell keepers, technicians — were collapsing at their posts as the negative signal overrode the harmony.

Lindley's voice cracked, panicked:

"Aldo?
Vittorio?
We're losing the lattice!
Something's corrupting the entire grid!"

Luc spun, rifle raised, scanning the room for an enemy that wasn't visible but felt.

"Where's it coming from? What the hell did they do when they were in here?"

Jasper growled even louder — staring toward the underside of the secondary console.

The Warbilizer pulsed...

The Border Collie barked...

When Light Implodes Inwardly

5 minutes beforehand

No warning.
No sound.

Just a violent collapse of space —
light folding into itself
like a neatly folded, origami star collapsing point-first.

Then—

Boom.
It burst outward in all directions at once.

The air split like a glass sheet shattering across infinity.

Sherri stumbled forward, boots hitting frozen tundra with
a jarring thud.
But now — for the first time — it had sunk in, the
magnitude of where she was –

And *when...*

Thirty-nine thousand years before her own birth.

Byron shouted her name — his face flickering like bad
film, half in this moment, half still in the last.

Jake hauled him upright.

Hannah spun, eyes wild, scanning the fractured horizon.

Snow whipping sideways in impossible vectors.
Lightning flickering in slow motion.
Auroras bleeding through cracks in time.

Shards of prehistory layered over modern echoes —
the world's skeleton exposed naked.

Sherri was now running for her life –they all were.

The ground beneath her wasn't ground at all anymore—just a constantly shifting kaleidoscope of fractured, spluttering time distortions, each step warping through *centuries in an instant*. Her foot landed in a snowy Ice Age plain, then a neon-lit cybernetic city, then a pristine meadow untouched by human hands—reality was bending and unfolding back in on itself, and they were at the epicentre of it all.

"MOVE FORWARDS – JUST KEEP MOVING FORWARDS NO MATTER WHAT!" Aldo bellowed over the comm system in a crackled tone – but only Jake was able to hear the message before it broke off.

"KEEP MOVING!" Jake roared, hauling his brother forward over the raging chaos surrounding them. Byron desperately clutched at his side, bleeding—from a wound that flickered in and out of existence. One second healing, the next gone, erased, then suddenly gaping open again and haemorrhaging...time itself couldn't decide if it had happened to him yet or if it had not.

Sherri's lungs burned as she vaulted over a collapsed, rusty metal girder—or what had *been* a girder. Now it was the exposed ribcage of a Woolly Mammoth. Before she could register any of this confusing turmoil, it *shifted again,* becoming a chrome beam extending from a futuristic skyscraper beneath her feet.

Everything was collapsing down, into, and back onto itself, over and over again in a confounding, rapid flux.

This place. This time. Their group. Nothing was supposed to be here, not anymore and it was rapidly being erased by the Warbilizer's poisonous chronology.

And in the very centre of all this, standing paralysed by the storm of the surrounding chaos, was the juvenile wolf.

A small, furry, golden-eyed anomaly in a war between two splintered realities.

Sherri did a baseball slide, coming to a stop, dirt and fermion-sparks flying up around her. The wolf was frozen, its paws flickering—one moment standing in a prehistoric tundra, the next in the middle of a suburban highway about to be run-over by the oncoming traffic, then a quiet, deserted beach.

This was it – *This was their moment...*

"Sherri!" Hannah's voice cracked out through the storm of chaos. She was grappling with the dog-flag, the same old one they'd made back home an eternity ago—but now *the paw print was gone.* Just a blank, white, canvas square on a bamboo pole –the only thing that was left of it, whipping wildly in the wind, as another flickering eruption of subatomic, lightning particles and ionic tendrils fractured across and through the space-time-continuum. Then came the angry, malevolent claws of spaghetti-like plasma that soon followed, fiercely trying to snatch-onto and tear-away at the flag that she was so desperately holding onto firmly with all her might.

"We're losing it!" Jake gasped, his voice raspy, distorting within the unstable soundwaves caused by the prolapsing timeline.

No. No, **not now!**

Sherri's mind burned, flashes of Uncle Frank's crazy theories detonating through her thoughts—The car accident, her wounds, Zeb, the Linear Displacement Generator, the Mandela Effect, all collapsing in real-time. The enemy had reached the fracture point first, trying to erase all of it, trying to overwrite history before the connection could be forged...or "re-forged"...or "pre-forged"—or ALL three versions of forging, smudged together as one.

The wolf should not really exist anymore now – But it still **DID!**

There it stood, with its tail wagging, doing that smiley panting-face that we all know and love ever so well.

LOVE can NEVER be destroyed! – You can't stop LOVE!

LOVE will ALWAYS exist!

If she didn't act now though, it quite possibly *wouldn't anymore*.

Jacinta, who was struggling on her own at the very end of the group, turned around, her pupils shrinking in horror. **"THEY'RE COMING!"**

Sherri spun around to look.

The Riftwalkers...

Shadowy, humanoid blotches not of this world, slipping through dimensional cracks like sick, living afterimages. Their forms hideously twisted and gruntingly bent, their bodies almost humanoid, but disturbingly not quite, their movements like glitches in the universe itself.

They weren't just here to stop them.

They were here to ***erase them.***

Jake screamed as one of them lunged toward him—it just missed grabbing him, recoiling back in a spasmodic, snapping motion. Yet, by coming that close to him, it had caused his entire body to become momentarily distorted, flickering between past and present versions of himself all at once. A baby / an old man / a foetus / a toddler / a nothing/ an everything –then back again to his normal self.

"SHERRI!" Byron roared. **"DO IT NOW!"**

The wolf.

Its tail wagged again...

Everything else; the storm, the collapsing multiverse, the creatures hunting them, the screaming past and future—none of it mattered.

Only this precious moment did.

Sherri stretched her hand out, reaching, waving, reaching —

She needed to touch it—she had to pat it with all the love in her soul, projecting our entire specie's collective love for them that we have. And in that impossible moment, she also needed to feel its love and loyalty reflecting back at her, forming a universal, cosmic bridge connecting humans with our furry best friends.

Her fingers brushed the wolf's head—

And the **universe exploded...**

For an infinitesimal instant, the quantum field stood
naked —
every particle unmade, every probability unbraided.
Time fell back into its primordial hush,
the silence before symmetry,
the breath before the first becoming.
In that hush, all things remembered what they once were.

And then everything began to reform again with light, love
and purity—

And the wolf was now the original female wolf.
Alive.
Golden-eyed.
Resurrected by the collapsing waveform.

Exactly where she had died before.

Exactly where she had stood when the sky above her first
broke apart and she fought to protect her human whom
she loved so unconditionally.

The first dog – The first human – The first pat...

She looked beyond the horizon and barked at something
very, very distant.

And, in Aldo's lab, 39,000 years forwards in time, a bark
reverberated in Jasper's ears and heart.

A Ball, a Cat, a Stick, a Squirrel, –But Never a Warbilizer

It didn't just smell repulsive —
it felt horrible too.

That bark from beyond, only seconds before,
had filled Jasper's spirit with courage — a pulse of
belonging, a reminder of who he was fighting for and what
the World meant in the heart and soul of a dog.

He stared at the ball-that-wasn't-a-ball
and barked at it, sharp and furious.

It didn't just smell wrong to his K9 senses —
it smelled like being left behind. It reeked of
abandonment.
That cold, empty hollowness dogs recognise long before
they understand it.

It smelled like the place where a pack should be… but
wasn't anymore,
a lonely, long-gone absence sharp enough to make him
whimper with anxiety.

It smelled like an unloved corner of the world,
the scent of being forgotten, neglected, unwanted,
unclaimed.

It smelled like a dry water bowl with nobody around to fill
it.

And deeper still—

it smelled like the memory of a pup left outside in the rain
and the cold,

that old wound that abused dogs carry in their chest when
something reminds them of the pain they never deserved.

And it *felt* like something worse—
the opposite of a pack, the reverse of being in a loving and
caring family,
a hollow, starving cold place where no warmth lived, no
love shone out,
a place so empty, nothing had wagged its tail in here for a
thousand years.

All of it hit him at once.

Too much evil and wrongness.
Too much "no love."
Too much "no heartbeat."

It hurt.

And that pain flipped instantly into fury —
a growl rising from someplace ancient inside of him,
a growl born from loyalty and devotion,
and from the fierce, inexplicable love dogs have always
carried for humanity —
even when humanity did not deserve it.

Dogs gave love anyway.
And they always would.

The Warbilizer felt him too.
It sensed him.
Recognised him.
Feared him.

Its relay shot backward through the lattice —
and the Hive felt Jasper's presence like a blade through its
organs.

The entire Nest screamed in terror.

Because Jasper was no ordinary dog.

Years in Aldo's lab had soaked him in harmonics.
He had learned frequencies no creature had ever held.
He had slept beside oscillators, curled beneath stabilisers,
wandered through fields that bent probability like paper.

He was a living resonance.
A breathing, fluffy antidote.
A dog-shaped nullifier of anti-Riftwalker energy across
every dimensional level.

And the AI of the Warbilizer suddenly knew it had met its
natural predator.

The Riftwalkers now had a fluffy, fanged monster they
feared beyond measure.

The Dog Who Broke the Dark

A humble dog, with a heart that was tuned to love, ended up being deadlier to the Riftwalkers than any weapon humanity had ever built.

Doc Lindley felt that truth rising through the floor before she understood where it came from — a low, trembling growl that vibrated her ribs and made every cable in the lab quiver.

"Luc," she whispered, eyes pinned to her monitors. "What is that…?"

Luc didn't answer. He already had his rifle raised.

Under the bench, the Warbilizer pulsed — a sick, stuttering heartbeat of negative-band distortion, like a parasite pretending to be part of the furniture.

Jasper saw it and felt it for what it truly was.

And that was enough.

The bark he had heard moments earlier — somewhere beyond time, somewhere threaded through the wormhole's breath — had lit something inside him.
Courage.
Purpose.
Belonging.

Now he stepped forward, growling deep in his chest.

Not a warning. A promise.

Years in Aldo's lab had tuned him like an instrument.
He carried harmonics like blood cells.
He was a *living remedy* to the Riftwalkers' energy.

And now he moved like a black and white wolf stalking its prey.

He lunged, seized the sphere, and shook it violently — that ancient dog-instinct that destroys snakes, vermin, and every enemy that has ever threatened the pack. It was precise and urgent.

CRACK.

The shell fractured. The Hive shrieked across multiple dimensions.

CRUNCH.

The Warbilizer caved inward, collapsing in his jaws like an old tennis ball turning into chewed-up dust.

Sparks spat.
Negative energy fizzled.
Dimensional circuitry disintegrated into pulp.

He dropped the remains onto the copper plate — a smouldering blob of wires, melted metal, and dying darkness.

He looked up smiling-panting at Lindley and Luc and gave them a very happy WOOF.

The Nest howled in agony.

And then—

the bells woke again – healthy and vibrant!

Resonance Restored

Vittorio staggered backward from his console as every monitor in the room burst into cascading colour — harmonic lines re-threading themselves in perfect, impossible unison.

For a heartbeat he dared not breathe.

Then—

Stability.
Alignment.
Resonance.

The bells were back to normal.

"Dio mio... yes!" he shouted, slamming his palms onto the desk.
"Bring up global feeds — *now!*"

Screens blinked into a twelve-panel world montage:

• Kyoto —

Monks who had been thrown to the floor rose again, gripping the ropes.
The great bell swayed, groaned...
and then boomed across the cherry trees.

• Machu Picchu —

The Andean team shook dust from their clothing.
Their sun-worn bell rang out, a thunderous note that echoed along the cliffs.

• Galway —

A fisherman wiped blood from his forehead, braced his boots, and heaved as the harbour bell began to sing again just like the ocean itself.

• Cairo, Reykjavik, Mumbai —

Everywhere, people rose.
Everywhere, bells answered back to each other.
Everywhere, the world stitched itself back together with sound.

The harmonic lattice surged upward and locked into place.

Vittorio spun back to his console, glowing.

"Lindley! We're fully back online. Confirm status."

Static fizzled—

Then Lindley's voice, breathless but triumphant:

"Device interference is gone. Jasper neutralised it. Grid is stable. We're ready when you are."

Vittorio allowed himself another rare smile.

"Then let's restore this world. Dr. Lindley... begin your seq—"

He stopped.

Her channel flickered.

"No... no, Jasper—stay still—just—just stay—"
Lindley's voice fractured, rising into panic.

"Lindley?" Vittorio snapped. "Report!"

A wet retching sound came through the line.
Metal scraped.
Luc shouted something muffled.

Then Lindley's voice — cracked, breaking, terrified:

"Vittorio... Jasper's collapsed. He—he vomited
something—black, like sludge—
I-I think the Warbilizer *infected* him—
He's not breathing right—
He's—oh God—Jasper—PLEASE—"

Her crying hit the mic like a knife.

The harmonics wavered.

Vittorio's stomach dropped.

"Lindley, HOLD ON—!"

The line cut.

Eurasia, Late Stone Age
– Upper Palaeolithic Period
–38,752 years BC
…and 10 hours and 2 mins beforehand.

The villagers had gathered around the strange newcomers in a wide circle — cautious, yes, but gentle, curious, welcoming.
Old women shuffled forward with bowls of fruit and strips of cooked meat to offer them. Children darted between legs to bring water.
Men offered to help Jake hold Byron as he laid him down, pale but conscious.

An elderly woman — sharp-eyed, ageless — pressed a warm cloth to Byron's wound.
She yelled orders to a young boy, who sprinted off to fetch more supplies.

Sherri watched with a swelling heart.

Then the female wolf moved closer.

Sherri saw the young man before the others did, and somehow, she knew exactly who he was – she felt his spirit as she looked at him to her right and then she turned to her left to see the female wolf standing there not too far away.

The boy whose grief had echoed across millennia.
The boy who had watched his new best friend's limp body being tossed into the river like garbage, as he ran away in abject dread and fear, screaming with grief into the cold morning's sky.

He stood at the edge of the crowd, eyes wide, breath shaking. He didn't understand how it could be so, but he didn't care either.

Because stepping toward him — slowly, tremblingly — was **her**.

The wolf he had loved so dearly.

The same animal he had cherished and befriended.
The same wolf the Riftwalkers tore from him in that act of savage cruelty.
Alive.
Whole.
Golden-eyed.

The boy's knees buckled.
His hands flew to his mouth.
A sob escaped him.

And then the wolf ran to him with her tail wagging –
whole body wagging, whining with joy.

They collided in a storm of fur and tears —
bond reforged in an instant,
sorrow transmuted into joy so pure it felt almost sacred to behold.

The boy buried his face in her neck mane, crying openly, shaking violently as she licked his cheeks, whined, pawed at him, trying to climb into his arms.

Other wolves approached — curious, gentle, nuzzling villagers, accepting pats and scraps of food from the children.

The clan watched on in awe.

And something opened inside of Sherri's soul.

A warmth —
the same warmth she felt during the long months after her
accident,
the warmth born of pain, and healing, and of summoning
grit,
the warmth of being remade.

The warmth of a dog being at your side.

The smell of a dog. The simple and beautiful smell of a
dog.

She realised it now:
that warmth was **purpose**. That smell was **life itself.**

She was meant to witness this moment.
To stand where the first pat had taken place.
To see the beginnings of its repair after it had been robbed
from us.

But still —
the wormhole did not reopen.

No bells.
No harmonics.
No light.

Just wolves, villagers, ancient snow...

And then—

**everything snapped to black. It almost made a
clicking sound.**

Not so much darkness —
nothingness – where even light was nothing.

The fire vanished.
The villagers froze.
The wolves halted mid-breath.
Even air and time seemed to fall away.

Then came the sensation —
their essences peeling away, thinning, dissolving
like threads being unwoven.

The children clutched at their parents' arms.
Hannah reached for Marvin and missed — her fingers
passing through him like mist.

But they all turned.

Every single one of them —
the kids,
the villagers,
the wolves,
the boy—

They turned toward **her**.

Toward Sherri.

The only thing still visible and solid in the dim, dark void.

Sherri stood suspended in the blackness,
alone, terrified, glowing faintly from the inside out.

Her glow flickered and trembled like a tiny candle in a
collapsing universe.

But it was a glow.

It was *something. And it held their focus and held them
together safely and in place, delaying the breakdown.*

They held on while the glow slowly began to diminish,
knowing they would soon be gone when her light went
out.

Everything was getting darker – something was breaking
everything down.

The Resonance Tape – Part II

The lab lights flickered like a dying heartbeat.
Jasper lay on his side, chest heaving shallow, black sludge dripping from his muzzle.
Lindley knelt beside him, hands trembling uselessly pressing a damp cloth to his mouth to wipe the horrible drool away.

"Come on, boy… please, please…" her voice cracked.

Luc paced in a tight circle behind her, one hand gripping his rifle, the other hand patting his pocket instinctively as he rapidly thought things through — then his fingers inadvertently patted the cassette tape.
Tears for Fears: Songs from the Big Chair.

His old lucky charm.
His private joke.
His one sentimental weakness in the entire World.

He froze.

A thought hit him like a jolt of static.

"…No way," he muttered.

"What?" Lindley snapped without looking up.

Luc didn't answer.
He was scanning the cluttered lab — coils, oscillators, dusty instruments, cables, relics from Aldo's audio-technicolour past…a dozen different LP players, tape-to-tape, 8 track players…

And then he saw it.

A tape deck.
A real, actual, huge, Philips stereo, tape deck player.
Wedged between two old oscilloscopes like it had been
waiting for this moment across time.

Luc grinned.

"Oh, you absolute magnificent bastard, Aldo."

He darted to the bench, slapped the tape in, and slammed
"PLAY."

Lindley's head snapped up.
"Luc — WHAT on Earth are you doing?!"

"My job," he said simply.
"And maybe... saving the bloody world."

The tape hissed.
Then that unmistakable synth line fired through the lab's
speakers like a neon spear of the 1980s.

Welcome to your life—

The opening lyric vibrated the copper plates.
The old tape deck thrummed like it had been plugged into
the bones of the Earth.

Jasper's ears twitched up.

Lindley gasped.
"Oh my god—his harmonic field—Luc, look!" A monitor
screen above showed a spike.

Luc knelt beside Jasper, touching his fur lightly.
"Come on, little sound warrior. You've still got business to
finish."

Jasper coughed hard — forcing the last of the sludge out.

His pupils dilated.
His breath steadied.
He pushed himself upright and gave Luc one weak but
determined lick on the cheek.

Luc swallowed hard and whispered,
"Good Boy!"

—Even while we sleep…

Jasper trotted — no, *marched* — back onto his copper
sound pad like a soldier returning to his post.

The old-school microphone crackled alive on its
suspension arm.
The harmonic rings around the pad ignited, one by one.

Lindley's hands flew to her console.

"Jasper's stabilised! His frequency's rising! I—I can start
the sequence!"

Luc stood over them, rifle ready, music blaring behind
him like a war drum made of pop-synth and swagger.

"Do it, Doc. Give the universe its favourite dog back."

Lindley hit the main activation switch.

The bell harmonics roared.

—Everybody wants to rule the world…

In Vittorio's control room, all twelve monitors spiked simultaneously.

He nearly fell out of his chair.

"My GOD—what is THAT spike?!"

Aldo's voice came through the comms, frantic.
"Vittorio? Are we back online?! I can feel the garage vibrating!"

Vittorio laughed — full-chested, relieved beyond reason.

"Back online?! We're BEYOND online!"
He slammed his fist on the console.
"ALRIGHT, ALDO — GO AHEAD AND OPEN THAT WORMHOLE UP FOR THE KIDS!"

Aldo yanked the levers forward in the Kirra garage.
The Kelvinator array screamed to life — sparks flying, air bending, the Omega Wave tunnelling into existence.

Back in the underground CERN lab, Lindley wiped tears from her eyes as Jasper stood tall, harmonics radiating from his chest like a concentric ring of divine, illuminated math.

Luc adjusted the volume on the tape deck.

Louder.

Louder.

—It's my own design
It's my own remorse—

He grinned at Lindley.

"Let's give the Riftwalkers a proper send-off."

She nodded, trembling with adrenaline.

"Start Sequence Theta—NOW!"

Jasper barked — one clean, perfect and beautiful, dog bark.

And the universe shook with joy and happiness.

It had its favourite dog back.

Frank's Little Errand

Frank hadn't told anyone where he was going after he left the Nest.
Not even Aldo.

He simply stepped sideways into the chrono-pistol's shimmering iris and vanished.

****HONG KONG**

(Time: Unknown.) **

He emerged inside a dim apartment overlooking Silvermine Bay at sunset.
Modern, immaculate, almost spotless — with a touch of beach kitsch décor.
Old surfboards hanging on the wall, old movie and retro surfing posters that were as old as time. Mostly clean but with a scruffy and comfortably lived in vibe.
His own Fortress of Solitude.

Frank didn't waste a second.

He crossed to what looked like an ordinary wall panel, pressed three points in a diamond pattern, and the panel hissed open.

Inside was an arsenal of exotic weaponry.

Rows of strange firearms gleamed under soft blue lights — pulse rifles, graviton flares, sonic throwing knives, two regular shoulder mounted RPGs that definitely violated at least six international arms treaties.

Frank exhaled through his nose.

"Home sweet home."

He grabbed a compact mag-dart repeater, a shockwave carbine, an anti-phasic stinger, and slung a graviton buckler onto his back.
Then he unclipped the chrono-pistol, cracked the chamber, and popped in a fresh power node.

Its display flickered:

45 JUMPS AVAILABLE

He nodded once.

"Plenty."

Frank fired the chrono-pistol at the air —
the portal blossomed like a bucket of water splashed onto a window —
and he stepped through once again.

BACK IN ALDO'S LAB

Luc nearly jumped out of his skin when Frank reappeared beside him.

Frank gently tossed a gleaming, unfamiliar rifle into Luc's hands.

"Catch."

Luc blinked. "What the—?"

"Just need your help for a few minutes," Frank said.
Calm. Crisp.
Like he was asking Luc to help fly-tip an old sofa by dragging it out onto the curb and leaving it further up the street a little.

Lindley stared at them.
"Frank, we're in the middle of—"

"You'll be fine," he said with a wink.
(Jasper didn't even look up. He was deep in his harmonic trance, eyes glowing like twin stars.)

Frank fired the chrono-pistol again, wider this time — a portal large enough for two grown men to stroll through.

"Renard," he said, gesturing.
"After you."

Luc stepped through without hesitation.

Frank followed.

The portal snapped shut.

**ORANGE SAND HONG KONG FACILITY

(The Night of the Attack — rewound.) **

The lab was still intact.
Still alive. The dogs were all resting happily. Staff and technicians were all in good cheer.
Only minutes before the massacre that so brutally wiped out the entire team and facility.

Frank and Luc materialised behind a row of concrete pillars.

Luc blinked.
"Where are we? … What time is this?"

"Before they killed our Hong Kong people," Frank murmured.
"And tonight… we don't let them."

He raised his weapons.
Luc did the same.

A ripple in the corridor —
shadows moving.

The Riftwalker's hired killers burst in, guns raised, laser sights arcing around, ready to slaughter the entire facility.

Except—

This time, two heavily armed temporal anomalies were waiting for them.

Frank fired first.

A neon-blue pulse burst across the room, slamming into a thug and throwing him backward into a table. His body instantly melted into a gloopy slop on the floor.
Luc followed with a burst from the gravitic repeater-rifle Frank had handed him —
the thug's weapon tore-up from his hands and smashed into the ceiling, while the thug was squashed down onto the floor with a cracking WUMPFF leaving a red, bloody pancake where he had been standing seconds before.

The attackers panicked.

Frank and Luc did not.

They moved like a pair of seasoned hunters, weaving between consoles and pillars, firing brilliant arcs of exotic energy at the murderous intruders, their shielding suits absorbing any stray rounds the panicked thugs managed to fire back at them.

A sonic knife whirred out from Frank's wrist rig — and jettisoned forward.
It sliced off one of the killers' legs — sent him shrieking to the floor as the blade dissolved into harmless motes of light particles.

Luc used a pulse mine the way a chef would splash salt over a large frypan.
One flick of his wrist — pop —
and three attackers were rolling on the ground, clutching their ears, begging the universe to stop vibrating their skulls into paste. Then they were still and silent.

Frank grinned mid-battle.
"Not bad accuracy, Legionnaire!"

Luc watched Frank fire a perfect shot through the corridor doorway, hitting one of the thugs directly between the

eyes and exploding his head.
“Likewise, cowboy!”

The last thug ran for his life.

Frank tapped his chrono-pistol.
A small portal opened in front of the fleeing man —
and the thug ran straight into the wall behind him.

Luc winced.
“That’ll leave a mark.”

“So will this.” Said Frank as he re-aimed the pistol
keeping it level and fired a thudding, glowing purple,
broad-beam laser at the man, instantly turning him into a
pile of smoking charcoal and ash.

Frank held the barrel to his mouth and gave it a comical
blow, then holstered the pistol.
“And now our guys and the dogs all get to live. All of them.
The whole Orange Sand team survives tonight.”

Luc exhaled.
For once, he almost smiled.

Frank lifted the chrono-pistol again, the chamber
spinning up with a soft electric whine.

“Alright,” he said, cocking an eyebrow at Luc and smiling
a cheeky grin.
“Time for you to go back to your very talented
sweetheart.”

Luc blinked.
“My what? Who says she’s my sweetheart?”

Frank gave him a sideways grin and a chuckle — the kind only someone who's seen too many timelines could get away with.

"All your wonderful kids do...ALL of the time."

Luc's face froze.
"What kids?"

Frank winked.
"You'll see."

He fired the chrono-pistol, the portal blossomed a bright orange candescence, and Luc was gone before he could demand any further answers.

Frank holstered the weapon with a satisfied shrug.
"Time waits for no man."

When A Decisive Invalidator –
Invalidates Decisively

Deep inside the Riftwalker nest—where timelines snarled like veins and every wall throbbed with stolen life—the Decisive Invalidator awakened. The countdown finished. It did not beep. It did not explode. Nor did it spectacularly detonate in any known or perceptual way.

It erupted into a pulsing wave of ordered signal and, slowly, it spoke words.

The Invalidator did not function as a weapon. It functioned as a calibration event.

At its core, the device generated a standing quantum field—a self-reinforcing harmonic lattice, tuned not to matter, but to consistency and integrity.

Frank had poured the goodness of his heart into the nuances of the device, never imagining that the universe would recognise its purpose so powerfully.

Every particle, every waveform, every probability-strand within its reach was sampled, phase-checked, and compared against a baseline older than spacetime itself: coherence. Not belief. Not morality. Agreement.

Much later, he'd realise that the breakthrough had not come from just calculative effort alone.

That night in Aldo's apartment, with schematics spread across the table in front of him and the fire burning low, Jasper had lain at his feet, breathing steadily, one warm flank pressed against Frank's ankle. The equations had stopped fighting him then. Small contradictions softened. Lines that had refused to close suddenly did.

Jasper lay by the fire, breathing slow and even — a small, steady thing in a universe that refused to let him be taken. Frank never questioned it. He only noticed that whenever the dog was there, the work seemed to settle, as if the room itself had quietly decided what it wanted to be.

Frank had thought it was fatigue giving way to focus. He did not yet understand that coherence had been present in the room long before the device ever learned to speak words.

It spoke in a crystalline waveform-lattice of **coherence and homeostasis — and of love**, a frequency older than language, older than worship. Multidimensionally loud, it permeated every surface, every object, every stolen geometry at once. There was no direction to the sound; it arrived everywhere simultaneously, bypassing distance entirely, as if locality itself had been temporarily revoked.

The wave did not push outward. It *resolved inward.*

Entangled systems across the nest shuddered as the signal passed through them, collapsing unstable superpositions, forcing probabilities to choose. Timelines the Riftwalkers had grafted, braided, and siphoned began to decohere, snapping out of phase as the Invalidator denied them the ambiguity they required to exist.

Where the signal encountered coherence, it passed harmlessly through.

Where it encountered contradiction, it corrected.

The Riftwalker nest—an architecture built entirely on sustained quantum violation—reacted like a body rejecting a foreign organ. Borrowed dimensions began to lose phase alignment. Stolen chronologies slipped out of lockstep. Probability wells drained as the Invalidator stripped away the tolerance that had allowed paradox to persist.

The sound was not heard with ears.

It was registered in fields, in charges, in the silent accounting systems by which reality keeps itself honest.

The timer released the signal.

The spoken words.

And the waveband.

The voice said:

"By the law that holds."

A ripple tore through the nest. The organic walls cinched inward like a suffocating lung. Riftwalkers convulsed as their stolen geometries twisted into impossible knots. Those nearest the device disintegrated at the surface, erased cell by cell, as if an unseen hand were un-writing them.

"By the pattern that endures."

A deeper rupture followed. Corridors folded like sheets of wet cloth. Egg-sacs imploded with sickening cracks. In-growth shadows peeled away from the walls and evaporated. Warp-throats collapsed, severing every exit. Riftwalkers hurled themselves at dying portals, only to liquefy against them like ink sucked into a drain.

"By the balance that remembers."

The nest began to come undone. Slowly. Methodically. A steady, tidal force dragged the creatures inward, peeling them apart in shimmering ribbons of un-light. Their frequencies destabilised, tearing loose from their bodies like static ghosts. One Riftwalker clawed the floor in terror before dissolving into dust that never touched the ground.

"You do not belong."

The destruction field widened. Across the world, a shiver passed through all living things. Bells in Bhutan rang on their own. A breeze sighed through forests that had been holding their breath for centuries. Wolves lifted their heads as if sensing a terrible burden slip away from the Earth.

"You were never invited."

The nest shook violently. Its walls buckled and fell inward. Time membranes split open like veils tearing in fire. Riftwalkers writhed and shrieked, their hive-mind voice cracking and splintering as their bodies crumbled into cascading folds of collapsing probability.

"You have overstayed."

A wave of pure unmaking blasted outward. Every frequency the Riftwalkers had stolen was ripped from their spines and hurled back into the void they came from. No timeline opened for them. No path unfolded. Every escape they'd once relied on slammed shut like iron jaws.

"Correction begins."

Their bodies tore like wet paper. Their limbs inverted. Their shadows screamed. Their dimensions buckled as gravity forgot what it meant to hold shape. Every unholy graft they'd inflicted on reality recoiled, snapping back with a vengeance older than any star.

"Balance is restored."

The nest's central chamber collapsed inward. Organic machinery twisted into coils, then strands, then smoke. The Riftwalkers, losing cohesion, flickered between shapes—skeletal, insectoid, mist—none lasting long enough to matter. Their hive-mind shriek became a layered, warbling howl that bent the air.

"All debt is reclaimed."

The Invalidator pulsed harder. Waves of harmonic force battered the creatures, stripping them of every stolen timeline, every grafted probability, every unnatural foothold. They began to melt, drip, vaporize, crumble— each one dying differently, yet none dying quickly or being spared from extreme pain.

"All trespass ends."

A burning light filled the nest. Riftwalkers convulsed violently as the very concept of trespass echoed through them—through every act of cruelty, every theft, every murdered wolf, monk, child, every life they had ever taken.

"There will be no repetition."

The field intensified, locking onto the very pattern of their existence. The nest's remaining structures collapsed like brittle bones. Strange, shrill, broken shapes skittered across the floor—half-body remnants scrambling for purchase before dissolving into smoke.

"Deviation is denied."

The nest thrashed as though the structure itself were trying to flee the signal. Riftwalkers shattered into flecks of darkness that sizzled away before hitting the ground. Fractures zig-zagged across every surface, ripping the entire dimension apart.

"The anomaly concludes."

The shrieking became one terrible chord—every Riftwalker crying out through every timeline in one last, hideous moment of unified panic. Their bodies collapsed completely, sloughing into liquid shadow that hissed and evaporated on contact with the Invalidator's field.

"This state will not persist."

The nest began to implode, folding inward like a dark star collapsing.

"This state will not recur."

The last walls twisted into nothing, falling into a single tightening vortex.

"It is finished."

The final Riftwalker dissolved with a wet, broken whine, a weak, wheezing flatulence into nothingness.

When Two Old Mates Catch-Up

Aldo was hunched over the wormhole console in Sherri's garage, hands flying across dials and switches he'd built out of scrap metal, copper coils, two hacked oscilloscopes, and something he'd cannibalised from a pool filter, as well as all the next-gen gear shipped from Frank.

The whole garage hummed like a Tibetan song-prayer.

He didn't hear the portal open behind him.

FWUMPF.

Frank stepped out of the shimmering oval and dusted off his jacket.

"Well," he said, surveying the room. "This brings back memories. Usually when we broke physics in someone's garage, it was *my* fault."

Aldo spun around, eyes wide.

"FRANK!"

The two men embraced in that good-old, full-bodied, back-slapping hug that best friends and family give to each other, almost to the point of causing cracked ribs and dislocated vertebrae.

"You magnificent bastard!" Aldo laughed. "You're alive!"

"You sound surprised?" Frank smirked.

"No. I'm mostly surprised you're on time."

Frank looked around the garage, squinting at the machinery.

"What—what have you *done* to my design?"

Aldo gestured proudly.
"Optimised it."

"You used hardwood," Frank said, poking the casing.

"Premium Australian hardwood…It's called Jarrah you know, and it's very expensive."

"And this—" Frank tapped a panel. "This is a… fridge thermostat?"

"It was lying around."

Frank nodded slowly. "Right. A fridge thermostat. To stabilise a wormhole throat."

"It works!"

Frank shrugged. "Well… of course it does. You built it."

Aldo grinned, eyes softening. "God, it's good to see you man!"

Frank's face warmed in a way he rarely allowed.
"You too, old friend."

They turned toward the glowing core of the machine — a swirling vortex tightening, brightening, harmonics climbing.

Aldo cracked his knuckles.
"Alright then. Enough nostalgia. Enough with the chit-chat and gossip."

Frank nodded and stepped up beside him at the console, carefully peering at a monitor he reached for a control lever.

"Let's get our kids home."

"For sure Kendrick - Let's rock this wormhole," Aldo agreed.

Side by side, they worked like a two-man orchestra:

Aldo flicked the harmonic stabilisers.
Frank tuned the frequency spreaders.
Aldo adjusted the phase coils.
Frank slapped the emergency bypass like he'd been doing it for decades as his full-time job.

The wormhole swelled — shimmering, vibrating — its ring casting pale gold light over the walls.

Then the harmonics surged.

First a hum.
Then a resonance.

—From Lindley's lab: the bells.
A twelve-note chorus weaving itself into the wormhole stream.

—From Jasper: a deep harmonic howl.
Not a dog's cry.
A cosmic melody.
A guiding tone.

The garage trembled as all three sources braided together into a single frequency:

The frequency that could reach **38,752 years BC.**

The vortex stabilized into a perfect funnel of shimmering light.

Aldo's voice broke.
"We're through. I can feel them...and just about see them in the tundra there."

Frank stared into the wormhole.
The swirling gold reflected in his eyes.
He inhaled slowly.

"Aldo... I have to step through and guide them back."

Aldo grabbed his arm.
"You sure? Wouldn't you be more help here?"

Frank gave a crooked smile.

"No one else knows the long way home like I do. Just in case."

Aldo closed his eyes for a moment — not in fear, but in trust.

"Then bring them back safely," he whispered.
"Bring them all home. Let's make this work."

Frank nodded once, stepped toward the swirling light...

...and vanished into the wormhole.

The Return of the Singing Monks

High in the Bhutanese mountains, the wind was thin and cold — the kind that tasted of damp stone, incense and mystical stars. Snow drifted in little spirals across the courtyard of the monastery, landing softly on the only remaining monk's robe.

Elder Sonam stood beside the great brass prayer-bell, his hands trembling, his robes heavy with grief. He had rung this bell for forty years, always surrounded by his fellow monks deep in prayer.

Now he rang it alone.

He touched its rim gently, almost apologetically, and whispered:

"Why am I left to pray when my brothers have been taken?"

His voice cracked.

"Why would heaven have decided to keep only me here?"

He lifted the mallet anyway — not out of faith, but out of love — and he struck the bell.

GONG.

The sound rolled across the Himalayas like a warm, soothing thunder.

He began to chant, voice thin but steady.
A prayer he had sung since childhood.
A prayer he thought he would never again sing in harmony.

As he chanted, a light bloomed on the courtyard stones.

At first, he thought it was the sunrise breaking early —
but no sunrise was ever this bright,
or this warm,
or this *gentle*...or early...

The light spread outward, filling the temple, flooding the
steps, reflecting off snow like liquid gold.

And then—

Shapes formed inside of it.

Robes.
Old, familiar faces.
Hands clasped in prayer.

One by one, the monks he had lost stepped through the
veil of radiance, smiling like men who had just woken
from a long, peaceful dream.

Sonam dropped to his knees, sobbing so hard he couldn't
breathe.

"Brothers...? Is it *really* you?... How...?"

The youngest monk — the boy with the chipped incisor
tooth who had always laughed too loudly — stepped
forward and lifted Sonam's face.

"Bla-ma," he whispered, "we were never gone. We were
only waiting to be remembered by people and the right
sounds."

Sonam clutched him, crying into his shoulder. Then the
others joined — arms around arms, heads together, robes
rustling like gentle wings in the mountain wind.

Then, with no cue and no hesitation, they began to chant.

Not because they had been instructed.
Not because ritual demanded it.
But because their hearts — newly restored, newly whole —
simply *overflowed*.

The chant grew, swelling in the cold mountain air,
weaving a resonance purer than any bell ever cast ever
did.
The prayer-bell vibrated without being touched, humming
in sympathy.

And then—

The sound lifted.

It rose up the mountains, into the thin air, and shimmered
like a river of music as it threaded its way into the open
wormhole far across the world.

Across continents.
Across time.

And into Sherri's heart.

Her glow brightened.
Her breath steadied.
Her soul aligned with the restored harmony of the world.

The wolves felt it.
The villagers felt it.
Even the sky seemed to soften in response to it.

Back in Bhutan, surrounded by his newly resurrected
family, Elder Sonam turned his face upward and
whispered:

"Let this light go where it is needed."

And sure enough —it did.

308

The Great Return

Her glow trembled like a tiny candle in a collapsing universe.
But it *was* a glow.
It was *something*. And it held them together, kept their atoms where they belonged, held the fraying seams of existence joined up for a few final heartbeats.

Then even that glow began to thin...
dimming...
shrinking...
flickering...

The darkness pressed in.

The universe buckled.

Something ancient and cruel was unravelling everything.

Sherri's light stuttered—

—and then the world exhaled. A long, silent pause followed.

Then suddenly, and ever so loudly, the world inhaled deeply...

A new chime rolled through the void.

Soft at first.
Then brighter.
Then unstoppable.

And in just a short cosmic heartbeat, the moment restarted itself again.

The darkness peeled back like frost rapidly melting under
a golden sunrise.
The ground re-solidified.
Time shuddered — paused — then eased itself forward
again exactly where it had left off.

Except now Sherri wasn't a flickering candle.

She was a beautiful, uplifting dawn.

Her entire body erupted into a radiant gold-white light —
warm, shimmering, holy in a way nobody could describe.

Villagers gasped and dropped to their knees, hands
clasped to their chests. The wolf pack encircled her, one
by one sitting on their haunches facing inward, heads
lifting skyward.

They all howled together. A beautiful, perfect circle of
wolves howling up at the heavens around a girl made of
light.

And from somewhere impossibly far away —
yet right beside them —
Jasper's howl answered back through the wormhole.

The harmonics struck like a cosmic chord:

Vittorio's world orchestra,

  Lindley's quantum sequence

  Jasper's harmonic howl

  Bhutan's resurrected monks chanting

  Almost every bell in the World

Tears for Fears: Everybody Wants to Rule the World

It was the combined sound of a universe remembering itself.

Light spread outward.
Sherri's glow intensified until even the granite mountains seemed to soften in her presence.

Hannah staggered backward and dropped the dog flag — then she snatched it up, again, clutching it with instinct. The pawprint on the flag had reappeared, bright and whole. She raised it high.

A young girl who often felt she lacked direction in life, now knew true direction like she had never felt it before, charging her soul through the flag.

That was when the barks began.

Not just one bark.
Not a few.

Hundreds.

Thousands.

Millions.

Billions.

A tidal wave of barking from somewhere behind Sherri — from a horizon that didn't exist minutes ago.

And then—

They came in an etheric, cosmic wave.

Dogs.

All the dogs.
Every lost dog.
Every forgotten dog.
Every dog erased from the world.

Pouring in like a glittering river of fur and paws and
wagging tails. Ethereal, radiant, luminous silhouettes of
every breed that has ever lived — every furball that has
ever wagged its tail, all shimmering like constellations
running on four legs.

Beagles bounding joyfully.
German shepherds tearing through the grass like heroes.
Old spaniels waddling along with glowing eyes of
gratitude.
Greyhounds and Golden Retrievers racing like streaks of
starlight.
Little terriers yapping with cosmic excitement.
Massive mastiffs lolloping forward with tongues out.

Every breed imaginable.

Some ran.
Some trotted.
Some limped.
Some floated.
Some were old but young again.
Some were pups again but carried the aura of long, happy
and full lives.

Collars jingled.
Tags sparkled.
Names were whispered in the air like fragments of prayers
being called out to them by their loving owners.

They streamed past Sherri — semitransparent, semi-solid. Thousands upon thousands per second, then tens of thousands — a torrential stampede of pure joy galloping toward the wormhole that now pulsed open above the tundra like a warm gateway back to their homes…back to their loving families and their precious owners whom they'd missed for a stolen eternity.

Hannah instinctively swept the dog flag backwards and forwards in an arc overhead, proudly, triumphantly. The dogs responded, turning as one, guided by her gesture — the ancient directional enchantment of the Scoot-Skittles dog-flag alive in her trembling hands.

The flag sang-out to them: This way – Over here – This is where you're meant to be!

The river of dogs became a sideways, bubbling waterfall of K9s, all stampeding with dog joy—
a brilliant stream of wagging tails and glowing paws rushing upward into the swirling light.

Every dog was going home.

Every soul had been restored.

Every heartbeat remembered.

Sherri glowed brighter still — so bright the wolves lowered their heads in reverence.
The villagers shielded their eyes.
Even the sunny sky seemed to be dull.

Then, as the final wave of dogs passed through the wormhole, the torrent slowed…
softened…
settled…

Until only two shapes remained. Tails wagging away madly. Happily panting and puffing.

Two Labradors.

Two golden, barrel shaped, adorable labradors.

The first lab looked younger than he had before — but still carried that old, wise gentleness in his eyes. He trotted forward first, tail swinging like a metronome of happiness.

Scoot.
Marvin's old dog.
His tail wagged so hard his whole back half wriggled.

Marvin burst into tears and fell to his knees as his old dog thundered up to him slathering him with licks and whines. He just hugged him and breathed in his smell and his fur – it was a life-giving essence he'd almost forgotten.

Sherri then gasped—
because several feet away, stepping gently through the etheric glow was her one and only...

Zeb.

Her Zeb!
Her missing heart.
Her beautiful Labrador.
Her childhood loyalty and love made flesh again.

Her best friend.

Zeb lowered himself into a full-body wag, trembling with joy, whining softly as he saw her and hurriedly waddled closer.

Sherri's knees buckled.

The wolves fell silent.
The villagers wept.
The universe held its breath, then cried tears of joy...

And a young girl and her lovely dog embraced once again.
Hugs, pats, pawing, licks and kisses...and a lot of belly
rubs.

And as the light settled,
as the last tremor of magic faded,
as the restored Universe exhaled into peace...

**Our world was now fully healed and wagging its
invisible tail again.**

The Long and Winding No-Through Road

The wormhole remained open in the tundra, a shimmering tunnel carved through reality, glowing away with a huge mouth of gold and fractal blue.

Then Frank stepped out of it.

He paused — hands on hips, chest puffed — and took an overly theatrical, drama-kid's inhale, followed by a long, soulful and satisfied exhale. His eyebrows climbed in sincere amazement.

Villagers. The most wondrously pure and happy looking group of people he'd seen in a long while.
Wolves. Beautiful, calm and friendly.
The gang of kids from 2025.
And two Labradors who absolutely did not belong here — yet somehow fitted in perfectly.

Sherri was kneeling beside Zeb, cradling his head in her lap, whispering her whole heart into his fur. But when the others noticed Frank standing there, she looked up — brightening like a sunrise.

She sprinted over and slammed into him with a hug that nearly folded him in two.

"Easy!" Frank laughed. "I'm a bit fragile! I'm practically a vintage piece!"

They both laughed, hugging again because once wasn't enough.

"Well," Frank said, throwing his hands on his hips and walking towards them all. "Time for you kids — and your two very out-of-place dogs here — to come home."

But then he froze mid-stride.

A few meters away, a mother wolf stood off to the side, watching over several chubby, impossibly fluffy pups that looked about three or four months old.

Frank blinked.
Then blinked again.
His face softened so fast it was comical.

He stood there motionless as tears welled up in his normally hard eyes.

They were absolutely the most beautiful things he had ever seen in an eternity of lifetimes.

"Oh, absolutely not," Sherri said looking at his expression, marching towards him as he gaped at the puppies. "I can see the wheels turning in your head right now."

But Frank had already walked over to them, knelt down, then sat cross-legged, and the pups — as pups do — swarmed him with reckless, wriggling love and abandonment. He scooped one up, a roly-poly bundle of fur, and cradled her like the crown jewels.

"I've been meaning to get a pup for a while now," he said, nose to nose with the bundle. "Have you *seen* how much puppies cost these days?! Any breed! Thousands! It's ridiculous!"

Sherri stared, horrified.
"You're not seriously contemplating what I think you're contemplating."

He beamed.
"You bet I am. And this little princess is the winner of my heart."

"But the Butterfly Effect! The Grandfather Paradox! You could affect so many things just by one small act—"

Frank raised a hand dramatically waving it around flippantly shooing away her words.

Sherri was on her soapbox. "Physicists say even just leaving your footprint in the sand could entirely change the future...they say if you step on a bug, you could create a whole new species due to that one bug missing from the food chain...We shouldn't really be here you know...it's pushing things..."

He raised his palm again, "Ahhhhhh Phooey!" and then added a long raspberry for emphasis.

"Let me tell you something fundamental about time-travel, young lady: ***there are no fundamentals to time-travel.*** That's all Hollywood guff. All that nonsense about squashed butterflies changing the future or accidentally preventing your dad from getting funky with your mum — or helping him to write a bestselling sci-fi novel - absolute rubbish."

He kissed the pup on the forehead.

"This furball is coming home with me."

"But—" Sherri persisted.

"—But nothing." Frank interrupted. "Most modern day theoretical physicists don't know their nostrils from their butt-holes when it comes to the real aspects of time-travel." He laughed a little. "Some do know a bit. Very few know a lot. But here's the truth: *most small changes never usually show up at all. Time-travel is a very, very nuanced thing."*

Byron yelled over from where he was laying down. "Because of the harmonics and scale of the action, right Uncle Frank? You need more than just jumping — you need the resonance too."

Frank laughed and pointed to Byron.

"Give that young man there a cigar! **Exactly!** Time-travel without the harmonics -good or bad of what's being done, is just stumbling over in style. Harmonics do the creating and re-stitching."

Frank removed from his pocket a small box with a modest speaker attached to it– and began speaking into it-

"Good people, we thank you for your friendship and kindness today"

The box then spoke in a very ancient language that would be almost untraceable by most modern-day, anthropological linguists –words that have long been lost to our species, heavily eroded by the sands of time, vanished vocab, phonetics and a syntax belonging to an incredibly distant human past...much, much longer than most of us would even realise...

The villagers all looked at Frank and smiled – they understood every word as clear as day.

A villager approached — an elderly woman with gentle eyes — holding clothlike fur she had been using on Byron's wound. She spoke softly, musical syllables shivering through the cold air.

The box transformed her speech into English:

"Your young warrior here is brave. He will carry the scar from his wound proudly. I have done my best to stem the bleeding. He seems to be okay for now."

Byron looked at her with a deep appreciation.

Frank bowed slightly. "Thank you." He walked over and knelt down next to Byron and removed a small spray can from his jacket.

"This should cover you until we get back kid." He raised the wadding and sprayed the wound prolifically. Painkillers, healing molecules and advanced antibiotics went to work as the nano-fibres sealed the wound thoroughly."

Still holding the puppy, Frank stood up and turned to face the women again and nodded "Thank you so much for helping to save him. He will be fine now."

The woman smiled and touched the pup's head, then spoke again.

The translator said:

"This creature... loves you already."

Frank smiled with his whole face.

He then lifted the translator box to his lips.

"Good people, we thank you for your friendship and kindness today."

The box spoke perfectly in their dialectical and tonal speech.
The villagers clearly understood everything.

Frank continued: "Please take good care of these creatures," he said, voice thickening with sincerity.

"They will be the most loyal companions you will ever know.

They will guard your children. They will keep you safe.
They will sleep at your doors, by your side, and on your beds.

Whenever you are alone in the world or feeling sad, they will be there to take away that loneliness and make you feel happy again.

They will follow you through hardships and joy.
They will teach you courage, patience, forgiveness… and give to you a love purer than any human heart could summon.”

The villagers listened, enraptured.

“When the nights are cold and dark,” Frank said, “they will sleep curled up against you, keeping your body and your spirit warm.
When grief comes, they will sit beside you without asking why you are sad – they will simply know that you are so and they will be there for you.
When your children cry, they will nuzzle them until their laughter returns.
And when you feel alone… they will remind you that you are never truly are alone when they are at your side.”

He swallowed.

“We call them *DOGS* — Doh. Guh. S.”

He modelled the pronunciation, slowly enunciating each consonant and the O vowel.
They repeated it perfectly, smiling at their new word they had learnt for their new furry friends.

DOG.

Villagers hugged Sherri and her friends goodbye.
The wolves nuzzled them.
Humans and animals — two families saying farewell.

Frank spoke into the neural link:

"Aldo — you there, mate?"

Aldo's voice came back, cheerful and crackling with static.
"I'm here. Ready when you are."

"Oh!" Aldo added, noticing the new pup through the
console's sensors.
"And Frank... what's that you've got in your arms there
might I ask?"

Frank grinned at the squirming fluffball.
"It's the start of a new chapter in my life."

Aldo laughed.
"Of course it is...And Butterfly Effect be damned hey?"

"You're darn tooting on that!"

Frank let the pup say goodbye to her mother — a soft lick
between them — then carried her toward the wormhole as
its light began to dance and ripple.

The future group gathered.

Byron didn't get jealous when Sherri turned and gave the
young Palaeolithic boy — the world's first human to
befriend a dog — a tight, emotional hug. Then she patted
the female wolf too – the first wolf – the first pat. The
three of them knew each other more than they knew.

She smiled and said:
"Dog."

He beamed and repeated the word proudly, patting the
wolf:
"Dog." His face was filled with love and joy and so much
life and happiness rolled into one.

Sherri's heart melted. She turned and patted her own
special dog with the same look on her face too.

Then she and Zeb walked over with the others toward the
wormhole.

The wormhole remained open there in the tundra,
shimmering away, a big passageway entrance into a light-
filled bonanza of quantum possibilities leading off into the
future.

Each of the group stepped steadily into it.

The wormhole swallowed each of them in one rushing
breath of light after the other.

Frank led the way, holding the fluffy wolf pup tight
against his chest. Zeb bounded beside Sherri. Scoot
padded along the shimmering floor like he'd done this a
thousand times before. The others stayed close, Jake
supporting Byron, Hannah gripping the dog flag —still,
Jacinta whispering it's okay—it's okay—it's okay.

So far, their experience of wormhole transit wasn't the
best.

This time wasn't going to be any different.

First came the jolts.
A hard sideways shudder that made everyone stumble.

Then the colour changed—
gold to blue,

blue to violet,
violet to some kind of dull, meaningless grey.

Frank frowned. "That's not good."

The walls of the wormhole flickered like a dying
fluorescent bulb.

Sherri grabbed Byron's arm. "What's happening?"

Frank's voice tightened.
"A few billion or so K9 pedestrians passing through this
wormhole earlier. I suspect a fridge thermostat your
Uncle Aldo used for what had originally been intended to
only be a small group of travellers might have badly
overloaded. I think it's about to—"

SNAP.

A sound like an exploding ice cube.
A flash of white.
A feeling of being pushed, pulled, inverted—

—and then—

Silence.

A soft grey nothing.

They landed in a weightless stumble on a surface that felt
like damp fog pretending to be solid. Byron caught Sherri
before she fell. Zeb shook himself, scattering droplets of
light instead of water. Scoot barked once—short,
confident—as if he'd been here before.

Frank stood slowly, squinting.

"Oh... hell."

There was nothing.

No sky.
No horizon.
No ground, except where they stood.
Everything else was a void of pale, shifting grey mist.

Except—

About twenty metres away, alone in the vast emptiness—

The "**NO THROUGH ROAD**" sign.

Leaning at the exact same angle it had always leaned away
at on the corner leading into Sherri's street. There it
stood, embedded in a modest, ten cubic meter island of
white beach sand like it had always done.
The same wind-blown sandy grains.
The same old, rusty sign. Same mottled white paint on a
hardwood post.

Hannah whispered, "It's still here...of all the things in the
world."

"Some objects just stick to one spot," Frank said, amused.

"The universe can rearrange itself all it likes. They know
they've got a cosmic reason to be there — and they refuse
to leave."

Now it was a signpost in the most universal sense of the
word.

And it was saving them.

They made their way toward it carefully, the ground
rippling like a waking dream. As they approached, the
little island of sand felt more real—grainy, warm, familiar.

The sign creaked gently, though there was no wind and it never normally creaked.

Sherri reached out and touched it.
It was solid.

Byron stared at the angle of the post, the tilt of the sign.

"Wait...I know this." His voice wavered with relief.

"This is exactly how it leans on your street's corner in the real world. So, if that's its normal lean...then *home* should be—"

He pointed. "In that direction, roughly."

The kids turned.
And for a heartbeat, they all saw it—

A flicker.
A shimmer.
Just a faint outline of Sherri's street and the houses: The coolabah tree. The roof of her house. The letterbox. The Colourbond covered driveway.

Like someone had pencilled reality lightly, but hadn't finished shading it in.

Zeb barked and trotted toward the house.
Scoot followed, tail high, totally unfazed.

Jake whispered, "They... they know where to go."

Frank agreed. "Of course they do. Dogs always know their way home."

Sherri's Garage

Aldo stared in horror at the smoking remains of the fridge thermostat.

"Oh no, no NO—come ON, you useless Cold-War-era relic!"

He yanked open drawers, rummaging frantically.
No replacement coils. No backup stabiliser.

Then— his eyes locked onto something sitting on a dusty shelf:

An old, silver, **Sony Walkman.**

Aldo snatched it, flipped it open, ripped out the batteries, unscrewed the back like a man possessed.

He held up a tiny copper-tuned frequency modulator coil.

"Oh you beautiful ancient relic—Frank is never going to let me live this down."

He slapped it into the wormhole throat stabiliser.
Sparks flew. The lights dimmed.
The machine groaned like an upset walrus—

Then steadied.

Aldo slapped the console.
"COME ON, COME ON—GRAB THEM!"

Back in Geneva, Jasper—still standing on his sound pad—
HOWLED his heart out.

The harmonics surged, and the wormhole shuddered into existence. It flickered violently, unstable and incomplete, only held together by the makeshift Sony Walkman coil and sheer desperation.

But it was open.

And because the kids and Frank were so close to home in their greyed-out, marooned dimension—drawn tight around the old **NO THROUGH ROAD** sign—the weakened wormhole finally had something permanent and solid to lock onto.

A fixed point.

A beacon.

An anchor.

The universe and the old sign worked together to do the rest.

Back in Limbo

The grey began to crumble.
Their outlines flickered.
The world around them shook.

Frank held the pup tighter.
"Kids, steady yourselves, we're moving again!"

They did.
The air vibrated around them – back where they had just
walked from, the old NO THORUGH ROAD sign began to
hum like a tuning fork.
Zeb pressed himself against Sherri's legs.
Scoot stood tall, ears forward.

Then—

A burst of gold light erupted everywhere.
A pull.
A sudden upward rush. They were lifted in a heartbeat.

Sherri screamed— they all did…
and then—

Sherri's garage...Again

The teleportation surge hit like a flashflood of gold and static.

One moment, the world was a fogged-out non-space — a grey nothingness, a place where even thoughts echoed strangely...

...and the next, the universe snapped tight around them like a closing fist.

Light burst inward.

Air rushed back into lungs.

And reality remembered what it was supposed to do.

They tumbled out of the garage wormhole and down onto the hard concrete floor in a heap of limbs, fur, backpacks, and startled yelling.

A heavy *THUMP* as they spilled everywhere.

Followed by—

—WOOF!
—OUCH!
—OWEE, MY ELBOW!
—WHOSE KNEE IS THAT IN MY BACK?
—IS EVERYONE HERE?!

And then...

Silence.

Not absolute quiet, but relief-silence.

The silence of people who have suddenly just realised
they're now safe.

When their eyes finally adjusted—

They saw it.

Sherri's old garage in all its magnificence.

Not as it once was — not as her dad's classic, old "Man-
Cave"
but as it had become in the days and hours leading up to it
becoming a wormhole generator:

A glowing tangle of coils.
Copper cabling soldered into spirals.
The Kelvinator fridge frame humming like a cathedral
organ.
Blueprints taped to the walls.
Workbenches cluttered with tools and half-finished
brilliance.
The cracked concrete floor now painted with stabilisation
glyphs and chalked-out harmonic equations.

Every part of it bore Aldo's hands
and Sherri's late-night determination
and Byron's scrappy build skills
and Frank's old-world engineering influence and his next-
gen equipment.

A slapped together, sanctum of science.
A shrine to hope.
The beating heart of a miracle.

And into that heart...
they had just crash-landed.

All at once.
All together.
Dogs included.

Beach sand spilled everywhere.
Grey dust ghosted off their jackets.
Two Labradors sneezed.
Scoot shook himself so violently he sprayed half the garage with beach sand.

Aldo staggered backward, wobbling, then dropped into a rolling chair and let his entire body melt like a man whose soul was leaving him through his loud, theatrical sigh.

"Ohhhhhh… my spine," he muttered. "I'm too old for frantically operating a wormhole rescue mission and I'm carrying too much weight to be standing for that long either."

Frank didn't respond.

Not verbally. But he gave Aldo a friendly salute.

Aldo held up the salvaged Sony Walkman coil—the little copper miracle he'd yanked from the ancient stereo device and shoved into the coupling node at that last second.

He kissed it.

A long, dramatic, heartfelt kiss right on the scratched metal.

"I," he declared reverently, "owe 1980, Sony and Akio Moirta a big thank-you note."

Zeb barked once — a bright, sharp, joyous bark.

Scoot wagged so hard his whole backside rotated like a helicopter trying to take off.

And the pup in Frank's arms — the one he'd insisted would not break the timeline — blinked sleepily… then yawned with absolute puppy satisfaction.

They were home.

They were safe.

They had won.

And as the golden hum of the wormhole slowly faded, and the last tremor of harmonics rippled through the garage walls like a heartbeat…

Every one of them standing in that room (Aldo still sitting) felt it:

The universe had stitched itself back together.

And it had also brought them all back to where they belonged.

To a world full of peace, love, family and friends…and dogs.

Sunset at Jack Evens Boat Harbour

The tide was coming in slow and glassy, pushing gentle ripples across the western, shoreline side of Jack Evans Boat Harbour. A couple of gulls strutted around the foreshore like they owned the place. Kids played, people strolled along the boardwalk. The sky hung low in radiant bands of apricot and soft orange, it was the kind of sunset that looked like it had been painted with the warm, loving hand of an old impressionist.

Sherri and Byron sat on the wet sand together where the water lapped around their ankles — close, leaning into each other, not quite arm in arm, but almost that way. Exactly the kind of closeness that could make your heart swell without warning.

Zeb lay just ahead of them on all fours like a golden sphinx, chest heaving, tongue lolling sideways in absolute post-swim exhaustion. His fur was soaked and shining with the last sunlight of the day.

Sherri nudged Byron with her shoulder.

"I swear," she said smiling, "if he goes in after the ball again, he's gonna sink like a stone. He's absolutely cooked." Byron laughed, then winced and touched his side.

"Well, I sort of feel cooked too. Whatever that spray was that Frank used on me…" He shook his head, still bewildered. "The doctor at Tweed Valley Hospital said I've only just got a nasty bruise and a little laceration. How is that even possible? That spear *went straight through me.*"

Sherri shrugged and brushed wet sand off her calves.

"Another one of Uncle Frank's inventions the world just isn't ready for. Or would get him immediately assassinated if he tried to market it."

Byron nodded.
"Yeah. That… that checks out…almost to the point of being a cliché."

They sat in silence for a moment, letting the evening settle around them. The harbour glowed like a pot of melted gold. A pair of dolphins surfaced briefly just offshore, drifting close to the shallows before slipping away again.

"Hey," Byron said, rubbing his hands together. "BBQ time? I'm starving."

"Well," Sherri said, turning to him with that particular glint she got when she was about to do something terrifyingly brave and terrifyingly honest at the same time, "there's something more important first."

Byron swallowed. "Uh… what's that?"

"Look at this sunset first," she said softly. "The peace. The quiet. Just take it all in."

He did. The water. The light. The sound of kids laughing somewhere behind them. The click of someone's fishing reel. The distant hum of planes over Coolangatta.

"Okay," she said gently. "Now look at me."

He turned. Hesitant. Shy in the way boys only ever are when they're in the presence of a beautiful girl before them… particularly one whom they're crazily in love with.

"Look into my eyes."

He did.
His breath caught.

“Now kiss me,” she whispered.

“Okay,” he said — voice tiny, terrified, hopeful — and he leaned in.

Their lips met in a soft, spellbound moment — the kind of kiss that doesn’t try to be anything more than the first one. Warm. Innocent. Perfect.

Sherri pulled back first, smiling against his breath.

“That’s enough for now,” she said, cheeks glowing. “Or we’ll stay here forever.”

Byron stared at her like she was something the universe had spent billions of years crafting on purpose.

“I couldn’t think of anywhere I’d rather be than with you forever,” he said quietly. Then he laughed at himself. “But also, I’m really starving… so let’s get going to the BBQ.”

Sherri burst out laughing.

They stood, brushing sand off their legs.
Zeb heaved himself up too — stiff, tired, but happy beyond measure — shaking water everywhere as the last light caught his fur.

Together they walked toward the boardwalk, the sky melting from gold to rose behind them, the dolphins resurfacing briefly as if to bless their path.

A girl,
a boy,
and a dog who had finally come back home.

Nothing Like an Evening Barbeque

The backyard of Sherri's house was alive with soul and happiness...and the smell of onions and sausages cooking away on a hotplate.

Fairy lights zig-zagged from the guttering to the fence posts. The barbecue hissed with that familiar and relaxing, evening vibe.

Parents stood in pockets of conversation, beer bottles and soft drinks in hand. Laughter rolled across the lawn, a warm summer's tide mixing with the gentle sea-breeze blowing in from the beach.

Dogs smooched and sat around everywhere — Zeb, Scoot, Jasper, other dogs of friends and family all mingled.

The little, tiny fluffy, wolf pup scampered around sniffing ankles and being constantly picked up, cuddled and smooched by everyone there. She was truly an irresistible, diplomatic envoy from the past.

Sherri's mum was mid-story with two other mothers, laughing hard enough to wipe tears from her eyes. Her dad stood with Frank near the barbecue, the two of them locked in a debate that somehow covered wormholes, surf tides, and whether Aldi sausages were secretly superior to Woolworths'.

At the salad table, Vittorio was carefully placing a large ceramic dish down among bowls of salad and plates of garlic bread.

"Lasagna," he announced mildly to no one in particular, adjusting it with quiet pride.

Behind him, two Orange Sand physicists hovered nearby, nodding appreciatively.

One of them leaned in, sniffed the air, and murmured something about Aldo's miracle spray can being "remarkable technology… but perhaps in need of a less sulphur-forward scent profile."

"It does have that farty eggs waft, I must say." the other added with a laugh.

Vittorio laughed too as he stepped over to them and joined in with the conversation on the means of travel to the BBQ they'd used earlier.

Jake, Jacinta and Byron's mum — Louise — arrived last, brushing her hair behind one ear as she shepherded her kids inside.

Aldo froze mid-sausage-turn.

Frank noticed immediately.

"Here comes the world-famous Louise –Byron's mum" he said, grinning. "Try not to combust Doctor Alderson, she's rather gorgeous."

Aldo swallowed. "I'm… fine."

He was not fine.

Louise approached, with an easy-going warmth in her stride, her smile striking like a match.

"Hello there Mr Frank Kendrick – Good to see you again!" She said jovially with a smile.

Frank laughed and nodded "Hey Louise, you must be the proudest mum around these parts – you do realise your kids helped to save our world?"

She huffed jokingly, "They haven't shut up about it since they got back. Thing is, *my* World won't be saved until they learn to tidy their rooms up more and they start picking up after themselves around the house."

"Good luck with that." Frank replied "They're teenagers. Easier getting World peace...although maybe...now...hmmm that could even be closer and easier."

"Oh! You must be Aldo," she said turning to face him, holding out her hand.

He took it — then panicked and accidentally shook it for way too long.

"Sorry — I, ah — I normally only talk to AI machines, physicists and border collies."

She laughed — rich, warm, delighted. "Well, I'm glad to be temporarily classified as either one of those...And I've read that border collies are the smartest dogs around."

"They are cosmically smart! Just like I'm sure you are too...when the kids aren't driving you mad?" He said awkwardly.

She roared with laughter and tapped him on the shoulder and nodded. He felt his nervousness wash away as he laughed along with her.

The sparks didn't just fly. They ignited.
Jake glanced at Jacinta. Jacinta glanced at Byron. None of them even tried to hide their delight. They loved Aldo.

Meanwhile, at the drinks table, Luc and Harriet stood shoulder-to-shoulder, impossibly at ease with one another — a couple forged through bullets, timelines, and Jasper's full-body harmonic shedding of soundwaves.

Luc approached Frank quietly.

"Frank," he said. "May I borrow your chrono-gun?"

Frank raised an eyebrow. "My boy... that is the most romantic request I have ever heard."

Harriet's cheeks flushed.
"Luc... what are you planning to do?"

Luc smiled, took her hand, and said two words.

"Everything - Everywhere."

Frank tossed him the chrono-gun with a wink.
"Bring her back in one piece — and try not to create seventeen paradox versions of yourselves."

Luc triggered the chrono-gate. A shimmering disc opened beside the washing line.

They stepped through.

FWUMP.

A soft gust of displaced air rippled the fairy lights.

Five seconds passed. Five. Four. Three. Two. One...

FWUMP.

They reappeared again — sun-kissed, wind-tousled, sand stuck to their heels, slightly damp from ocean spray, and absolutely tanned and glowing.

Luc's shirt was half-open. Harriet's braid had pine needles in it. They looked like two people who had just lived a hundred perfect lifetimes together.

Harriet held up her hand.

A ring glittered — silver, simple, elegant, timeless. Massive, the size of a Junior Mint.

Aldo shouted, "CONGRATULATIONS!"
The whole yard erupted into cheering and clapping.

Louise hugged Harriet. Jake whooped. Frank gave Luc a high-five and a slap on the shoulder.

Frank then raised his voice, gesturing grandly.

"Hang on! Everybody stay right where you are — we're not done!"

He marched inside quickly and returned with an old ghetto blaster the size of a small suitcase.

He smacked the side of it. "Who's ready to time-travel properly?"

Frank grinned at Luc "Hand it over to Aldo right now, young man."

Luc grinned and handed over the old Tears for Fears cassette to him.

Aldo accepted it reverently.

He popped it in.

A hiss. A click.

Then—

'Welcome to your life...'

The opening synths of *Everybody Wants to Rule the World* shimmered into the air.

Jasper climbed up onto the picnic table like it was his personal concert stage and howled on the downbeat.

Everybody started to sing along too.

Zeb joined in — a deeper, old-man Labrador bass note bark.
Scoot added the joyful mid-range wuffle.
The puppy joined in with howling puppy notes.

Everyone was crying and laughing and singing at the same time.

Harriet leaned into Luc. "We have to use this song at our wedding...don't we?"

"Oh, we so really have to!" he murmured, kissing her forehead. "It's our personal, national anthem now."

Frank took the puppy back from Sherri's arms and held it up to his face. With a wide loving grin that made him look 20 years younger, he kissed it on the nose.

"She's your Butterfly Effect," Sherri said, nudging him. "She did change something in the future: your grumpy spirit!"

Frank chuckled, soft and happy in heart and mind.

"Look how much she's changed you Uncle Frank – and there you were saying change was impossible and what a load of rubbish all that time-travel, Butterfly Effect theory was BLAH BLAH BLAH."

Frank gave the puppy a snuzzle with his whole face as it licked him and nuzzled him back.

"I stand by my call on the matter...as does she."

"So, have you given her a name yet?"

"Mariposa." Frank beamed a massive smile *"It's Spanish for butterfly"*

Sherri nearly fell over backwards laughing, as did Aldo and the other kids. It was their inside joke.

The song soared. Everyone sang the lyrics. Jasper howled higher.
The moon climbed up over the roofline, washing the backyard in gentle silver.

Aldo walked over to his special dog after the song had finished and gave him a big hug – "Okay Sinatra, that's enough singing for you, give your voice a rest and come and have some of the burnt sausages I've saved for you."

It was joy. Pure, unfiltered, well-earned joy.

The critical turmoil that had been erupting around World had abated in a breath.

And beneath the music and laughter and the hiss of sizzling sausages, something deep and gentle settled into Sherri's chest — a warm, luminous peace that felt like the

World had finally found its rhythm again and everything had found its way back to where it belonged.

Something beautiful and gentle locked itself back into place.

A sense that the universe — and everyone's place within it — had finally realigned, steady and right for once.

Under the Coolabah Tree

The barbeque was still roaring out the back, laughter rising and falling like soft tides. Frank was being teased mercilessly about becoming a "dog dad," Luc and Harriet were leaning into one another as if they'd been in love for centuries, and Aldo was absolutely besotted with Louise — sparks flying everywhere, like two flints striking in the dark.

But Sherri had slipped away quietly.

She walked out to the front lawn, to the old, raised mound beneath the coolabah tree — *their* spot.
Her spot.
The place she'd sat a thousand times, wrapped in eucalyptus shade, watching Jake and Jacinta and Byron playing away in the cul-de-sac, back before the universe split itself open and handed her an unbelievable destiny on a cracked dinner plate.

Zeb padded over and sat down beside her, tired from swimming all evening, his fur still damp, smelling faintly of salt and sunlight and joy. He flopped against her, settling onto his haunches in that sphinx-like way he always had, leaning his body against hers as if he'd never left — because now, he would never leave her again.

Above them, the full moon hung bright over Coolangatta, no longer sinister, no longer heavy with stolen souls — just a warm, soft lantern in the sky. A healed moon. A free moon.

Sherri draped her arm around Zeb's shoulders and rubbed his velvety ears. He closed his eyes and leaned harder against her, panting in that lopsided, slightly smelly,

shameless dog-breath way that only made her love him
even more.

"Well…" she murmured, voice warm and cracking with
everything she'd been through.
"Man's best friend…"

She kissed the top of his head.
"…and this girl's best friend in the whole world too."

Zeb wagged his tail — a slow, heavy, contented thump-
thump-thump against the grass.
She laughed contentedly at the sound of it.

And somewhere far beyond Coolangatta, beyond the cul-
de-sac, beyond time and space and every stitched-up
thread of reality that we can't even begin to comprehend…

**the Universe watched them with unconditional
love…**

…and it wagged its cosmic tail

—thump-thump-thump.

Afterword

This story sure didn't begin with a plan.

It arrived quietly, randomly over time — through memories, questions, and the lingering sense that something important had been misplaced in the world.

I didn't set out to write about time fractures, secret experiments, or even the fate of dogs. I followed a gut feeling instead: that some bonds matter so deeply they echo across generations, cultures, and time itself.

The idea came to me on one of those emotionally exhausting days — a really rough one where comfort only arrives later on in the evening.

Old 80's music playing away. Sunken into my sofa. And my dog, sensing exactly where I was at, climbed up beside me and rested his head on my lap.

As one of my favourite songs from my youth played, I caught myself realising that something about it wasn't quite the way I remembered it. The words were close... but not the same anymore. It was a small thing, easily dismissed — and yet it stirred a larger, unsettling question.

What if something precious could be altered or erased — and we barely remembered it had ever been there at all?

The First Pat grew from that feeling.

From love. From loss. From loyalty.

From the comforting smell and feel of my dog next to me.

From the simple, enduring truth that real connection leaves a mark on the universe — and on our hearts.

If this story found you when you needed it, even briefly, then it has done what it was meant to do.

Thank you for reading my book.
— Mark

About the Author

Mark Rengel lives in Coolangatta, Queensland, Australia, with his wife, two daughters, and his spiritual advisor — Arlo, their Border Collie.

He juggles part-time work, house-dad duties, and completing a Bachelor of Education, while continuing his long-standing commitment to storytelling and creativity.

Mark's life has taken him far beyond Australia.

Over the years, he has lived and worked across Asia, studying and teaching in China, Hong Kong and Japan, spending time in a Buddhist monastery, training in traditional martial and healing arts, and travelling widely through remote regions of the world. These experiences continue to shape his writing, infusing it with curiosity, compassion, and a deep respect for connection — human and otherwise.

He now hopes to write as many fun and inspiring novels as he can, drawing from the rich, winding journey that has brought him to the present.

www.ingramcontent.com/pod-product-compliance
Lightning Source LLC
Chambersburg PA
CBHW051008180726
48291CB00006B/2023